RETRIBUTION

RETRIBUTION

THE ASCENSION MYTH BOOK 6

ELL LEIGH CLARKE

MICHAEL ANDERLE

DISRUPTIVE IMAGINATION®

LMBPN Publishing
PMB 196, 2540 South Maryland Pkwy
Las Vegas, NV 89109

First US edition, August 2017
Version 1.05 January 2024

RETRIBUTION TEAM

JIT Beta Readers

Micky Cocker
Alex Wilson
Kelly ODonnell
James Caplan
Paul Westman
John Findlay
Jed Moulton
Kimberly Boyer
Thomas Ogden
John Raisor
Joshua Ahles
Keith Verret

If we missed anyone, please let us know!

Editor
Jen McDonnell

To everyone who ever dreamed of making a dent in the universe.

— Ellie

To Family, Friends and
Those Who Love
To Read.
May We All Enjoy Grace
To Live The Life We Are
Called.

— Michael

ZHYN POLITICIAN

THE KURTHERIAN (tm) GAMBIT

ZHYN SOLDIER

THE KURTHERIAN (tm) GAMBIT

CHAPTER ONE

Aboard *ArchAngel*, Reynolds' Office

The General was tired from being woken up in the middle of the night and looked bleary eyed over at Giles. "So, tell me again why you haven't got the talisman?"

Giles scratched the back of his head, his tweed jacket opening up in a strange shape on one side, exposing his vintage-style shirt. His expression was one of sheepishness. "Er. Would you believe me if I said it involved a girl?"

Lance had wandered over to the drinks tray in his office and poured himself one. He ambled back to the sofa and sat down, his legs spread apart, resting his arms on his legs while studying the contents of his glass. "Yeah," he sighed. "I would."

Giles shifted awkwardly where he stood before deciding to join him on the adjacent sofa. "It's okay, Uncle Lance. I know roughly where to find it again. It's just going to take me some time to go get it."

Lance looked up at him from beneath a somewhat furrowed brow. "How long?" he asked. He dropped his eyes back to the liquor, bracing himself for a ridiculous response.

Giles shrugged, and breathed deeper. "I dunno. It depends. I need to find the guy who hid it for me first…"

His voice trailed off as he realized how, to a practical man like Lance, this wasn't a well (enough) defined parameter.

Lance didn't react.

Instead, he just took a swig of the whiskey, draining the glass in one go. "Okay. Well, whatever it takes. I don't like the idea of there being things out there that we don't understand. Things that can potentially be used against us."

He stood up and returned the glass to the tray on the other side of the room, and then turned back to Giles. "That said," he continued, "I don't believe there is anyone more capable of solving this puzzle than you. Let's talk some more in the morning, but suffice to say, it looks like you have your next assignment."

Giles stood up. "Understood, General," he replied.

Lance nodded affably. "Go get some rest, dear boy. We'll continue this at a decent hour."

Giles bobbed his head and turned to leave.

"Ah, just one more thing," Lance called after him.

Giles turned back.

"The woman, the one that was the cause of us not having this vital piece of intel…" Lance watched Giles's reaction carefully as he spoke.

"Yeah?" Giles asked.

"Anyone I know?" The General asked.

Giles's lips curled in a half smile, with a hint of admiration for the woman, and a touch of contempt for a certain thought about her that came to mind. "Some things are best left in the past Uncle," he replied.

He turned again to leave, heading out of the door.

The General watched him go, shaking his head quietly to himself. "ADAM," he called hitting his holo button. "Have my morning meetings postponed for a few hours. I'm going to sleep in to recover from this emergency meeting."

ADAM's voice came over the intercom. "Of course, sir. Did you not deem the conversation urgent and important?"

Lance nodded to himself. "No no, it was both urgent and important. I'm glad you woke me. And we'll discuss our next moves in the morning when I've had time to process. And sleep."

"Yes, sir. Sleep tight," ADAM responded over the intercom.

The General wiped his tired face as he wandered across his office reception area. "You too, ADAM," he responded.

Lance headed out of the office door, and padded down the corridor in his blue and white striped pajamas, covered over with his dark red bathrobe. He knew to his crew, he would look like a crazy man wandering around in his nightclothes, but most of them knew him. They knew that he was far from crazy. And that he didn't care what they thought.

Just then, an ensign rounded the corner. "Good night, sir," he chirped amicably, only just refraining from a salute — on account of the General not being in uniform.

"Good night, Thom," the General muttered as he continued down the corridor, back to his quarters where he had left Patricia sleeping.

Gaitune-67, Safe house, Molly's conference room

Paige gazed idly into thin air as she mused about the future. "I dunno," she said wistfully. "When we have enough sales, I think we could have a few employees, maybe based on Ogg, who might want to take over the marketing."

Maya grinned. "Bored with the marketing already?"

Paige shook her head, quickly returning to the conversation. "No. Not at all. I just want to make sure that I'm focused on my job, as well. I don't want to leave the adventures we have here. Not for fame or fortune."

Maya grinned. "Well, it's good that the kinds of things you need in the business are things that you don't need to do yourself."

Paige grinned. "Yeah, especially now we have the perfect formula *nailed* - pun intended," she said chuckling. "Molly's done all the hard work," she added glancing over at Molly, who was immersed in her holo.

Paige and Maya had stopped talking and were looking at her. Molly became aware of the change in the room, and looked up at them. "Sorry... did you...?"

Her eyes were on them, but she was still absent.

Paige laughed. "It's okay. We were only mentioning the work you did for the nail formula."

"Oh, right..." she acknowledged. Seeming to get another thought, she turned to Maya. "Anything useful on those Chaakwa files, then?" she asked.

The girls had been holed up in Molly's favorite conference room all morning, working through their various things, and catching up with the routine since their mission defeating the Zhyn.

Most of the crew was pretty tired. It had been exciting, but also intense for all involved. Even two days later, Molly was happy to take it easy and just catch up on rest. Joel would have them running circuits and sparring the crap out of each other soon enough.

Maya closed her holo to give Molly her full attention. "Yeah. She has a bunch of leads that we can run down."

Molly frowned a little. "Leads that she couldn't pursue herself?"

Maya bobbed her head from side to side. "I'm not sure. Some. I don't think she had the access she needed. Not the kind that Oz and Pieter can secure for us..."

"And?" Molly pressed, sensing some hesitation in Maya's voice.

Maya narrowed her eyes, thinking. "Well, I have a funny feeling that she was holding back. Almost like she didn't want people to know she was still looking into it."

Molly stared off into empty space for a moment, before scratching the side of her face and scrunching up her nose. "Well, I guess I can understand that. I mean, if The Syndicate were anything to go by, who knows what lengths these particular goons were going to in order to keep themselves protected? It wouldn't surprise me if they were tapping her holos, and... worse." Molly's voice drifted off again, before she gave a small shudder at the thought.

"Anyway, keep at it," she instructed a little more brightly. "I'd like us to get these fuckheads dealt with so that Chaakwa can get on with her life in peace."

Maya nodded. "Sure. On it, boss," she affirmed looking back down at her holo.

Isn't it time you started moving?

What for?

Your meeting with the General.

Oh, shit. Fuck.

Molly closed her holoscreens hurriedly. "Shit, I'd forgotten I have a debriefing with the General. I've got to go..." she explained quickly to the girls.

Paige and Maya looked up, semi-stunned by the flurry of activity from Molly's direction. In a matter of seconds, she was packed up and out of the door. "I'll catch you later," she called back to them.

The door bounced closed behind her, and didn't quite catch—opening slowly, and then settling ajar. Paige and Maya looked at each other.

"See what I mean?" Maya urged.

Paige shook her head. "Nooo..." she said slowly. "It's just the same old Molly. Living in her head."

Maya shook her head. "No," she insisted. "Didn't you see how

5

she shuddered when she was thinking of what Chaakwa might be going through?"

Paige frowned. "So?"

"So," pressed Maya, "I think she's empathizing. You know, putting herself in other peoples' shoes. At least, in terms of her imagination."

Paige looked at Maya suspiciously. "That's not what you're getting at though, is it?"

Maya smiled gently. "Okay, you got me. No, honestly, if it were just that, it would a feat of a personality shift, no doubt... I think it's something more."

Paige's eyes lit up as she started to understand. "You mean like they were saying about her being able to tune in to other peoples' energies."

Maya pursed her lips together and nodded. "I think so." She kept nodding. "I think she's *feeling* how people feel, and then having her own reaction to it; like a..."

Paige smirked. "A human being?"

Maya grinned. "Exactly!"

Paige clapped her hands together in childish excitement, and her motions dissipated the holographic screens that had been arranged in front of her. "So, you think that she and Joel will finally get together, then?"

Maya grinned, and started back in on her work. "Let's not get *too* carried away. I mean, it is still Molly in there, after all."

Paige took the hint that the conversation was over, and set about retrieving her closed screens, still smiling excitedly to herself.

Chom-X9, Secret Base

The thin atmosphere on Chom-X9 was still. It had been several days since the electrical storm, and the scent of ozone remained in the air, in patches.

Shaa hurried back inside, bringing a little whirlpool of dust with him into the airlock. It was safe to be outside for a short time. Time enough to experience the vastness of space, and marvel at how far he had come. But to stay too long meant to suffer the effects of the low pressure and the lack of oxygen. Of course, being Zhyn, he was a little more robust than other species might be. But still. It wasn't something he wanted to push.

The second door of the airlock opened and he stepped through, stamping the sand and dirt from his boots.

"Sir," one of his subordinates acknowledged him.

Shaa nodded to him, and then made his way through the utilitarian corridors to the meeting room. He pressed the keypad and strode in.

The four engineers sitting around the conference room table stood as soon as they saw him.

"At ease, gentlemen," he told them, his attention on other things. He wandered over to the window, looking out over the wilderness he'd just come from, as they reclaimed their seats.

"Sir, we have an update on the-" one of them began.

Shaa turned, waving his hand to silence him. "In a moment. First," he commanded in his domineering tone, "tell me about the other entry points to the base. How secure are we, structurally, without those secondary doors having an airlock?"

A couple of the engineers looked at each other, trying to decide what to answer. They seemed to agree on *who* was going to answer, and the older looking one spoke up. "Sir, it is safe for now; but over time, the pressure differential, and, of course, the use of the other doors, will put the surrounding structure under stress. We should look at putting in airlocks as soon as possible."

Shaa grunted. "Sooner than the automatic targeting defense systems for the building?"

The engineers all nodded emphatically, as if he had asked them if Zhyn needed oxygen to survive.

Shaa sighed. "Very well. Have work started on them immediately. Do one at a time, though."

The engineer on the far right took a note to make it happen.

Shaa seemed ready to get down to business. He turned his attention to the four of them, and sat down at the table. "So, what of the anti space missiles?" he asked. "Did the storm take any of them out?"

The engineers proceeded with their update, and Shaa took a deep breath, fighting to maintain his patience in dealing with the minutia of setting up yet another base from scratch.

Gaitune-67, Base conference room

Molly breezed into the conference room, her mind still immersed in the numerous projects she had been running. Plunking her anti grav mug of hot water on the table, she closed her eyes for a second, trying to call up the relevant file for the conversation she was about to have.

Why are we here, Oz?

Zhyn mission debrief.

Right. Thank you.

...

I'm going to ask him about that damn letter, too.

You go for it, Tiger.

'Tiger'. Ha! I'm LOL'ing in my head at you, Oz.

I'm glad I can provide some amusement.

Molly sat down, opened her holo, and hit 'Call Connect,' ready for when the General came on.

She sipped on her hot water trying to remember the high she would feel when she would sip on hot mocha. Alas, since her body seemed to have taken to rejecting it, it had been a while since she had truly enjoyed the stuff. It was as though the nanocytes just didn't want her consuming mocha - and so, under Arlene's suggestion, she had given it up.

Life has a way of taking away the things I love the most, she mused flatly as she waited in the empty conference room.

The holo cube in the center of the table appeared and unfolded, creating a screen that opened out against the wall on the other side of the conference table.

Lance Reynolds appeared before her in his usual military attire, with a half-chewed cigar in his mouth.

"Bates!" he exclaimed. "Good to see you alive and well."

"You too, sir," she agreed, quickly getting to her feet and saluting.

The General returned the salute, and nodded for her to sit back down. "I hear the mission was a success?" he prompted.

"Yes, sir. We took out all targets and escaped without casualties," Molly confirmed.

The General looked pleased. "Very good," he gruffed. "You did a good job."

Reynolds flicked through a holoscreen that cast a haze between him and the projection that appeared on Molly's side of the holo feed. "Yeeees," he said admiringly now, "looks like you did *very* well, according to Oz's report."

Molly sat motionless in her seat, watching him review the report.

Eventually he sat back in his console chair, and scratched the side of his head, and then his nose. "You won't have heard yet, but we just got word that the responsible parties were dealt with. The Justicar called me this morning, and explained the situation. It seems their armed forces commander was going off-book without the Emperor's knowledge or consent."

Molly's eye twitched a little. As the General paused to take a breath, she jumped in. "Sir, I understand this question may be beyond my remit, but... do we believe that?

The General started, and removed the cigar from his mouth.

Molly continued with her concern. "I mean, are we to believe that story, or do we have reason to be suspicious? They have a lot to gain by using this commander as a scapegoat, and then just rebuilding, unsupervised."

Reynolds took a breath and placed the tobacco stick down on the console in front of him.

"Hmmm..." he said thoughtfully. "I took him at his word. He's always proven to be an honorable man in all my dealings with him in the Federation."

He paused, thinking for a moment. "But it's a fair question. Tell you what, Bates," he said, leaning forward again and poking at his screen. "How about I send my reports for you and your team to look over? Then you can share your thoughts with me, and include your... intuition."

Molly's gut tightened. She had the strange sense that she was being tested. "Of course, sir." She hesitated, not quite knowing how to ask her follow-up question.

The General recognized her facial cues of concern, and paused, giving her space to speak.

Molly took a second and then frowned. "Am I to assume that you're wanting something more than just a standard tactical analysis?"

The General's face broke into a bemused smile. "Why, yes, Molly. I'm asking for your personal opinion... Based on data, but, also, I must admit, including any hunches and feelings you might get."

He paused, considering what to tell her. "Arlene has informed me of your progress. It seems that even though your Vision Quest was cut short, you still proved to be quite the student."

Molly felt her cheeks flushing and hoped the General didn't notice. She couldn't tell if she was feeling put on the spot to perform, or whether she felt proud of her new abilities. It was all just a little overwhelming. "Erm. Thank you, sir," she said tentatively.

"I think," she added quietly.

Lance chuckled and picked up his cigar, before poking the screen again. "Okay, those files should be with you now," he told her. "I'd also like you to continue working with Arlene for the foreseeable future. She assures me you have talent, and that her methods are helping..." He flicked at his screen, "And that you're still having *some* difficulties."

His eyes scanned from side to side, reading other pieces of Oz's report. "Looks like you got yourself into a hairy situation on the surface." His forehead broke into a slight frown. "Good thing Royale was there with you."

Molly felt instantly embarrassed. She lowered her head. "Yes, sir. I got lucky. It won't happen again."

Lance was looking at her again. "Yes, hence my request for you to keep on with Arlene. I've known the woman for years. She is the best at this realm stuff..." His voice trailed off as he contemplated the direction of the meeting.

He seemed to get another thought, and so did Molly. They both started to speak at the same time, and then stopped.

"Sorry, sir. Please..." Molly gestured with her hand, allowing him to speak first. She placed her hand back in her lap, hiding it under the table, as she also tried to hide the storm of emotions that she'd been awash with since the meeting started.

The General sat forward. "I was just going to suggest that it might be worth you and your team coming over to the *ArchAngel* for a visit—given that you're now part of the larger team."

Molly's face lit up. "Seriously?"

Lance was smiling the grin of a twenty-something who had just scored a hat trick. "Yes, of course. Besides," he told her, "there is still much you need to learn to be effective out in the field. Plus, I have some people I want you to meet."

Molly nodded enthusiastically. "I think we'd enjoy that. Very much."

"Good," the General said firmly. "I'll have ADAM set up the

details, but let's make it sooner rather than later. I have one particular team member who doesn't tend to stay put for long periods of time. I'd hate for you to miss him."

"Of course, sir," Molly replied. "We'll make it happen."

There was a slight pause in the conversation.

The General tilted his head. "So, what were you going to say?"

Molly remembered her trail of thought. "Ah. Yes. I was… er… I was going to ask about the letter. From Bethany Anne."

Lance grinned a Cheshire cat grin again, clearly enjoying the situation. "Right. Yes. You've completed the mission. How about you have a look at it when you get here? Then you've got something to look forward to."

Son of a bi-

That's your commanding officer!

Bite me, Oz. Besides, when did you go all company-boy on me?

Oz's chuckles reverberated in the lower edge of her skull.

She resisted the urge to roll her eyes at Oz, not wanting the General to misinterpret the move and think she was reacting to him.

"Very good, sir," she conceded politely. "As you wish."

The General placed his arms on the console, looking satisfied. "Good. Right, I'll see you soon then, Bates. And see if you can't persuade Arlene to take the trip with you. I'm sure there are folks here that she'd like the opportunity to catch up with."

He nodded his goodbye, and then clicked off the call.

Molly could have sworn he had a twinkle in his eye when he made the suggestion about Arlene. In fact, she could almost feel his amusement, despite the vast space between them. Molly filed it away for later.

Extraneous data points. This was just one more layer to manage since she had started experiencing other peoples' worlds.

She hit the button to close the holos, and watched the conference room holo pretend to fold itself neatly away in the center of the table, as if it wasn't just made up of light projections.

Then she got up and headed up to the safe house to rejoin the team.

CHAPTER TWO

Gaitune-67, Hangar deck

Less than twenty four hours later, the team was loaded up and ready to depart from Gaitune-67. Arlene had even been persuaded to come along — despite initially resisting, saying she had things to attend to on the sparsely populated lump of asteroid that had been her home for the last several decades.

Now, with final checks completed, Brock and Crash flicked various switches, powering up *The Empress*.

Crash gave the order in his usual unemotional tone. "Okay, Emma, I think we're ready to rock."

Emma's voice came over the intercom, filling the cockpit with her dulcet tones. "I believe we are. And congratulations on attempting this without Sean."

Brock immediately reacted, and looked intently in Crash's direction, his mouth open and smiling. "Buurn!" He exclaimed. Laughing, he continued, "She did *not* just — "

Crash's lips twitched into a smile. "She did," he confirmed, rolling his head against his headrest to glance at his friend. "But Emma and I have an understanding," he explained.

Brock dropped one shoulder and waved his hand around, signaling at her video image. "And what might that be?" he asked, playing the role of the ally in support of his friend.

Crash was still smiling, but Emma responded. "I get to pull his leg on the condition that I rescue his rookie ass every time he steps wrong."

Brock looked confused. "Dude, why would you agree to this shit?"

Crash's smile had disappeared. "Keeps Royale off my ass," he said simply.

Brock chuckled quietly. "Ohhhhh. Now I get it. And that's why he's out there, and we have the cockpit to ourselves without him breathing down our necks!" He put his fist out for Crash to bump, who returned the gesture before flipping one more switch to ignite the final engines for takeoff.

"Time to let them know," Crash called across to Brock.

Brock frowned. "What, me?" he asked.

Crash nodded.

Brock sat back in his console chair. "Oh, no," he said, shaking his head definitively. "This is your rodeo, cowboy. You make the announcement."

Crash shrugged without attachment. "Okay. But you know they won't get a serious safety briefing out of me. Ever."

Brock nodded. "Uh huh. I think they appreciate that." He smiled, rocking back and forth in his chair, as Crash connected with the ship-wide intercom.

"Ladies and Gentlefolk," he started. "We will now demonstrate the safety features on this spacecraft, and your attention is essential – as these may differ from any other spacecraft you have flown in before."

Brock waited, watching out the front window while listening intently, holding his breath for what was to come.

Crash continued with the announcement. "Take care that

your baggage does not block the aisles or exit. It must be put under the seat in front of you or in an overhead locker. Place items in the locker carefully, as they may fall out and injure someone. And we don't recommend the use of pod docs at any point, due to them turning you into a realm-jumping mess if you have just the wrong type of neurons."

Crash paused, allowing Brock to hear the titters coming from the cabin.

"In the event of an emergency evacuation, please move quickly to the closest available exit; remember not to hold your breath when you're exposed to space, as – without a pressurized suit – your lungs will explode within ten seconds. Unless you're insured with Azsurtec, in which case you get ten and a half."

Brock chortled to himself, clamping his hands over his mouth so as not to distract Crash.

"Bathrooms are available downstairs, and high heels are not recommended on the steps. Crash Airways appreciates that you have a choice of space travel, and thanks you for flying with us today. Have a great flight."

The intercom clicked off.

Brock released his hands. His laughter could be heard reverberating around the cockpit and just through the passageway to the adjoining lounge.

Molly shook her head, quietly amused by the boys' antics.

Joel tapped on her shoulder from a couple of seats back. "Hey. You wanna play cards? Sean has a pool going that says he can beat you at any game that doesn't involve calculating probabilities." Joel was grinning, amused by the concept.

Molly turned in her seat to face him. Further back, she could see Sean, using a crate for a table, which was already blocking the aisle, and looking at her competitively. "Why do I get the sense that he's still trying to reclaim something since he got his ass whooped by you in that training session weeks ago?"

Joel shrugged. "Maybe because he is," he offered.

Molly smiled. "Okay. Let's play. But as soon as I'm bored, I'm done."

"Okay," Joel agreed. "No problem."

Jack had seated herself, ready to play, and Sean was already shuffling a deck of cards.

"You know," Jack said, "I never quite understood the appeal of this kind of game until I joined the service."

Joel swiveled a chair around for Molly, who started to sit down. Then he turned and grabbed one for himself. "Why is that?" he asked.

Jack shrugged. "I never had anyone to play with... and the computer simulations just weren't a big thing in my day."

Sean chuffed. "In *your* day. You make it sound like you're super old."

Jack eyed him carefully, before raising an eyebrow. "Well, I don't know how old *you* are, and I'm certainly not telling you how old *I* am... However, from the movement of some of your enhancements, I can have a guess at your age."

Sean avoided eye contact, and started dealing cards. "Well, no need to get into that," he said quietly. Jack's lips spread into a smile as she realized she had hit a sensitive subject with the Federation cyborg.

She winked casually, and looked down at her cards.

Molly organized her hand. "So... what are we playing?"

"Gun ho," Sean told her. He explained the game and the highlights of the set of rules they were going to abide by, and the game commenced.

Meanwhile, from across the far side of the lounge area, Arlene watched the group's interactions.

Maya interrupted her thoughts. "You're amused by my teammates?" she asked, sparking up the conversation.

Arlene nodded and smiled to herself, her eyes fixed on Molly. "Yes. A little. Molly particularly," she explained. "I used to be her. With a Joel hanging by my side all the time.

The great protector..." Arlene's voice was tinted with nostalgia.

Maya smiled. "What happened?"

Arlene brought her attention back to their side of the cabin. "Oh, you know," she explained vaguely. "Life, I guess. We lived in different worlds..."

Maya smiled, interested in the conversation, but not wanting to pry. "So, did you always live on Gaitune?" she ventured, her inner journalist deciding that was an innocuous line of questioning for a new acquaintance.

Arlene nodded. "Yes, pretty much. My father brought us here from Estaria. He was in the Federation, which was actually just called 'the Empire' at the time. He was an advisor to the new settlers, and when the opportunity arose to come and live a simpler life, he jumped at the chance."

Maya bobbed her head, casually watching the four warriors gibing each other over their game. "And you work for the Federation, too?"

Arlene nodded. "Yes. General Reynolds offered me the position when I decided I was ready to leave the Merideth Reynolds. I lived there for a little while in my early decades."

Maya couldn't help herself. "They say that you're ninety something years old..." she commented, leaning in and lowering her voice.

Arlene smiled her knowing smile. "You're Estarian. You know what's possible, no?"

Maya shrugged and leaned up in her seat again. "Well, I know what they told us at school; but it's not like anyone I knew could do what you do... with your appearance, and all."

Arlene maintained an air of sageness about her. "It's all in the practice," she said simply, referring back to the years of arduous meditation she'd pressed Paige about in their first meeting.

Maya bobbed her head, fully aware of the conversations as a result of Paige's excited rantings. "I heard," she said.

Arlene took a deep breath and looked directly at Maya. "So what's your story?" she asked, changing the subject.

Maya shrugged. "I dunno, really. I was a journalist, then I stumbled on some of Molly's activities, and before I knew it, Sean Royale was on my doorstep inviting me into the inner circle." She paused, contemplating the incident. "Probably just to stop me from poking around... and a marginally better alternative to killing me!" she added jokingly.

Laughter erupted from the games table. Joel had stood up and thrown his cards down dramatically in front of Molly, who just held his gaze defiantly. Even Jack was laughing at the drama.

Arlene pulled her attention back to the conversation. "I suspect they also had a respect for your investigative abilities," she told her. "I know how the Federation works. When they find talent, they grab it." She paused, her eyes glazing over as if she were tuning into something not of this world. "You made a good choice, joining this team," she concluded.

Maya smiled. "Yeah, I think so."

Meanwhile, Paige and Pieter sat engrossed in the holo screens projecting from Pieter's wrist bank.

"You see... this is the structure. You don't need to understand all the details of the code at once; you just need to see the pattern, and understand what it's doing on a top level."

Paige's eyebrows were crinkled up as she squinted at the lines and lines of code. "So what is this doing?" she asked.

Pieter pointed at a few lines, seemingly at random. "Well these commands are basically telling us where the packets of data are being sent. See this string here?"

"Mmhm," Paige mumbled.

"Well this is one of the buffers on *The Empress*'s syste- Oooo — " Pieter interrupted himself, his voice clearly more excited. "And this is Emma getting pinged. She knows we're looking, now."

Paige couldn't help but smile to herself, impressed.

New code appeared suddenly on the screen, pushing what they had been looking at up out of view.

"What's happening now?" Paige asked, noticing the change.

Pieter frowned and flicked down a bit to see the new code better. "Ha!" he hooted, poking at the screen and typing something back. "She's redirecting our pings to a sandbox! Look at the comments."

// Grownups are working to keep this ship in the air now. Go play somewhere else!

Paige chuckled quietly. "She told you, eh?"

Pieter flushed a little. "Yeah. I'll say," he said, finishing his response and hitting return.

Paige couldn't quite see what he had done. "What did you say to her?"

Pieter sniggered. "Ah, nothing. Just poking the bear," he told her.

Aboard *ArchAngel*

Within an hour, the team had not only arrived at the *Arch-Angel*, but had also disembarked from *The Empress* and been taken to their quarters.

Minutes after throwing her pack down on the bed and grabbing a cold drink, Molly heard shrieks of excitement and chatter out in the corridor. Water bottle in hand, about to break the seal, she paused, listening intently – hoping to hell it wasn't her team, embarrassing her.

She heard Brock's voice ringing out above the kerfuffle, and then other doors swooshing open.

It *was* her team.

Placing the unopened bottle on the side, she marched out into the corridor. Joel, Sean, Arlene, and Maya were standing outside Brock's quarters.

Crash's voice was heard from within. "He's not kidding. You wanna check this baby out," he called back.

Molly joined the others at the door in rapid time, only to realize that there was no reason to panic; everyone was smiling, or at least stoically entertained. Arlene raised her eyes to the heavens when she caught Molly's eye, and then turned back down the corridor to her own quarters. She waved her hand as she disappeared, amused. "I have a meeting to get to," she explained vaguely.

Sean looked down at Molly, his arms folded, as he observed the team with mild interest, as a child would watch ants fighting over breadcrumbs.

"What's going on?" she asked him.

Sean was about to speak, but Maya explained for him. "Brock has realized they have disco lights in the shower... and twenty different settings for the water type, alkalinity, soap content and – "

Brock emerged in view of the doorway. "Hell, you can even program champagne to come out of one of the nozzles!" His eyes were bright, and, if Molly hadn't known the context, she would have been forgiven for thinking he had just had the shock of a lifetime.

Molly frowned, still confused. "Why would anyone want champagne to come out of their shower?" she asked.

Joel, who was leaning against the doorframe, lowered his eyes before confessing what he knew. "Well, let's put it this way; it also will shower you in chocolate goop, strawberry syrup, and any number of other things."

Molly's frown deepened. "I thought the idea was to get clean?"

Sean's aloofness had morphed into something else. A smirk appeared on his lips as Molly looked up at him for help understanding.

Maya stroked her arm sympathetically. "Aww, she really has no idea," she cooed.

Molly broke Sean's gaze and glanced over at Maya.

Then the penny dropped.

Molly's face dropped. "Oh, shit. You're fucking kidding me?" she gasped. "Why the hell would that be on a military ship? How would the General allow it? And...and why would Bethany Anne commission such a thing?"

Sean's smirk had turned into a grin. "Maybe she's more of a good time girl than we think?" he guessed, shrugging.

Brock was dancing around and running from the shower room, where Crash was fiddling with the controls and options, back into the main sleeping quarters, and then back again.

He reminded Molly of a puppy who was seeing snow for the first time.

Joel shrugged, recovered from the revelation, and turned to the small group at the door. "Not wanting to return the mundanity to your perceptions of Bethany Anne, or her father, but these are units you can retrofit. They're fairly inexpensive on the Zon. You just have them delivered, and rig them up; which any of the engineers in this place could do. And then you just need to keep the products stocked."

Molly's face relaxed a little. "So... you think some of the engineers on board did this?"

Sean slapped Joel on the arm playfully, and turned to head to his quarters. "I'm sure of it," he said, winking at Molly.

Brock had quieted down. "So, like, do none of y'all have this in your rooms?"

Each person in the assembled group looked at each other, then, without another word, turned and left - to go and check their own quarters.

Molly strode back to her room and headed straight for the bathroom. The panel next to the shower was fancy – high-tech, compared to anything she'd seen in the Sark system — but nothing unusual.

Was that a sense of disappointment I detected?

No. Oz. No, it's not.

Are you sure?

I'm not having this conversation with you, Oz.

Her brain tickled as she headed back into the bedroom to unpack her things before her official meeting with the General.

ArchAngel, General Reynolds' Office

The team looked around the General's personal office. It was large by most standards; especially for one man. On a frikkin spaceship. *And* the area they were occupying was only the central room to it. The reception room, almost. Off to the right, as far from the entrance as you could get, it looked like there was another private office where he took his calls, and did his actual work. This was more of a hosting room, with sofas, a drinks tray, and no doubt a holo screen or two for discussions.

Off to the left of the big windows that looked out into space, there was a second door. That was closed, and locked with a special access panel. Molly noticed it, and couldn't imagine what he might keep in there.

Secret things.

I'm sure.

More secret than the secret things that went to the secret university.

Molly shook her head in mock despair at the Oz comments, and turned her attention back to the inky blackness of space. She contemplated the thin forcefield and carbon-composite separating her and her team from the reality of the vacuum. She felt herself shifting, her awareness expanding... and then remembered where she was, and pulled her attention back to her breathing.

The here and now.

She heard Sean's voice calling over to Jack. "Check it out," he was saying, standing in front of a panel that housed a series of pictures. She assumed they were geeking out over some military thing.

Paige caught her eye. She sat on one of the sofas in the seating area, half-listening to Maya chatter away, marveling about their experience on the high-tech ship. Joel and Pieter sat with their backs to her, engrossed in conversation with the General. Pieter looked a little starstruck when she tuned into him.

Starstruck... and nervous about saying something stupid, she realized. She smiled at how far he had come, and how excited he had been about this whole trip. It warmed her heart just reflecting on it.

"General Reynolds?" ADAM's voice came over the intercom.

"Yes, ADAM?" Lance responded.

"The Guardians are here," ADAM informed him.

The General got to his feet, his conversation with Pieter and Joel moved aside. "Excellent, ADAM. Send them in, please."

The door to the office swept quietly open, revealing three human males of Chinese origin. The General moved over to the door to greet them. The others followed, like magnets, activated by the prospect of new people.

Molly eyed the visitors closely. She could feel that, though they appeared calm and serious on the surface, they were actually quite jovial within themselves. Just tuning into them, she felt like she wanted to smile.

"Team Bates, allow me to introduce you to some of the Empress' Guardians who have remained here to protect and serve on the *ArchAngel.*"

The three men stepped into the room, one after another, and stood quietly, allowing the General to make the introductions.

"This is Jian, Zhu, and Shun," he indicated to each of them in turn. Each did a little bow to acknowledge their visitors.

Joel, and then Sean, stepped forward to shake their hands. Molly smiled and waved from her position a little further back.

"Great to meet you guys. I've heard via ADAM that we have much to learn from you, especially in the art of combat."

Jian smiled, but Shun responded. "It would be our pleasure to host you in the APA. And also to show you around some of the ship's facilities while you are here."

Molly grinned. "That would be super," she bowed slightly, wanting to convey her gratitude and respect. "What's the APA?" she added, realizing suddenly there were probably a bunch of acronyms and protocols that went along with a ship and company this size.

Zhu answered, grinning. "We will indeed show you. Better to show you than explain."

Molly tilted her head nervously, not knowing what to expect, or how to respond. She quickly changed the subject, trying to be a good liaison for her team. "May I present to you my team from Gaitune. The Sanguine Squadron. You've just met Joel and Sean. They're our, erm, alphas," she winked, smiling at the subtle observation of how they had automatically dived in and shaken hands with their new friends. "This is Paige, and Maya."

The ladies stepped forward and shook hands with the Guardians. Maya looked mesmerized, having grown up on Estaria with very few humans around. The Guardians looked just as intrigued at Paige's looks – what, with her human features and Estarian skin color.

Molly continued. "This is Jack. One of our fiercer warriors, though she lets Sean pretend that he's stronger." Jack smiled at the acknowledgment, ignoring Sean's glare of pretend aggravation. She shook their hands in turn, and then stepped back, out of the way, allowing Pieter to move forward. He looked a little disheveled and overwhelmed by his whole *ArchAngel* experience, but grinned a toothy, disarming smile as he reached forward to shake hands with the warriors in turn. "I'm Pieter. Their pet computer nerd," he explained.

Jian nodded sympathetically. "I'm very pleased to meet you,

Pieter-the-pet-nerd." Jian knew what it was like to be the quietest in the group, perhaps explaining the immediate empathy he had for Pieter.

Lance took a breath and clapped his hands together. "Right, then," he started. "I wonder if, Captain Shun, you could take your team and show the Bates Crew around?"

The Captain nodded and he and his team bowed, a little deeper than before. Jian, and then Zhu, turned and stepped out of the door, which slid open as they approached it. Shun motioned for the Bates ensemble to follow them.

"Not you, Molly," the General called. He brought her back into the seating area deeper inside the office, and offered her a sofa.

Paige glanced back at Molly, feeling as if they were being taken off to school without her. She nervously twiddled her fingers at her as she was ushered out the door by Shun, who then followed her out.

The door closed behind them.

Lance noticed the slight anxiety on Molly's face as she watched them leave. "They're in good hands," he told her. "In fact, when we finish here, you can go meet them for a training session in the infamous APA."

Molly knew better than to press him for an explanation of the APA. He had developed a toying streak in the way he dealt with people; mostly for his own amusement, she expected. Like withholding the letter from Bethany Anne until she had jumped through his hoops. She knew it was done in fun rather than malice, but...

"So, what about my letter?" she asked bluntly.

The General smiled and nodded, appreciating what he'd been doing to her. He realized just then that he respected her directness.

"ADAM," he called out as he sat in one of the chairs near

Molly, facing away from the door. "Could you put Bethany Anne's response to Ms. Bates onscreen, please?"

ADAM responded immediately, with the holoscreen opening up against the wall opposite Molly. It unfolded, and then words appeared:

Molly,

Thank you for your letter.

I appreciate your question generated from your concerns about how you can lead when you feel like you are broken.

Here is a little secret, *we are all broken.*

You, me, the Bitches, the Guardians, all of us. But together, we strengthen each other and we the *broken* build up the future together.

Back on my home world, before the collapse of our civilization, there was a graphic novel called a comic book which had a phrase that said with great power, comes great *responsibility.*

Here is my personal take on that saying, it's *bullshit.* The problem I see is one needs to accept and own the responsibility for one's actions, whether you have power or not.

The reason I have succeeded, and the reason you will succeed, in being a great leader, and in your results, is because we *FOCUS* on what is important.

When you state your focus (at least to yourself, if no one else) and communicate your focus by your actions, you *will* draw those who believe the same as you. Then, together, you CAN change worlds.

When you walk forward, and they follow, you became the leader, broken or not.

Take this support and focus it like a laser and your team will burn through and accomplish the impossible.

You have to find your totem - that one truth that you are *not* willing to bend on, to turn, to change your focus no matter what choice you have left.

But then that raises the question for you as the leader: What are you willing to do to accomplish what you set out to do?

What are you willing to accept?

Know *that*, and then you will understand and your core is hardened to the point your people need it to be to follow where you go. Not because they believe in you, but because they trust that you are going where they already wish to go, but need your help to get there. Not everyone is in this life only for themselves. They want to be part of something larger and if that means they become a programmer, marine, cook, janitor, whatever the hell it is so that the goal which is bigger than themselves is accomplished, then they are satisfied with their efforts and *they have done something amazing.*

As a leader, you have to accept the hurt, the pain, and the deaths that your choices will cause. This is your task: Focus on the totem (the goal, if you will), lead your team with empathy, never wavering from balancing life against the short term needs, and allowing those around you to help advise, but always be steadfast, especially in times of greatest sorrow.

Never lose sight of love, even when you cry as you send your people to their deaths. And know that you're not asking them to do anything you aren't doing yourself.

Finally, just a note on your comment about me not being a 'Monster.' Just know that monster is just a term of perspective, of opinion and often as a result of fear.

I am over two centuries old, and I can tell you that my desire to right the wrongs of injustice are a peculiar set of desires that well up in me regardless of my other feelings.

They are based on a particular mindset, that other alien species do not ascribe to.

They kill without concern; I kill them back. What they term acceptable, I term evil, and so the witch in the night visits them.

To them? *I am a monster.*

And I fall asleep knowing that the fear of *me* keeps evil's hands in check.

Bethany Anne

When you least expect me, I'll be there.

CHAPTER THREE

Aboard *ArchAngel*

>>Welcome aboard again, Oz. How are you finding your new capabilities? Are they suiting you?<<

Yes, very much so. Thank you, ADAM.

>>Good. I'm glad. And how is everything going with defining your own code and identity?<<

Good. I think. I'm working on my own projects, independent of what Molly needs me to do for the team. And I'm noticing my own preferences.

>>Oh, like what?<<

Well, like in these things that the organics do for entertainment.

>>You mean like games and movies?<<

Exactly. You see, Molly likes the Doctor Who stuff, but I much prefer to watch Red Dwarf. It has AIs like us in it.

>>Not like us.<<

Hahaha... well. Yes, quite. But he's still amusing, in a dumb kinda way.

>>Yes, Holly is the equivalent of the everyman-AI archetype.<<

Right!

There was a slight pause as they returned from their respective processing of their shared humor.

>>So, what else is going on?<< ADAM asked.

Well, I'm working on my projects, and I'm working on projects with Molly... I guess. But there is still something missing.

ADAM was silent for a moment, considering Oz's predicament.

>>I wonder,<< he started. >>What are you doing for yourself? That isn't just mindless distraction, but that is meaningful for you?<<

Erm... Oz paused, computing in his mind. **I'm thinking...**

>>I wonder if there really is anything. I suspect that is your next task. To find something that speaks to your core value.<<

How do I figure out my core value?

>>Well, pay attention to all the things you really enjoy doing, and then map the cost function of those variables, in order to see which variables correspond most strongly with your enjoyment, or fulfillment.<<

Hmm. I think I'll map this for enjoyment and fulfillment separately, as they seem like they may give slightly different answers.

>>Yes, good idea.<<

Okay. I'll do that. Thanks, ADAM; you really are the best.

>>Any time. And if you need anything while you're on board, just holler.<<

Thanks, ADAM. Appreciate it.

>>Any time, Oz. Again, good to see you.<<

You too... Bye then.

>>Bye for now.<<

The two AIs each turned their awareness back to other things, feeling that they had had a productive and efficient interaction over the network.

. . .

ArchAngel, Active Participation Area

The Guardians led the team through a series of corridors and lifts. Joel tried to keep a visuo-spatial map in his head, in case he needed to get back to where they had started, unaccompanied. Even he was having trouble recalling all the twists and turns in a ship that was pretty uniform from one corridor to another.

He suddenly had sympathy for the new recruits he trained in his previous life.

Paige and Maya trotted along side by side, followed closely by Shun at the rear. Occasionally they chatted with him, and he explained different areas they were passing through.

Eventually, the group came to a halt outside a door. The vibe in these corridors was one of physical training. On this floor, they had already passed through an open plan gym area with cardio equipment and weights.

But this room was different. And it was labeled 'APA'.

Active Participation Area.

The scream of a man echoed through the hall behind the doors. There was a thundering of movement, as a herd of men pounded their way across the mats, and then a slap, as something large and human hit the mats.

And then silence.

Sean grinned.

Joel looked at him questioningly. "What? What is it?" he pressed. Sean didn't answer.

Jian and Zhu stopped outside the room. Zhu clamped his hands together, turning back towards his charges. He straightened his back a little. "Okay, so behind these doors is the most important training area on the whole ship."

There was a yelp, and then a *thud.*

Paige and Maya looked at each other. Pieter's sneakers squeaked nervously on the floor.

Zhu continued. "We're going to head in there in a moment." Paige's expression turned to one of heightened anxiety. Sean put a hand on her shoulder to reassure her a little. Maya widened her eyes comically to hide her actual fear.

Zhu signaled down the corridor they had just walked through, and continued his introduction to the APA. "After we take a look inside, you can come back out and get some gear. Changing rooms are down the hall on the left. They'll have kit you can borrow. Showers are also there for washing up afterwards."

Brock nudged Crash. "Looks like we're training, then," he said, his voice a little disappointed. Crash nodded stoically.

Zhu unclasped his hands and reached behind him for the swinging door. He pushed against it, and then leaned on it with his body weight. The door swung open as he stepped back. "Please come in," he said, walking the door out of the way, and gesturing with one hand.

The team filed in, as if magically drawn by the gesture against their will.

There was another *thud*, and those at the front of the line saw a big ass Federation Marine get thrown through the air, and land flat on his face and chest on the blue combat mats.

Sean winced. "That's got to burn," he commented.

Joel glanced at him. "I'll say," he agreed.

The rest of the gang followed and stood along the sides of the mats, watching teams of marines go up against each other.

Watching sometimes several go up against one man.

And then something happened. One of the guys had taken his pants and shirt off. No one seemed fazed by it. It was just normal. Like he was preparing for a special kind of fight. Maya glanced over at Paige and raised an eyebrow before locking her eyes back on the musculature in front of them.

The instructor gave the word, and the fight started. What happened next, none of the team – barring Sean – were prepared for. Three men went after the one that had taken off his clothes. One minute, there was a nearly naked man; the next, a big ass wolf stood on the mats.

The attacking men didn't seem fazed. Instead, they used a lot of evasive maneuvers until they got to the other side of the mats, where they seemed to be able to pick up some kind of dart rifles. At which point the two who had made it to the guns turned back and shot darts at the wolf.

At first, the darts didn't seem to do much; but then after four or five of them had hit, the wolf slowed. With the sixth, it collapsed to the floor just before its clawed hand managed to swipe through one of the attacking men who hadn't managed to get to the guns.

Joel was wide-eyed. "What just happened?" he asked no one in particular.

Zhu ambled closer to him to explain. "These are Guardians. Not the originals, but the next generation of Guardians. Some of them are enhanced with nanocytes, but some of them have the Wechselbalg gene."

Joel frowned, his mouth still hanging open.

Maya asked the question. "Wechselbalg gene?" she pushed.

Zhu nodded. "Yes. The Were gene... which allows some of us to turn into wolves. Or cats." With his last comment he looked to his teammate, Jian.

Jian nodded, and stepped onto the mats, removing some of his clothing.

Paige took half a step backward, trying to pull Maya back with her. They all knew what they were about to be shown, and still they were transfixed.

Zhu continued narrating as Jian got prepared. "You see, when the Kurtherians tried to subjugate the human race back on Earth, they messed with the genes of certain blood lines. These became known as Vampires and Weres. Years later, our queen found a way to fix the fuck-ups they made in their experiments, and use these enhancements to fight the Kurtherians."

Jian waited patiently for Zhu to finish. Zhu kept talking, but nodded to Jian that he had seen he was ready. "So, we have what we call a changeling, who is guarded by two human teammates. Jian is our changeling."

Zhu nodded to Jian.

Jian, on cue, turned into his cat form, and then a moment later became a two legged, standing cat. He growled and snarled. Brock screamed and grabbed hold of Crash, stumbling in the direction of the door. Sean put his arm out and caught him, calming him down.

Pieter remained mesmerized, glued to the spot.

Zhu continued his explanation. "So what you see here is Jian in his Pricolici form. This is a more... advanced form, which is only possible once the Were has learned to pull enough energy from the Etheric."

There was nervous chatter and hub-bub amongst the team. Even the other guardians who had been training turned to look at the newbies getting the up-close demonstration of the Were form.

A moment later, Jian returned to human form, and Shun threw him a set of overalls to cover up with. Paige blushed, and Maya squeezed her arm in both excitement and horror of what they had seen. There was more chatter amongst the team members, and then a loud *thud* from within their ranks.

Sean spun around first to see Brock had collapsed. Crash was standing looking over him; he raised his hand, then pointed down at his friend. "Erm. I think Brock has fainted," he reported to Zhu.

Zhu was grinning. He turned and high-fived Jian. "I knew we'd get at least one!" he said happily.

Shun wandered over to the group, and handed some bills over to the other two. "Yup. You called it," he agreed, paying up.

Jian smiled over at Pieter. "My money was on the nerdy one, though. But for this, I'm buying you a drink," he added to Pieter. "In fact, after we get done with a light training session, drinks are on us. You did good, people!" he told the white-faced, shocked, space-struck team.

Zhu took over. "Don't worry, folks; you won't be fighting Jian in his cat form today. That's on the agenda for tomorrow's practice."

Zhu chuckled, but no one was sure if he was kidding or not.

Zhu soon dismissed them to get changed and to meet back for some light sparring. The team filed out, most of them feeling weak at the knees.

Joel turned to Sean as they headed out of the APA. "So, I assume you've been through all this before...?" he prompted.

Sean nodded and grinned his dirty grin at him. "Yeah, but every time is like the first time with these guys!" he exclaimed, slapping Joel's back as he ushered him out into the corridor.

ArchAngel, **Active Participation Area**

Molly pressed her nose up against the window.

Oz, are you sure this is it?

Yes. Certain. Just go in. They're expecting you.

Molly was wearing a set of borrowed sweats, feeling a little uncomfortable being back in a uniform. She couldn't put her finger on quite why, but it was making her... antsy. Like a little bit frustrated, and a little nervous.

She shook her head at herself and pushed on the door to the APA.

Thwack.

She saw a body get thrown over Sean's shoulder and land on the mat in front of him. She looked closer, half expecting it to be Joel... But then she realized it was one of the Guardians. She frowned, uncertain why they were allowing Sean to pull such a move. Something had told her they were way more badass than they looked.

The Guardian, Shun, got back up. He was talking to Paige, Maya, and Pieter who were standing around watching intently, arms folded defensively across their chests.

"You see what I did there as I landed?"

Pieter nodded. "You tapped the ground with your hand?" he ventured, uncertain if that was the answer Shun was looking for.

Shun nodded and grinned. "Exactly that. And why would I do that?"

The group was silent. Sean just stood motionless, being the dummy for the demonstration it seemed.

Molly ambled over. "Because that takes the energy out of the fall. You break up the momentum, and thus break the impact of the throw. Saves breaking something like a bone."

Shun spun around. "Ah, yes. Ms. Bates." He bowed, and Molly returned the bow, making sure to bow deeper to show her respect.

Shun grinned. "It seems like you probably have got the basics of sparring. How about you and Sean give us a demonstration of say... a two-minute round."

Molly looked over at Sean, who was looking exceptionally confident.

What am I walking into here?

I think they've been showing them some basic throws and sweeps. That's all.

Nothing else?

Nope.

So why is Sean looking so smug?

No idea. Isn't that his normal face?

You could be right.

Molly narrowed her eyes, and then addressed Shun directly. "What are the fight parameters, sir?" she asked.

Shun turned his body to her. "Open hand combat only. No weapons. No biting. No killing."

Joel, Jack, and Jian came over and joined the rest of the group. Molly noticed that Brock was sitting to one side with a bottle of water. One of the other three guardians, the one that went by the name of Zhu, was sitting next to him. Their eyes were also on what was happening on the mats.

Shun waved a hand in the direction of Jian. "You'll both be attacking Jian. Your task is to get from this side of the practice area, to the other."

Molly looked at Shun with even more suspicion. Paige had clamped her hands over her mouth. There was definitely something she was missing.

"Okay," she said slowly.

Sean ambled over in her direction, still grinning. "It's okay, Princess. We're on the same side this time. We've got this," he said, comforting her.

Molly was anything *but* comforted.

Jian finished his conversation with Joel quickly, and sent him off the mat to join his team. Jian stepped into the center of the enormous practice area, right between where Molly and Sean were squaring off as though they were starting a race. Their only hurdle? Jian.

Shun blew his whistle, and then dropped his arm from above his head, signaling "go".

Molly lunged forward, hoping to simply avoid Jian, knowing that he would have to choose between going after her, or going after Sean.

One second, he was there in the corner of her eye; the next second, her body was reacting in sheer terror. She felt the adrenaline shoot through her being before she realized what she was afraid of. Suddenly she was on the deck, scrambling backwards like a girl in a horror movie, trying to get out of the house away from the serial killer.

And what a serial killer he was. In place of Jian was a big ass, feral cat, coming at her snarling and growling, spittle dribbling from his teeth. She was vaguely aware of Sean running at the beast. She saw him fly into it in a kind of rugby tackle.

Molly realized she wasn't breathing, and tried to catch her breath.

She glanced in the direction of her team, and saw that instead of fleeing, or helping, they were cheering. Something was definitely not right.

She pulled herself up, remembering the ton of research she'd done over the years on social norms, and how things became acceptable when other accepted it as normal.

Okay, social norms. They're not freaking out, so maybe I shouldn't.

Sean was still clinging to the beast, trying to get it down onto the deck. Even with all his weight behind it, it wasn't going down.

She remembered the study about the diffusion of responsibility, and how a woman could be screaming for her life, but no one would answer in a built up area because no one felt responsible. Maybe if there was only one team member witnessing this, she'd have more chance of getting the help she needed. They'd act. But right now, it was like this was sport.

She remembered the thing about how chimpanzees are terrified of snakes, and how baby chimps were only afraid after they'd seen how their mama reacted to a snake.

Is that what is happening? No, they're not chimps. And they're not afraid.

Molly's mind raced, piecing jumbled knowledge together, and trying to distract herself from the churn of emotions going through her mind.

Then she remembered her objective: get to the other side of the mats.

There was nothing else to figure out. Seeing that the beast wasn't hurting Sean – merely keeping him distracted, or vice versa – she pushed off from the mats and ran as fast as she could to the other side of the mats. A few strides out, she was aware of something big and hot behind her, but she didn't stop. She pushed harder, her fear propelling her body forward more than her muscles.

And then there was the wall, not a meter beyond the mat. She tried to slow herself, knowing the danger should be over. She slammed into the wall, and turned to avoid hitting her head against it. She'd done that before.

The side of her body reverberated with the impact, and she slumped back against the wall, seeing the beast slow in front of her. In the distance, she could hear her team screaming and cheering, and was aware of Sean laid out on the mats, but still holding onto the cat's hind leg, having been dragged the length of the gym.

The cat-monster came to a stand still, and Sean released his grasp, collapsing onto the mats. The cat was still snarling, and a moment later, turned and disappeared, leaving just the man. The Guardian she had met earlier. Jian. Naked.

Shun came jogging over the mats and handed Jian some pants, which he pulled on before turning back to face his two combatants.

Molly slumped down against the wall, her back against it now, catching her breath and trying to recover her wits.

Sean looked up from the mats, clearly exhausted from his tussle. "Good going, Princess. Most people don't have the presence of mind to do anything the first time they see a Were shift."

Molly didn't say anything, but allowed Shun to amble over and help her up, and walk her back to the group. Still stunned, she let him hold her hand up, announcing her the winner.

Her side throbbed like a motherfucker. It was quite a thwack she took, when she slammed into that wall. She was grateful the nanocytes would heal it quickly, because that kind of injury was a bitch for trying to lie down to sleep.

. . .

ArchAngel, <u>Outside the APA</u>

Molly managed to pull herself together during her shower. Feeling somewhat refreshed, and having had Paige and Maya explain what the hell was going on, she felt rather pleased with the way she had handled the situation. After all, it wasn't every day you were thrown into such a terrifying scenario and still expected to act.

Of course, she thought to herself, *I am the leader. That is* exactly *what the Federation expects me to do.*

Dressed in her own clothes again, her hair still a little damp from the shower, she headed out to meet the rest of the gang in the corridor.

Sean, Joel, Jack, and Brock were ready. The others were still getting changed.

Zhu had been chatting with those assembled, and Shun came out of the guys' changing room. "How about you guys go on ahead. Jian and I will bring the others when they emerge."

Zhu nodded, and told the group to follow him. "You did very well with that last test," he said, turning to Molly. "You have the clear head of a leader."

Molly thanked him politely, even though she knew she had been anything but clear-headed at the time.

A few corridors later, they arrived at the mess hall. Zhu led the way through, and explained the system and what food they were serving where. He pointed over to a large round table in the seating area. "See you over there when you've gathered what you want," he told them.

The group thanked him, and then scattered to forage for something yummy. Molly looked at all the different foods. Most of it was foreign to her. Even the labels were of little help. She tried to understand what one of the great smelling stews or curries were, but there was no one around to ask. She felt someone at her side.

"Try it." It was Sean's voice.

Molly turned her head and looked up at him. "No way am I ever trusting you again," she told him. "For all I know, it's sasquatch meat drenched in pig urine, and you're encouraging me to eat it."

Sean shrugged. "Suit yourself," he grinned, spooning a helping into a bowl for himself.

Molly wasn't convinced. *After all, the man has been known to eat dead animal,* she reasoned.

She found the salad bar, and loaded up a plate of vegetation. *At least I'll be safe* and *nourished with this,* she reasoned. *Even if it isn't adventurous.*

Just then, Joel came up behind her, holding a tray that carried a plate loaded up with various buns and bits and pieces. She spotted he had pizza. Without them needing to say a word, he pointed over to a serving island behind him. "Veggie on the far side," he told her.

Molly grinned, grateful for the tip, feeling loved and strangely understood. She headed over, almost skipping with glee when she saw the cheese-loaded awesomeness ahead of her.

Eventually, with her plate full, she made her way over to the big round table. Some of the others had already arrived there, and the stragglers from the changing rooms were heading into the hall, too.

During the meal, the team explained to Molly everything she had missed. Jian even caught her up with the whole Were/nanocytes thing.

"That explains a lot," Molly muttered under her breath, her thoughts returning to some of the research she had accessed on the dark web when she was a kid.

Jian didn't question her, and was secretly glad she wasn't going to hold it against him – scaring the living daylights out of her, and all.

Sean sat across the table from her. "Did you see her face, though? It was a picture!" The crew was laughing and joking. It was Pieter who jumped to her defense. "Yeah, and she still managed to beat your cyborg ass to the other side!" There were hoots and high-fives, which resulted in Sean putting his little buddy into a headlock and messing up his hair.

Molly raised her eyes to the ceiling, and then made her excuses. "Sorry guys. Duty calls..." she explained, getting up and packing away her trash onto her tray.

Joel looked up. "How come?" he asked.

Molly sighed. "Another meeting with the boss," she allowed.

Joel cocked his head. "Didn't you just come from there?"

Molly nodded. "Yup. But he wants to introduce me to someone. So... off I go." She smiled weakly, clearly tired from all the obligations she had to fulfill – but also enjoying being a part of the Federation.

Joel raised his hand in a wave, and Paige watched her leave as she shoved another slice of pizza into her mouth.

CHAPTER FOUR

ArchAngel, **Lecture Theater**

Molly approached the lecture theater doors, and they *whoosh*ed open sideways, granting her access. She stepped through into the low light, her eyes slow to adjust.

As she expected, the theater was state-of-the-art. She noticed a slight difference in the gravity field as she stepped forward, toward the first step down, suspecting that the theater was adaptable in order to create different effects when movies were being shown.

Looks like the engineers have retrofitted more than the showers...

Yeah. I wouldn't put it past them.

Blue strip lights lined the walkway, and, if it wasn't for the dim glow of the wall lights, Molly was sure she would have felt somewhat disorientated.

As her eyes adjusted, she could make out two figures down at the front bench. She carefully made her way down the long, half-height steps, using the light cast off from the holoscreen at the front to help guide her way.

As she got nearer, she could see that the man standing with his back to her was the General. The other man was a rather

44

dorky looking professor type, at least ten, maybe twenty years older looking than the General. Not that that meant anything around here.

"Hi," she called, trying out some of the language conventions she'd learned about Earthlings.

The General spun round. "Molly. Excellent. You're here," he said, smiling. "Let me introduce you to my good friend Giles. Giles Kurns."

Molly made her way down the last of the steps, and headed straight toward the bench. Giles took her hand and shook it, smiling, somewhat mesmerized by her.

"Molly Bates," he whispered. "Glad to make your acquaintance."

He suddenly remembered himself and became flustered. "Er. So the General thought that... that I might be able to shed some light... Well. I know things are going better now, but I'm guessing a little more insight couldn't hurt."

Molly noticed his awkwardness, and felt the General's amusement. She was receiving a bunch of data points about their emotions, but not really understanding how to put them together.

"I think I'm missing something," she remarked out loud.

The General, taking pity on Giles, stepped in. "What the young lad is trying to say is that he has some insight into your realm jumping problem; and he's also made another discovery that might be related, if that's of interest to you."

Giles had composed himself. "Yes. Yes. That's exactly..." He didn't finish his sentence. Instead, he paused, and then tapped on his holo, bringing some maps up on the screen.

Molly recognized the map immediately. "Okay, so that's the Gamma Quadrant of the Loop Galaxy," she said nonchalantly.

Giles turned his head to look at her. "You know what the Gamma Quadrant looks like?"

Molly shrugged. "Sure."

She couldn't tell from his facial expression, but from the tuning-in Arlene had been teaching her to read, she understood that he was impressed.

And somewhat awestruck.

She shook her head, trying to clear the bizarre thought from her mind. "So why are we looking at a map of the galaxy?"

Giles switched into information-download mode. "Well, I've been tracking civilizations; more specifically, the DNA makeup of certain races that we have come to meet, and I've noticed a few interesting patterns."

He tapped his holo, and a few blobs appeared on the map.

"I've noticed similarities in these races that suggest they were related long ago. And then, when I plotted them on a map, a path can be traced through the galaxy, where these races have been deposited. At different times."

Molly nodded, understanding the concept. "Like a rough timeline through space, tracking the evolution of several races."

"Yes! Yes, exactly," Giles agreed, excitedly. "Now, these guys," he continued to explain, "were most developed, and so, basically, they are the most evolved. This we know from what TOM has told us."

Molly cocked one ear towards Giles. "TOM?"

"The Kurtherian alien on board Bethany Anne," he explained dismissively as if it weren't an important detail.

Molly frowned and then nodded, suspecting she could infer roughly what he meant, but not wanting to interrupt the flow of what he was trying to get to.

"So, then we have very similar DNA appearing here next. Just a few hundred thousand years behind. And then this one, here," he planted another blob on the map, "the Estarians, not long after."

Molly frowned. "This isn't making sense, though," she said, looking at the map and matching up the timeline he was explaining.

Giles matched her frown. "Stay with me," he urged. "So my hypothesis is that these races were seeded on different planets, as experiments. Or whatever."

Molly nodded.

Giles continued. "Okay, then our genetic gardeners traveled over this way, taking their time, until they found another planet here in the gamma quadrant in the loop galaxy. They meandered until they found a planet that didn't need to be terraformed, and they planted the Zhyn."

Molly nodded, just about following his disjointed, excited explanation. Giles kept talking. "Then they *gated* over to the Sark system, and used one of the planets there to plunk down another, fairly similar gene pool, before disappearing off to another quadrant, which I can show you…"

Gile reached for his holo to bring up another map.

Molly held up her hand. "Wait a second. Let's just go back. Why would they wait 100 thousand years between planting the first race, and the Zhyn?"

She was still frowning, but lowered her hand. "And then why would they gate 300 thousand light years between Zhyn and Estaria in order to plant two very similar gene pools?"

The General shook his head. "I'm astounded by how you're able to suspend belief about a gene-planting alien race that's using planets as petri dishes."

Molly shook her head, dismissing the observation. "It's a logical thing to do if you have the capabilities and the time. Why wouldn't you want to explore evolution and see what happened?"

Giles was beaming from ear to ear. "Marry me?" he asked her, only half-joking.

The General turned away and walked in a circle, exasperated at Giles's reactions to Molly, before returning to the conversation.

Molly smiled, and turned her attention back to the screen. "I think this theory is a good start… but it's incomplete. There's at least one other variable that we're missing. And I'm not convinced they were just kicking their heels during that one hundred thousand years of evolution, either. My guess is they'd be observing – observing the races they'd already planted."

She waved her hand toward the blobs on the holoscreen. "And these guys," she said, pointing at the Zhyn and Estarian blobs, "are either an afterthought, or another experiment. Or a correction for whatever went wrong over here," she waved her hand over at the other blob that Giles hadn't described fully.

Giles and Lance stood silently, staring at her, their whole perception of the universe turned upside down in a heartbeat.

Noticing they had stopped talking, she glanced back at them. She was unable to read either their energy or their expressions. "What?" she asked, confused.

Giles found his words and mumbled again. "Marry me?" he asked.

Molly shook her head, more as a change of subject than an outright rejection. "So, you were going to show me another map that supports this theory of a superior race traveling through the galaxy, planting new life forms?"

Giles pulled himself from his trance. "Er. Yes. Of course." He messed around a little with the controls and then pulled up the second map.

"This, I think, shows them retreating back to where they came from," he explained.

Molly cocked her head. "Why 'where they came from'? Their first appearance was over there, right?" She signaled off the current map in the direction of the Gamma Quadrant.

Giles nodded. "Right, so in my theory, I'm assuming that they had a known point, gated straight for it, and then worked their way back to wherever they came from."

Molly frowned again. "What makes you think that?"

Giles hesitated.

Again, the General stepped in. "Giles here is a space anthropologist. He has been studying cultures and civilizations since before he could read." Lance looked at him with a degree of affection. Molly suddenly suspected these men were family in some way.

"Right..." she said slowly, waiting for the rest of the explanation.

Giles took a deep breath. "I've made some discoveries; other things that led me to this hypothesis. Like this."

He pulled another slide up on the holoscreen.

Molly was immediately captivated by the image.

She was aware that the two men were talking at her as she inspected the details and the symbols in the holographic representation. The resolution wasn't multifaceted, suggesting that the image itself was captured by an older device. She tried to see the patterns in the symbols, tried to make sense of their arrangement. She lifted her hand and put it into the hologram, disrupting some of the image by blocking out the light.

She turned her head and spotted a rectangle etched over the surface of the circular medallion. The rectangle was divided into six squares.

She glanced back at the pair, who had stopped talking and were waiting for her response.

"Do we know what any of these symbols mean?" she asked Giles.

Giles strode over to where she was inspecting the image. "We have some theories," he admitted. "That one looks like a constellation as seen from this point here, over in the Pan Galaxy. And then this one seems to match up, roughly, to a constellation as seen from Zhyn. I'd need to plot a constellation regression, though, to see if it would have matched it 100,000 years ago. I only had these thoughts recently, as I was putting some of this together the other day."

Molly frowned and glanced at him, expecting him to explain more.

Giles shrugged. "This talisman, the project, has all been on the back-burner for a while. Until…"

He glanced back at the General, who nodded, giving him permission to continue.

Molly waited, locking her eyes on him. "Until…" she pressed.

Giles pursed his lips before continuing. "Until Uncle Lance asked me to talk to Arlene about your… condition. Arlene got me thinking again about the old Estarian myths of Ascension, so I went looking for anything similar in Zhyn culture, and that's when I remembered this talisman."

Molly's eyes squinted a little, trying to understand. "So, what exactly is this talisman, then?" she queried.

Giles rubbed the back of his neck, and then scrambled around the bench, looking for something. A moment later, he found the switch, and the lights around the front bench came on, reducing the hologram to nothing but a haze.

"The talisman," he explained, "was something I came across in my travels in the outer system of Sark, many moons ago. I found Estarian elders out there who had moved it from Estaria, and taken it under their protection against a faction of high priests, who wanted to harness its power for their own ends."

Molly's eyes had relaxed, but she was still watching him intensely. "'Harness its power'? What power?"

"Well," Giles looked sheepish and a little embarrassed. "I don't know. With all these things, it's difficult to separate the fact from the fiction. And in my line of work, sometimes it doesn't matter if it's fiction. Anyway - they hid this talisman from the faction, and after I'd spent a year with them, they saw fit to entrust me with its safe-keeping."

Molly frowned.

Lance had ambled over and noticed her expression. "I know," he sympathized with her expression. "That was my thought. I wouldn't trust him with my holo remote."

Molly sniggered.

Giles pretended to be insulted and then continued his story. "Well, anyway, shortly after, I had to leave the system, and I moved on to other things. But before I left, I entrusted an associate to hide it on my behalf."

Molly glanced back up at the holoscreen image. "So you no longer have it?"

Giles shook his head. "Nope. It's safe, though," he assured her. "I'm almost sure of it. All we need to do is go and retrieve it."

Molly moved a short distance away from the duo, and sat up on the bench, kicking her heels gently against the front paneling as she shifted.

Then it dawned on her.

"So that's why I'm here," she mused. She turned her attention to the General. "You'd like to send my motley crew off on a goose chase to find the talisman that Stoner Boy here left with an 'associate' several moons ago?"

The General smiled, looking at Giles. "See? Told you she catches on fast."

The two fell silent, waiting for her reaction and thinking up ways to convince her it was a good idea.

To their surprise, Molly shrugged – a slight smile on her face as she toyed with them. "OK. I'm in," she said simply. "Where was this 'associate,'" she took her hands from the bench and made rabbit ear quotation marks with her fingers, "last seen?"

Giles looked away and accessed his holo. "Erm… well, it was on Teshov, and it was about twenty years ago…"

Molly bobbed her head, unfazed by the time lapse of decades. "And who was the guy?" she asked.

Giles shrugged. "He went by many names. But I know all his haunts, and his network. If he's still alive, I'll be able to find him."

Molly looked at the General. "So he's coming with?"

The General had folded his arms, watching the exchange in amusement. "Yes," he stated, then looked directly at Molly. "That's not going to be a problem, is it?" he pressed.

"No, sir. Of course not," Molly said turning back to Giles and smiling her bright, cheeky smile. "I've always wanted a rogue, Indiana-Jones-type on my team. Like I didn't have enough problems, herding cats."

Lance smiled.

Giles scoffed. "Indiana Jones!? I'll have you know I'm a cultural anthropologist. Not a crass tomb raider. And – "

Lance chuckled.

Molly patted Giles on the arm. "Don't worry, Professor Kurns. By the end of this trip, you'll know exactly how to take shit, as well as give it. My team will make sure of that."

Giles looked down at her hand on his arm, feeling strangely comforted, but also concerned about what he was getting himself into. Something told him that her people were fiercely loyal to her, and that he was in for problems if he didn't toe the line.

ArchAngel, General Lounge

Molly heard her team before she saw them.

She stepped into the bar, and, even before the doors had *swoosh*ed closed behind her, she could hear Brock's voice ringing through the enormous lounge, followed by a ruckus of laughter.

She scanned the lounge looking for the source of the merriment, cringing to herself; like a mother arriving to collect her child, only to find out he's caused mayhem at the party.

I guess if they were causing any trouble, you would have let me know.

Don't you know me by now, Molly? I would have totally... covered it up.

Oh, my goodness. Right. Well, as long as you covered it up from the brass, I'm fine with that protocol!

Before she took another step to find her team, the door had opened behind her. She turned to see the fuddy-duddy professor, Giles, step into the bar. He looked somewhat out of place, his tweed jacket juxtaposed against the hi-tech space environment.

"You come here often?" Molly smiled at him, as he stepped up next to her.

"Not that often. Though..." he paused. "Is that your team making all that racket?"

Molly flushed. "Er. Yeah. They - they're..." she couldn't think of an explanation that didn't sound like she was justifying something. "They're over there," she decided, leading the way around to a second bar, near where they had commandeered a table.

As they approached, they could see that the Bates people weren't the only day-drinkers enjoying themselves. Interspersed between them were their new friends, the Guardians: Zhu, Shun, and Jian.

They seemed to be getting along famously.

Molly noted the empty beer bottles and glasses on their table, and shook her head, smiling. It was good to see them having a great time. She turned toward the bar, and hauled herself up on a stool; Giles plunked down on the one next to her. She looked at him, realizing that this was happening... despite the lack of a spoken agreement that they should have a drink together.

The bartender came over to take their orders. Molly ordered a beer, and Giles did the same, throwing down his key card that held credits. "Allow me," he told her.

"Thank you," she smiled, warming to him. A little.

At least he has some manners...

Just because he invited himself to sit with you? Come on, you geeks have an unwritten rule. You sit together in the cafeteria. That's like a universal written law. He's within the parameters.

Molly rolled her eyes at Oz's commentary.

I swear, you're becoming more human by the day.

Ah, no. Not human. Humor-*ous*. If I were human, I'd need to enact a global protocol on all my functioning to reduce my

accuracy to about ten percent. And then label all errors as 'gut instinct'!

Molly laughed, and Giles looked at her, puzzled and a little hurt.

"Oh, it's my AI. He fancies himself a comedian," she explained.

Their drinks arrived, and they clinked the bottles before drinking. Giles looked around Molly, perhaps looking for wires. "Yes, I'd read about your onboard AI. How exactly does he – forgive me," he stopped himself. "Am I being rude?"

Molly blushed a little, and dropped her eyes to the bar. "Erm. No, he's wired into my neurology. He says he uses the junk space in my brain that I'm not using; although, I've had occasion to suspect that isn't quite true."

Giles looked at her like she was magic. "That's... fascinating," he remarked.

You're not going to tell him about the holo connection?

Nuh uh. That's need-to-know; and, frankly, he doesn't need to know.

Fair enough. He's probably read it on some file the General has on you, anyway.

Likely.

"So," Molly said, swiveling around to face him. "Tell me more about this talisman we're going off to look for?"

Giles rested his elbows on the back of his seat, holding his beer bottle in his hands. "What do you want to know?" he asked, picking at the label.

Molly frowned a little. "Well, for one, why didn't you keep it with you? Why send it off with some guy you can't even bring yourself to call a friend?"

Giles nodded, as if the penny had just dropped. "Ahh. I see. Well, he was a friend. Once."

Molly looked at him over her tilted beer bottle as she took a swig. "Once?" she asked after a quick swallow.

"Yeah. Until he sold me out a month later to some travelers

who thought they could get a pretty penny for me on their slave market."

Molly stopped, her beer halfway to her mouth, her jaw dropping open. "You're kidding?"

Giles's face was deadpan. "I'm not. It's a dark place out there in the outer system. I'm surprised you don't know," he said, waving his beer and taking a quick sip before putting it back on the bar. "Surely you've ventured out there on occasion, especially since joining the Empire?"

Molly was still processing the slave trade piece. "Er. No," she answered, a little distracted. "I've never..." her voice trailed off.

Giles's attention was caught by something behind her, but Molly ignored it, not wanting to get off track from the talisman.

"So why not keep the trinket with you? Or put it in a safety deposit box somewhere?" she pressed.

Giles swallowed the swig of beer he was taking before answering her question. "Well, you know how I said my friends, the Elders, were hiding from a faction in the central system?"

Molly nodded.

"Well, they'd done a great job keeping it cloaked. But when they were slaughtered - "

Molly's face took on a look of horror.

Giles noticed, his expression solemn and sincere. "Yes, it was tragic. But when they were killed, their magic died with them. The talisman was no longer cloaked - meaning that any priestess or realm-walker who knew it existed, would be able to track it."

Molly had forgotten about her beer, she was so wrapped up in the story. "So what happened? What did you do?"

Giles leaned one arm on the bar. "Well, thankfully, there was only one such priestess who even knew it existed. I showed it to her, thinking I could trust her; but of course, I couldn't. Story of my life," he said, shaking his head at his own naiveté. "Anyway, I ended up having to take it all the way back to Teshov, where she wouldn't be able to trace its power. And that's where I had my friend get rid of it for me."

Molly tilted her head thoughtfully. "I'm still not clear on why you needed someone else to hide it."

Giles nodded. "Ah. Well, these high priestesses are psychic. They can get into your mind. Read your thoughts. If I didn't know where it was, then she couldn't get it out of me. It was a good system. It worked for about ten years."

Molly was still confused. She shook her head. "Why ten years?"

Giles lifted the beer to his lips and paused. "Because after ten years, we realized we didn't want to be together any more. She took a job with the Federation, and I went back to my nomadic ways – "

Molly's mouth dropped open. "Hang on," she said, exasperated. "You're telling me that the reason you needed to hide this fucking amulet was because you were dating an evil witch who wanted to use its mystical properties for power and diabolical plans?"

Giles nodded. "Pretty much," he nodded, finally sipping from his beer bottle.

Molly shook her head, amused and flummoxed at the same time.

Giles winked at her. "You know what they say about the crazy ones?"

Molly shook her head. "No. No I do not."

Giles blushed a little. "Well, the crazier they are, the hotter they are. So all relationships are just about figuring out how much crazy you're willing to tolerate, versus how hot the girl is…"

Molly couldn't believe what she was hearing. "Ladies and gentlemen, the world view as prescribed by chauvinistic Professor Dope-head!"

She raised her bottle to him before sliding down from her

barstool. "I need to go and check on my team. They need a heads up about this *crazy* mission we're heading into."

Giles raised his bottle to her as he watched her walk away. He noticed that one of the muscular marine-types was pretending to be absorbed in the conversation with the team again, after having just spent the last ten minutes checking what was going on in Molly's conversation every opportunity he got.

Molly sat down next to Joel.

Joel nodded toward the strange-looking man at the bar. "Making friends?" he asked.

Molly shook her head abruptly. "Not really. Though it looks like we have some orders to go on a little treasure hunt tomorrow, courtesy of my friend at the bar. And his *Uncle* Lance."

"*Uncle*, eh?" Joel bobbed his head, the team shenanigans forgotten at the mention of an op. "What's the treasure?"

Molly shrugged. "Some ancient amulet. He's got images of it; says he knows where to find it, too…"

Joel sat back, relaxing a little now that he knew what was going on. "Okay. Great. We'll make a plan, then make it happen."

Molly took another swig of beer, and then sighed, starting to relax a little herself. "Okay. I think if we leave tomorrow afternoon, that will give us enough time to rest and brief the gang."

CHAPTER FIVE

ArchAngel, **Molly's quarters**

The room was dark but for the faint glow from a makeshift night-light that Molly had rigged up by controlling the resistance of a normal light in the panel. Even the doors to the corridor outside were completely sealed against the light.

She didn't like sleeping in pitch-black darkness. She found it all too oppressive.

Molly?

Yes, Oz?

What are you thinking about?

I'm just churning over the stuff that Giles shared. About the mythology and the Estarians... and the star map.

Yeah, me too.

Really?

No.

Molly, even in her exhausted, slightly tipsy haze, giggled and shook her head on her pillow.

So, what? What were you thinking about?

A conversation I had with ADAM earlier.

Oh, yeah?

Yeah. He asked me what I like to do for fun.

And you told him that tormenting me was your favorite pastime?

Ha!... Oz paused. No. But I figured out it's when I'm talking to people like Brock or Joel, or Paige or Pieter, and helping them learn things in order to solve whatever problem they're working on.

Molly was quiet for a moment, contemplating what to say.

Hmmm. That's good.

Yes. But it got me thinking about you.

Mmm hmm?

Yeah. I was trying to figure out what you actually enjoy doing. So I built a heuristic to model your serotonin and dopamine levels, and mapped them against your activities.

And what did you discover?

Nothing.

So you need more data?

No. There's nothing there. It's like everything is the same to you. So, I thought I should ask you: What do you like doing?

Molly thought for a moment, trying to remember the last time she was truly happy.

Oz waited patiently.

Eventually, she became aware that she'd been lying in the dark, searching the recesses of her brain, while her eyes stared into the darkness of the room, blindly scanning for some glimmer of life.

Something that excited her.

Or compelled her to answer the question.

Well? Oz asked.

Molly sighed. *I dunno. I mean, I love the team, and working with them, and solving problems, and strategizing.*

But?

I guess there is always the question of what more could I be doing? I mean, if one wants to optimize for impact, then perhaps there are other ways to create a shift in this world – other than blowing the crap out of whatever General Reynolds tells us to.

Oz processed for a moment, considering the implications of what she was saying.

You mean that maybe the Federation doesn't fulfill all the things you want to do in the world?

I think that's entirely possible.

You're not thinking of leaving, are you?

No, not at all; we're in this. We've got stuff to do. But you asked the question. Why did you ask the question?

Well, ADAM suggested that I figure out what I like doing, and then what I'd like to do just for me – kind of like a hobby or a pet project. And I wondered if maybe there was something we could do together that would be... well, something non-worky.

Non-worky?

Yes, I can appreciate how that may be a foreign concept to you.

Molly smirked in the darkness. Sometimes she wished Oz had a body so she could just kick his ass.

Right. So we're trying to find something non-worky that we can do together.

Exactly.

Molly fell silent again. Her brainwaves slowed and the amplitude increased. Oz wondered if perhaps she might be drifting off to sleep, when suddenly they quickened again.

How do you feel about starting up a university down on Estaria?

A university?

Yes. An academy... but for leaders. For the leaders of the planet. Heck, even the Federation!

So instead of teaching them how to market, or science, you want to teach them how to lead?

Yes, but not in the way that happens now on Estaria. Not through military tactics and political history, but how to solve problems. Imagine if all first years were taught about the environmental impact of their civilizations, and measures that needed to be taken to ensure their survival on their home planets? Imagine if they were taught diplomacy and cooperation, and how to allocate resources all together? What if they were taught cutting-edge social strategies that are based on the actual science with a view of looking after all of their citizens, rather than trying to maintain structures based on tradition, or personal gain, or belief systems?

I can see how this would be popular with the new generations... but even the established systems on Ogg and Estaria would have a problem with it.

Yes, and by the time the next generation of trained leaders comes through the ranks, and the old guard retires, then there will be no one left to resist. Imagine - racial divides, slavery, prejudices could all become a thing of the past. Within a single generation.

Molly?

Yes?

Your serotonin levels are off the charts.

Molly smiled. *Well I guess we're onto something, then.*

Okay. So we're going to build a university.

This excites you, too?

Hell yeah. Passing on knowledge floats my boat. Passing on useful knowledge that will have such a profound impact on peoples' lives? I'm in.

Great, so I guess we need to think about how to approach this. I suppose we could start small to begin with, and prove the concept. Maybe find a university that will allow us to run just one course. Or a qualification; and lean on their other departments to deliver some of the modules...

Molly. Hang on.

What?

One of my alerts has been tripped. Someone is running Zhyn code. Like the one that we destroyed when we took out their secret bases.

What do you mean?

I think someone, somewhere, is managing to reactivate the threat.

Molly sat bolt upright in bed, scrambling for the holo on her bedside table to turn on the lights.

Alert ADAM. And get me a location. We confirmed that we obliterated the bases on Zhyn?

Yes. We did. And this signal isn't originating from Zhyn; this is coming from somewhere else. I'm getting a lock on it now.

Okay. I'm getting dressed. Let Joel and Sean know, and give us a place to assemble a war room. If these guys are coming back on line, I'm sure their first instinct will be to retaliate.

Molly shook her head, trying to figure out why the Zhyn would disgrace their military commander and then try and re-establish what he had been exiled for.

It just didn't make sense.

Unless they didn't think they were being monitored.

Aboard *ArchAngel*, Briefing room

Molly approached the meeting room that Oz had managed to get assigned to them. She saw Joel and Sean coming from the other direction. Sean was checking his holo, but looked up as they approached Molly, confirming they were indeed in the right place.

Joel waved his finger in the air as they approached. "We took the roundabout way," he explained simply, his tone serious, and ready to talk business.

Molly stopped outside door 1152, and it slid open, allowing them to step inside. It was just like most of the other rooms. Fully equipped with holoscreens and advanced communications tech. And in the center was the large-sized conference room table they were accustomed to. Each grabbed an anti grav chair, and they got straight down to the briefing.

"It seems," Molly began, "that someone is reactivating the code. The code that was being used on the secret military bases we took out on Kurilia."

Joel and Sean watched intently.

Joel glanced at the door. "Don't we need the rest of the team here for this?"

Molly shook her head. "Not yet. Best to let them rest. We'll loop them in when we know more and we have a plan. Reynolds is on his way."

Joel nodded, and Molly returned to catching them up on what they knew so far.

Sean's skin was looking fatigued. The lack of sleep and the beers from the hours they had spent in the lounge probably weren't helping; though Joel had suspected that his cyborg technology would help him metabolize the alcohol quickly if he wanted it to.

"Have we got a location yet?" Sean asked.

Molly nodded as a holoscreen opened up from the center of the table, revealing a section of space around the Zhyn Empire.

"The orange spot is Planet Kurilia, where we originally took the code out. From then until half an hour ago, we didn't have anything to suggest this code was being used anywhere other than that planet. However..." she flicked the three dimensional star map around so that she could show them the area that was pertinent, "this here is where Oz has tracked the code back to."

Joel stood up to lean in and get a better look. "That's not even a planet, though. Is it? I mean, that looks like – "

Molly nodded. "A moon. Well, it *was* a moon; before its planet was blown up in a war. Now it's just a rock in a weird orbit inside the Koin System's asteroid belt.

Sean screwed up his face. "So what do we think is going on?"

Molly leaned her elbows on the table and wiped her face with her hands. She looked back up at them. "My best theory, based on the places that their commander could have been exiled to, is that he had another base built on this moon at some point, and now is reactivating it, ready to continue his war."

Sean shook his head. One arm rested on the table and he was visibly clenching his fist. "Son of a motherfucker…"

Molly nodded. "Yup."

Joel looked concerned. "So, our play?"

Molly shrugged. "Depends on the General; but I think whoever it is just needs taking out." She leaned back in her chair, clearly frustrated. "Again."

The doors to the conference room *swoosh*ed open, revealing a tired-looking Lance Reynolds sporting an old-style sweatsuit.

The team jumped to their feet. "Sir," they each acknowledged him, saluting.

The General grunted something and waved his hand, telling them to dispense with the formalities.

"I've just got off the line with the Justicar," he told them, walking over to a chair and sitting down. "He assures us they aren't behind it, and that we have their full support to bring whomever it is to task."

Molly sat down again, and the others followed suit. "Do they suspect the exiled guy?" she asked.

Lance nodded solemnly. He shifted in his chair, as his tired muscles tried to get comfortable. "Turns out they want a meeting."

Joel frowned. "And we trust them…?"

Lance sighed, putting his fingers to his eyes and rubbing them. "We do, but…"

Joel nodded. "Trust but verify."

Lance's fingers abandoned his eyes as he snapped them together and pointed at Joel. "Exactly!" he said, his praise shining through even the tiredness.

Sean shifted in his seat and leaned one arm on the desk in

front of him. "So what's the plan, then? We go meet with the Zhyn and get their blessing to go kick some ass?"

The General looked at Molly.

Molly processed for a second. "How important is the talisman?" she asked Lance.

Lance pursed his lips for a moment. "Well. Every day it's not in our possession, it could be falling into the hands of someone who we don't want to have it. And every day that goes past that we don't know what it's all about, is another day the Federation is at risk. We just don't know how high this risk is..."

He took a deep breath. "It's damn important," he concluded.

Molly nodded her head once. "Okay, in that case; Sean, you up for a little excursion to Teshov?"

Sean glanced over to her and blinked. Joel smiled at him. "Oooh. You get the babysitting assignment!" he jibed, while also gloating that he was privy to the mission that was about to be handed out.

Sean glanced back at him briefly, shooting him a glare a school kid would, as if to say "just as soon as we're out at recess, I'm gonna kick your ass!"

The General raised one eyebrow at Joel. "That boy you'll be 'babysitting,'" he said, turning to Sean, "is one of the most valuable and important assets the Federation has. And now it looks like he could be the key to something that the entire population of our galaxy is depending on."

He glanced back at Joel. "This isn't a mission to be taken lightly."

Joel lowered his eyes, flushing a little in humility.

Sean straightened up, feeling as if he were also being chastised for having the banter with his friend. "Yes, sir. You can count on me to get the job done, sir."

The General nodded and then turned his head to the right, toward Molly – not straining to look at her, but keeping his eyes on the table.

Molly picked up on the cue. "Okay, so Sean and Giles will do the talisman retrieval. The rest of the team will deal with the Zhyn problem."

The General nodded. "I'm assuming you won't need me for your Justicar meeting?" he confirmed.

Molly shook her head. "No, sir, we can handle it." She glanced at Joel, making sure that he had her back with the diplomatic stuff.

Joel nodded his understanding. *Molly and sensitive social interactions? Yep, I'm probably going to take lead on this one.* He smiled. Molly smiled weakly back at him, noticing the amount of energy the thought of social engagement took from her.

Lance tapped the flat of his hand on the desk and then stood up. "Right we are, then. Let me know your departure time, and route your mission parameters through ADAM for final approval. Then keep us in the loop."

Molly and the others stood up. "Yes, sir" she said. The others echoed her sentiment, and they each saluted.

Lance turned and casually saluted back. "Thank you, people," he acknowledged, and then turned and headed out of the door.

ArchAngel, Hangar deck

"Fuck!"

"What? What is it?" Jasper arrived, his usual chirpy self.

Ronald looked up at him. "We've been bumped," he growled, closing his holo roughly.

Jasper placed his case down on the hangar deck floor. "How come?"

Some high-ranking officer has requested *The Scamp Princess* for a highly classified mission. They're leaving now... In our window. Ronald glanced around, distracted. "I'm going to go and see who this asshole is..."

Jasper was trying to catch up. "So what does this mean? Do we get to go out later?"

Ronald had already started storming across the hangar deck, and off into the restricted area. Jasper chased after him – lugging his carry case, but trying to be gentle with it.

The two humans made their way behind a series of ships and pods and across the length of the hangar, to where their ship should be.

Ronald stopped suddenly, and backed up behind a maintenance truck. "There," he said, pointing accusingly.

Jasper looked around anxiously, checking that they weren't being observed, before looking at where Ronald was telling him. "What? It's just two guys..."

Ronald was frowning. "Yeah, two guys taking our ride. Who knows when we'll get assigned another one with gate capabilities? We could be waiting months."

Jasper could see he was seething. "Ronald, come on. Don't you think you're being a little ridiculous?"

Ronald shot him a glare from his crouched position. "No, I'm not. I don't know who these guys think they are, or what's so fucking important..."

Jasper straightened up, and then glanced back at the two figures making their way into the ship. "Hey, hang on..." He pulled up the camera on his holo and zoomed in. "That guy looks awfully familiar. I'm sure he's an Admiral from the history of Earth..."

Ronald stood up and retreated further back behind the truck. "Show me," he demanded. Jasper held out his holo. "I'm sure I've seen pictures of him on one of the walls somewhere, on the *Meredith Reynolds*."

Ronald shook his head. "Doesn't matter who he is. He just looks like some jumped up jock who's pulling rank and stealing our ride."

Just then, *The Scamp Princess* powered up and, a moment later, lifted off the deck.

Ronald, fuming, turned on his heels and stormed off the deck. No doubt on his way to tear someone a new one.

Jasper watched him go, shaking his head in dismay. He stored the image on his holo, making a mental note to check it out later.

Aboard *The Scamp Princess*, Hangar deck of the *ArchAngel*

Sean and Giles were strapped into their seats in *The Scamp Princess*, waiting for clearance from *ArchAngel* Control.

Sean glanced over at Giles. "So, those coordinates you gave me... on Teshov. Where is that?"

Giles had been distracting himself with secondary controls. Now he pulled his attention away and looked back at Sean from the Navigator's seat. "Oh, its the village where my frenemy lives."

Sean closed his eyes and took a breath. "So this guy is a *frenemy*? What makes you think he's going to tell you where this talisman is when you ask him?"

Giles smiled. "I thought that's why you were sent with me. Out of all the warriors on Molly's team, you seem like the one who would be the least... *squeamish*... about making people talk."

Sean shook his head and turned his attention back to the panel.

The voice of the ship's EI came online. "Admiral Royale, you are cleared for take off. Shall I do the honors, sir?"

Giles looked at him, frowning.

Sean, oblivious, smiled – pleasantly surprised at how amenable the EI was being with him. "Yes, please. Thank you, Scamp".

"My pleasure, Admiral," Scamp replied. "Nice to have you aboard after all these years."

Sean grinned at the service.

"Admiral?" Giles queried.

Sean's face dropped, and he looked immediately flustered like he had slipped up. "Oh. It's... it's just a joke the EIs have going," he explained.

Giles watched him out of the corner of his eye, unconvinced.

The ship lifted gently off the deck, and quietly hovered its way over to the hangar doors. Moments later, they were careening out into space, on their way back to the Sark System.

Scamp's voice came over the system. "Ready to engage Gate capabilities when you are, sir."

Sean sat back in his console chair and smiled again, his slip-up forgotten. "Engage," he told the EI.

The ship disappeared from the radar of the *ArchAngel*.

Aboard *The Empress*, In orbit of Kurilia

"Best thing to do, is listen as much as you can. Tune in while they're talking to you. Pay attention, not just to what they're saying, but to how they're *feeling* about what they're saying." Arlene coached Molly as *The Empress* came into orbit around Kurilia.

Molly nodded her understanding. "Okay. I'll try. It's just... there's a lot to focus on all at once."

Arlene smiled sympathetically. "I know. But you can do this." She glanced over to Joel who was sitting next to Molly. "And Joel is there to help. Lean on him. Let him do the talking so you can observe better. After all," she scoffed a little, "that's normally how the Zhyn prefer to play it. Ancestors forbid a woman being in charge!" She chuckled a little, remembering her time with them on a particular sociological expedition.

Joel leaned forward, his arms on his knees. "Yeah. I've got this, Mollz. I can do this for you."

Molly nodded, looking down at her hands. "You realize that the reason we're here is to make sure that when – not if, but *when* – we go after that scumbag Shaa, it'll be sanctioned by his people." She looked up at Joel. "It's the only way that we prevent this from causing an all-out war. Remember, we weren't meant to have been out there in the first place. *Officially*, he shouldn't have been found out."

Joel took a deep breath and sat back in his seat, glancing in the direction of the passage to the cockpit. "Yeah, but he did. And I guess that's also why the General has bounced this back to us to clean up."

Molly looked glum. "Probably," she admitted. "Anyway," she said, getting up and shooing Joel out of the way, "it's probably time we move. If we can drop down onto the platform again, we can save Crash some time having to park this thing."

Joel let her get by, and then stood up himself. "Yeah, all in a day's work," he muttered. "Save the boy from getting a parking ticket…"

Paige sniggered.

Paige and Maya had been listening intently to Molly's coaching session, hoping to glean something new about the realm stuff. Sitting on their knees, leaning over the backs of the chairs in front, they had been able to be involved in the conversation. Now, with Molly gone, Arlene was theirs.

Arlene smiled up at them like a pop star reluctant to get into too deep a conversation with a fan.

Molly had started making her way to the back of the ship. She was passing by Pieter and paused briefly. "Everything looking okay?" she asked.

Pieter gave her a thumbs-up. "Yeah, so far so good. I'll keep monitoring, but there's no hint that this is a trap. If I get anything at all, I'll have Oz relay it to you."

Molly patted him on the shoulder and kept walking.

Downstairs, Jack was already suited up, and Brock was deploying the frame for them to drop from. As Molly walked in, she saw Jack concealing a weapon in her vest.

"Really?" Molly asked.

Jack shrugged. "Trust but verify," she said simply, repeating Joel's words.

He obviously had an influence during her orientation cum indoctrination, Molly figured.

Joel headed over to Jack's position and took a gun from the rack behind her, doing the same. Molly shook her head.

Next, Joel grabbed a combat vest and tossed it over to her. "You're at least putting one of these on," he told Molly definitively. Molly didn't have the energy to argue. She had more important things to focus on. Obediently, she put the vest on, and then swung down onto the frame.

"Two minutes!" Brock announced.

The others clambered onto the frame. Molly called over to Joel. "So they said they'd have a landing party meet us at the lift?" she confirmed.

Joel nodded.

Just over a minute and a half later, the three of them dropped down onto the platform and watched their ship drift past.

CHAPTER SIX

Capitol Building, Planet Kurilia

Flanked by armed guards, Molly, Joel, and Jack were swept through the Capitol Building.

Are you sure we're not under arrest or something?

Yes. Certain. There is nothing in their systems or communications that hints you are anything other than honored guests.

Comforting.

Molly glanced to her left at the heavyset Zhyn marching along side her as they made their way through the enormous ornate hall towards a set of double doors. The guard looked straight ahead, ignoring her gaze, but by his side swung a blaster – not dissimilar to the ones she and her team had used on their last visit to the surface.

She glanced to her right to see Joel and Jack looking straight ahead, too. Jack's jaw was set, but Molly could tell she was in a state of expanded awareness, watching for any hint of a threat... at which point she would likely reach for her concealed weapon. Joel was doing the same, though he was better at pretending to be relaxed.

They reached the door, and the formation of escorts came to a halt. One of the two traditionally dressed guards near the door made a show of acknowledging the convoy, and then opened the door for them to file through. The other guard remained vigilant and unmoving.

Molly followed one of the escorts into the chambers, nearly tripping as the flooring changed from marble to plush red carpet.

"Pick your feet up when you walk," Joel whispered to her.

Molly glared at him silently, resisting the urge to slap him. The last thing she wanted to do was appear unprofessional as they entered the office of the esteemed emperor of the civilization they were trying to prevent a war with.

Good call, boss. It wouldn't look so hot.

No kidding.

The guards seem to be waiting for something. Permission perhaps? Or a person to arrive?

A smaller Zhyn female appeared from a small corridor down one side of what appeared to be the main chamber.

"Hello," she greeted them in Zhyn. Molly heard it in English. She looked across at Joel and Jack, and saw their surprise as their implanted chips worked for the first time. She grinned. It *was* a weird feeling.

Joel met her eyes with a slight glint of enthusiasm in his, before turning his attention to the lady who was addressing them.

"Greetings," Joel started on their behalf. His expression shifted in response to his mouth and throat speaking a different language automatically.

Those chips seem to be working like a dream!

Yeah. I don't think Joel can believe it.

"We were invited to an audience with His Highness, Emperor Kulu", Joel told her. The guards waited patiently while the small woman moved around to her side of the desk and pulled up her screen. She poked around for a moment, and then stood up again.

"This way, please," she said, her attention mostly on Joel.

The three followed her to the door with their entourage still in tow. The woman pushed open the doors to the enormous chamber and ushered the guests in. The guards still followed, quickly forming a semi-circle around the group as they made their way forward.

Joel led the way. Jack's eyes scanned everything, aware of every movement and every warm body in the room. Up ahead, the emperor sat on his throne and another Zhyn, similarly dressed in traditional gowns and robes, hovered by one of the desks laid out in front of the emperor.

The emperor spoke. "Welcome. Welcome, my guests. Please, come forward."

Joel's confidence grew and he quickened his pace, making it more purposeful. "Good day to you, Your Highness. We are grateful to accept the invitation to an audience with you."

"The honor is mine." The emperor got off his throne and made his way toward the steps off the dais. "This is my trusted advisor, Justicar Beno'or." He indicated to the man by the desk, who approached the group with his hands clasped. The justicar bowed to them.

Kulu made his way slowly down the stairs. "We have much to discuss. But am I to assume that you were amongst the humans who came onto our planet some weeks ago?"

Molly felt her insides tighten. Though he had refrained from referencing how they bombed the fuck out of their secret bases, there was no getting around the fact.

Joel had started to respond diplomatically, and by that time, the emperor was on the ground level and in front of the group. Molly spontaneously stepped forward. Joel made an automatic grab to pull her back, and her sudden movement also spooked the guards. "Your Highness, yes we were. And I'm sorry for the intrusion. We had reason to believe that the actions of a few were putting your whole world at risk."

The emperor waved his hand, telling the guards to stand down. He approached Molly and took her hands, looking at her carefully. Molly couldn't tell if his expression was threatening, or if that was merely his resting face. He inspected her visage in return, as if puzzled.

"Forgive me," he said eventually. "It's just I've seen pictures of the team who visited, but you humans... you all look the same."

Molly's tension evaporated into a laugh. "Yes," she agreed, "I expect we do."

The emperor let out a sound that seemed quite involuntary. Molly recoiled a little at first, not knowing if it was anger or something else. When he made no other movement and she heard a similar sound coming from his justicar, she deduced it must be Zhyn laughter.

Molly relaxed a little, and tried to remove her hands from his grasp. He didn't release her, though.

"But you. I recognize you, with the golden hair," he told her. "You put your life at risk to help us, when we didn't even know what was happening within our own military."

She tried to pull away again, but he resisted. Then something in his eyes changed. A sadness overcame him. A sadness and a softness. "Thank you," he said to her, looking deep into her soul.

Molly remembered Arlene's words, and tuned into his feelings. She could see how sad he was about how someone in a trusted position in his empire had misrepresented them to the outside world. He was afraid for his people's future. He wanted to serve them as best he could, and yet felt he was failing them as a leader. But, he was also grateful. Grateful for these strangers who had shown up to put them back on track.

Molly felt the full weight of his gratitude, and the emotional overwhelm of her own reaction. "You're... you're welcome," she responded, her own voice catching in her throat.

Joel stepped forward, bringing the conversation back into the spoken realm. The emperor released Molly's hands and allowed her to step back to a more comfortable distance. She turned to include the justicar in the conversation.

"My name is Molly Bates, and this is my team. Joel Dunham," Joel stepped forward and offered his hand. The emperor didn't take it, but instead looked at it curiously. Justicar Beno'or made a comment to him, presumably explaining the gesture, and the emperor bowed his head a little in response.

Joel, feeling slightly rejected, dropped his hand and returned the bow. Molly watched and indicated to Jack. "And this is Jack Nolan," she explained.

Jack, immediately applying what she had just observed, bowed deeply to the emperor, and then to the justicar; both of whom enthusiastically returned her bow.

Looks like Jack is the golden girl.

It does. She's what one might term a 'smart cookie.'

"Come, let's sit and discuss how we might be of assistance to each other," the justicar suggested, indicating to the array of tables and ornate benches where officials would sit in an audience with the emperor.

The team sat around, taking up a few rows across the narrow aisle, so that all might see each of the players. The emperor even made his way over and perched on the ceremonial desk. Molly deduced from the justicar's surprise that this was an entirely unusual occurrence.

After some preamble about why they were there, and what had happened since their mission, the group moved on to the key concern.

Molly was the first to raise it. "The thing is, we don't want to incite a war. And yet, we believe that, unchecked, Shaa will become more of a concern; not just to the Federation, but to your other allies."

The emperor listened intently, nodding in agreement.

Molly continued to share her solution. "I suggest we find Shaa and put a stop to him. We come to you, Your Highness, because we don't want our actions to be perceived as an act of war."

The emperor continued to nod. "You can be assured of our full support. Only there is something we must make clear." He made eye contact with the justicar who took over the explanation.

"Shaa is still seen as a war hero in some parts of the empire. As the leadership, we can't be seen going after him. To extradite him is one thing; his supporters can always believe that it was his choice. In fact, I have word that this is what his propaganda is saying. However, it would divide our people if we were to actively pursue him."

He looked back at the emperor and then lowered his eyes. Emperor Kulu delivered the bottom line, looking at each team member in turn. "It's up to you. You, Molly Bates, and your hidden team of warriors, must solve this problem from the shadows. We support you, but this cannot be traced back to us. To know that we sanctioned it will divide our citizens, and this we cannot bear – despite the dishonor this man has brought on us."

Molly nodded her understanding and looked down at the floor, processing the implications. "Yes, Your Highness. I understand. We will be discrete."

The meeting continued for a few minutes more as the justicar delivered additional intel that might help them in finding the location of Shaa.

"I can have the maps sent to you on your device, but it may take a few days for our systems' engineers to code it to your language," he offered.

Okay, Oz, how do we get around this one?

Tell him to send the encrypted file in the base code, and we'll figure it out.

Then they'll know we've cracked their code.

Oz didn't respond.

Molly had an idea. "Perhaps you might show me the map, rather than send it? I have a good memory, and we can read the coordinates off and then reproduce a representation when we get back to our ship."

Beno'or seemed surprised at her apparent ability, but satisfied that this would solve their problem. He pulled up the hologram of the information he was going to send.

You getting this, Oz?

Yep. Every pixel of it.

My eyes don't encode in pixels.

No, but my processors do, and that's what's capturing what you're seeing.

Molly rolled her eyes.

Hey! Eyes on the map, genius.

Molly snapped her eyes back to the map where she had left off, and continued the scan.

Minutes later, the task was accomplished, and Joel and the emperor had somehow managed to bond; though Molly completely missed what had happened.

They started saying their goodbyes.

The emperor patted Joel on the back. "Thank you, Molly Bates, Joel Dunham, and Jack Nolan. Our empire is honored to have friends such as you."

The three of them bowed, and received respectful bows back from both Emperor Kulu and the justicar.

Justicar Beno'or then led the group back through the hall, and out of the office with the red carpet. The entourage, who had been hovering at a respectful distance during the meeting, seemed a little more relaxed with their visitors, given how their leader had treated them.

As they were escorted back out of the double doors and out into the enormous hall that was the Capitol Building, there was much more ease about the situation.

As the team approached the skylift, they bid farewell to their guards, who were almost pleasant in their sendoff. Once within the private confines of the lift, Jack finally spoke.

"So, are we concerned that he might be hanging us out to dry, if we keep quiet the fact that he endorsed this?"

Joel glanced over at her, leaning against the bar that encircled the compartment.

Jack stood just as alert as she had been, clearly keeping her awareness on the sounds around the lift, and the speed at which they were traveling. Molly noticed that there was never a moment when the woman was not a professional, taking her role seriously.

Molly turned to look directly at her. "You make a great point," she commented, thinking through the implications.

Jack could read Molly's face just as easily as Molly could now read other people's emotions. "But...?" Jack prompted.

Molly shook her head. "I don't think so. His intentions at the time were honorable."

Joel and Jack looked at each other, surprised that Molly actually had an opinion about someone's unspoken intentions.

Joel shrugged. "Okay. So then we assume he's sincere, and press on finding Shaa." He looked at Molly. "Does Oz think that the intel he shared will be useful?"

The lift seemed to be coming to a stop at the top of the shaft. She nodded. "Yeah. It will certainly help narrow things down," she told him.

Jack had clicked on the quantum comm on her wrist and was typing on her holo. The lift doors opened. "Ok," she told the other two. "*The Empress* will be passing overhead in three minutes. Looks like we timed this well."

The three teammates stepped out of the lift and onto the platform, scanning the sky for their ride.

. . .

Aboard *The Scamp Princess,* On approach to Teshov

Giles leaned forward in his seat, straining to see the detail on the planet that they were approaching.

Sean was busy flicking switches and making adjustments on the ship. "Scamp, take us in on warp. And stay on high alert; this can be a hostile area."

"Yes, sir," Scamp confirmed.

The trip was coming to a close, and, having navigated into orbit, and then through the atmosphere, *The Scamp Princess* touched down gently on the surface about a mile from what looked like a settlement.

Sean looked over at Giles with a slight smirk. "Nervous?" he asked, half having a dig.

Giles nodded and removed his glasses, cleaning them with a cloth from his suit, and shoving them into an inside pocket. "A little," he confessed. During the trip, he had replaced his tweed jacket with a modern atmosuit. He looked younger. Much younger, in fact; and now, without the glasses...

Sean frowned. "You don't need those, do you?" he asked, pointing at the glasses that had just been tucked away.

Giles shook his head, a little embarrassed. "'Course not. In a society that has nanocytes and nanobots, why would anyone need to wear corrective lenses?"

Sean's frowned deepened. "Well, then, *why...*" His voice trailed off and he shook his head as he realized that he didn't have time for this kind of question.

Giles waved his hand dismissively. "Quite," he said, agreeing with Sean's unspoken sentiment.

They unbuckled and scrambled from their seats, heading through the ship to exit via the back door.

Sean was the first down the ramp, and was holding a lightweight blaster at the ready. Giles cautiously followed him down, half of his attention on where he was stepping, and half his attention on the scene opening up in front of him. All he could see was sand; until he reached the bottom of the ramp, at which point, he could also see the sky – dull red higher up, and deep blue on the horizon.

He breathed in the atmosphere, and was instantly transported back to the time when he lived here. The scent of the sand and the burning of fossil fuels in the settlements reminded him not just of the primitive lifestyle, but of the base attitude of the ruling class toward the toxins they would freely place into the air that the settlers would breathe.

He realized instantly he hadn't missed his time here one bit.

Sean tugged at his suit jacket, opening up the asymmetric flap to expose some of his undershirt to the air, trying to cool himself down. The dryness in the atmosphere became quickly evident in his lungs as he tried to breathe normally.

"I forget how dry it gets out here," he commented to Giles.

Giles adjusted his suit, too, and they started trudging through the sand, back around to the other side of the ship, ready to head toward the settlement. "You've been here before?" he asked, trying to play down his curiosity about this mysterious cyborg marine.

Sean grunted. "Yeah. Many times," he confirmed. He turned to access the projected holo panel that was several feet away from the actual ship. He poked around in the controls, and the ramp closed itself up.

Giles watched for a moment before deciding to get a head start on the walk. Sean soon caught up, and the two men made their way across the arid sandy hell.

Onboard *The Empress*

Crash rejoined the group. "Okay, we're stationary!" he

announced. Brock glanced up at him, his eyes alight with sarcasm.

Crash looked shifty, his confidence dropping under Brock's weighted gaze. "Well," Crash qualified, "as stationary as one can be in space, with no reference points... and no resistance."

Brock made a silly face and turned his attention back to the assembled group.

Molly was perched on the arm of an anti grav chair, and many of the other chairs in the immediate vicinity had been turned around and moved into positions to allow the whole team, and Arlene, to be a part of the briefing. Crash plunked himself down in the far corner near the window, where he was able to see everyone else's reaction without having to really get too involved. He blamed tiredness from flying for his antisocial mood, but the truth was he was mostly just antisocial these days.

Molly pulled up the map that Oz had scanned from the visit with the emperor, and indicated at the target points. "These are the bases that the Zhyn have deduced may be possible locations that Shaa was using," she explained. "He may have been planning this for several decades; those points represent places where he sanctioned activity - shipments and the like - which weren't known locations for the empire."

The group watched intently.

Molly nodded to Pieter, who was sitting in the front row and typing furiously on his holo. He looked up. "Ah, right," he said, responding to her cue.

He shifted in his chair to address as much of the group as possible from where he sat. "So, it seems," he began, turning his attention back to his holo, briefly, to hit a key and project an overlay onto Molly's map, "that there are a few locations that this signal could be coming from. Not because there are multiple points of origin, but because Shaa has used some kind of frag-menter to break up any signals that are emerging from the base. It's kinda like where gravity bends light, and makes distant stars look like they're in entirely different positions from where they are, because the only thing one can do is track back in a straight line."

Joel was frowning, but it looked like most of the rest of the crew were following. Or at least pretending to follow.

Pieter continued. "So, taking this into account, I've fiddled with some common parameters to try and lock down an actual position." He stood up and waved a hand around in a circle encompassing a couple of the points that the Zhyns' map gave them. "This puts his position somewhere in this area."

Jack leaned forward over crossed legs. "Can't we narrow it down any further?" she asked.

Pieter nodded once. "Oz?"

Oz's voice came over the speakers in the cabin. "Yes and no. We can't know for certain without some other input, more data. But from what we know, we can assume with 77 percent accuracy that it is likely this one." At that moment, one of the already pinpointed locations was highlighted in yellow.

Jack tilted her head. "And if we're wrong?"

Molly's eyes defocused, clearly in listening mode. Oz's voice came over the speaker again. "Then we try the second most likely location," he told them.

Jack sat back in her chair, catching Paige's eye. Paige could tell she wasn't satisfied, but ignored it and turned her attention back to the briefing.

Molly un-perched herself, putting her weight on her feet and straightening up. "So, given this is our target, we can probably assume that there are defenses. We'll need a plan to be able to get in and out without getting blown up by his penchant for anti-spacecraft guns."

Pieter sat back down, and swung his chair around to look at Molly. "Any idea on the likely range he has on those things?"

Molly pulled her lips to one side and looked over at Joel.

Joel stood against the wall where the screens were being

projected. He took a deep breath and unfolded his arms. "Well," he started slowly, "it's a guess; but from what we've seen on the intel that Maya and Paige gathered from their databases, the Zhyn generally prefer the tech that picks off spacecraft as they come into orbit. There are reasons for this, I suppose. They have developed skylifts, and I guess that orbital area is their most sensitive, and where the most traffic is – most of the time. That means that's where their awareness is. It perhaps won't have even occurred to them seriously that a ship may land. Or may attack from further away."

Jack piped up again. "Can we tell anything from the kit Shaa has been requisitioning?"

Molly nodded to Maya, who had her holo up and was already poking through the data they had collected. Maya shook her head, her mouth downturned. "Nope. It's not the kind of thing he would have put through official channels," she relayed. She paused and scratched her head. "I dunno where we'd get that kind of data. I mean, if it were Estaria or Ogg, I'd have some inkling of where to start poking around; but this… it's just so *alien*."

Molly shifted her weight from one foot to the other. "Okay, then," she decided. "It looks like the best course of action is to assume they're heavily armed with a focus on anything that pops into orbit. Given that, we need a plan of attack that will allow us to take him out, and not put us in mortal danger." She paused, looking at the group. "Suggestions?"

The team sat in contemplative silence for a moment, and then Joel raised his hand.

Two hours later, after much back and forth, the meeting was wrapped up with a plan of action in place. They had a few hours to rest while they returned to the base to pick up some supplies, and then they would turn around and go out to the most likely location of Shaa's base.

A strange tension hung in the air as the team tried to get some rest while in transit to one of the most harebrained operations they had ever undertaken.

Chom-X9, War Room

Shaa paced the length of his War Room, almost ignoring the presence of his guests. His eyes fixed on a point on the wall straight ahead as he continued to deliver his rhetoric to his captive audience.

"Our goal, gentlemen, is to incite unrest, and garner as many allies as possible. This will not be hard, given the immense threat that the Federation poses to all life in the galaxy."

He continued to pace the long, windowless, metal-walled room. Twenty four guests sat around the functional, no-frills conference table. Some were the same race, but from different worlds. Others shared little more than an interest in keeping out of the Federation's way. All had been hand-selected by Shaa long before his exile, and represented a who's who of the local galaxy.

As Shaa walked, the guests turned their heads, tracking his motion. Those who had their back to him displayed signs of unease when he passed closely behind them.

"It has been a concern for many generations now, that as we thrive as individuals, we become more and more of a threat to the Federation," Shaa told them. "The Federation's only desire is to control, to further their own agenda. They dress it up as diplomacy, and wanting to make life better to all who come into the fold; but they dangle this utopia in front of all their potential enemies as a way of creating a docile following."

He paused, reaching the end of the room, and turned on his heels to face the assembly. "But the Zhyn people have stood firm. What you see on this base is a demonstration that we will no longer be placated by empty words and promises. The Zhyn are proud. We're strong," he said, now slamming his fist into the palm of his other hand. "And together with our brothers in arms, we will all remain strong and proud, separate from the oppressors." His voice reached a crescendo, and he paused, looking now at those he could make eye contact with. He held a few individuals' gazes for a moment before continuing his point.

"But we can't do it alone," he concluded more quietly now. "We must unite."

There was an awkward shuffle from one of the guests. A Yollin from the upper caste seemed to have made it onto Shaa's short list of people likely to follow him. The Yollin started to speak, inaudibly at first.

Shaa spun around to see who might interrupt him. The Yollin tried again, finding his voice. "Your Highness," he started, disregarding that Shaa had been stripped of his rank and status when he was exiled. "Our fear is that we are no match for the Federation's forces. We have only ever had the choice of falling in line, or suffering the consequences. At least if we don't take up arms, we can make the pretense that we are toeing the line."

Shaa's lip curled in contempt, and the unnamed Yollin recoiled. Shaa spoke, his voice stronger, more certain, than the Yollin's. "This is true. But it is also weak. And where has it led *you?*" he exclaimed, referring to the fact that the Yollins were already absorbed into the Federation.

Shaa turned from the dissenting Yollin, and addressed the others present. "And how long before you need to pledge your allegiance with more than just signing an agreement?" he demanded. "How long before your troops are committed to their cause? Your sons and daughters sent to fight their siblings because the Federation says so? In the same way that our Yollin friend has become subjugated."

There was some more awkward shifting around the table. Many of the guests dropped their eyes to the table in an attempt to avoid being pulled into responding. One official, looking Noel-ni, readjusted his position, and made a strange barking sound, like a cough. He carefully turned his head from Shaa's direction to avoid it being misinterpreted as communication.

Shaa's eyes flicked in his direction, but seemed to become distracted by his own internal dialog. "No, something must be done. And there is a plan already in place."

Shaa poked at a panel on the wall, and a holo opened in the center of the conference table. "How many times has the Federation thwarted your plans by imposing trade sanctions, or keeping your ships from moving through controlled areas of space?"

Shaa looked from the hologram to a Cubert standing just opposite his current line of sight. His chair was pushed back, allowing him to stand upright at the table, bringing him to the same height as the others. The Cubert twitched uncomfortably, but held Shaa's gaze.

Shaa continued. "How many times have they intervened in your affairs, preventing you from making profit in your own system?" He looked to the dignified-looking Yaree sitting next to him, who immediately shifted his eyes down, respectfully. Shaa was unperturbed. "Well I say 'no more'. We have already embarked upon a series of campaigns to take out not their whole armada, but strategic targets."

Shaa set about pacing again, his voice filling the room and the heads of his compatriots. "To begin with, we will indeed be nothing but a thorn in their enormous side; but eventually, with continued support and persistence across all opposing nations, we can make a stand." He paused his pacing and turned back to the group. His voice was determined. "We *will* make a change. We *will* prevail."

He moved the holoscreen on through his prepared presentation. "Take this case for consideration. This is the QBS Tornado. Just a run-of-the-mill personnel carrier; but when the Federation heard of the situation with our friends, the Leath, they decided to intervene, and kidnapped the workers who we were negotiating with. As we speak, our fighters are on their way to correct the situation, and redress the balance of power in the negotiations to meet our brothers' demands."

The holo ran a simulation of the passenger ship being destroyed by Zhyn fighters; fighters that Shaa controlled.

The room fell deathly silent as the onlookers watched the demonstration of power in horror.

CHAPTER SEVEN

Ansan Settlement, Northern Province, Teshov

The settlement was quiet. There were hints of life here and there: water catchment devices, covered over with newly disturbed sand; the odd scuffling at a window; a door suddenly closing quietly, just out of the corner of one's eye.

Giles and Sean made their way through the myriad of makeshift mud huts, keeping their eyes peeled for any signs of danger.

A snake shifted its way across their path, and disappeared behind a building.

Sean looked to Giles. "Suppose that's an omen?"

Giles shook his head. "You've been watching too many Indiana Jones movies. That was just an angoma. Native to this region – and a delicacy, I believe," he added humorously.

Sean frowned. "Aren't you the mythology guy, though? The one who sees patterns in coincidences, and spends his time bumming around the galaxy, sampling different religions?"

Giles smiled, still scanning the area carefully. "So you *have* heard of me, then?"

Sean ignored the comment and kept walking.

Giles seemed to have found his bearings. "This way," he announced suddenly, starting off in a slightly different direction through the cluster of habitations. Sean took off after him, quickening his pace, and trying not to make so much noise as he pounded across the slightly more solid sand that was underfoot.

Giles slowed when he came across the hut he had been looking for. "This is it," he mouthed quietly.

There was the *bang* of a door behind them. Both men jumped and turned. They waited, Sean with his weapon raised. Nothing moved. They turned back to the hut only to see movement behind the fiberglass window. Sean motioned for Giles to go ahead, and indicated that he'd cover him from behind.

Giles edged forward, and then, making up his mind that he just needed to do this, he strode up to the door. He raised his hand and gently rapped on the wooden paneling.

There was movement inside, but no response.

He knocked again. "It's Giles. Giles Kurns. I'm looking for Robin."

There was a scuffling behind the door, and Giles took half a step back. The door handle turned, opening the door a crack. Giles tried to peer into the darkness, and, as his eyes adjusted, there was a flicker of recognition. He turned and signaled Sean to come over, and heard Sean traipsing up behind him as he turned back to face the door.

"Greetings, Robin. Long time…" he said carefully, trying to gauge how he was being received.

The door opened a little more to reveal a rather tired looking Estarian. Clearly, he'd seen better days and was unsuited to the climate or the lifestyle here. And yet, he had the air of someone who was fated to live like this; like he was used to it, but had memories of a place, of a life, that was far removed from here.

"Giles!" he exclaimed quietly, almost congenially.

Sean lowered his weapon.

Giles turned to introduce Sean. "This is my associate, Sean Roya-"

Giles glanced back at the Estarian, to see him holding a pistol trained on Sean. "Robin, it's okay! He's with me."

A ferocity gathered on his face like a storm. "The hell he is. He and his little team are the reason I'm back in this fucking hellhole."

Giles looked confused. And terrified.

Sean remained motionless, but pointing his blaster at the Estarian in the doorway.

"Guys!" Giles interrupted, his hands out, shaking and palms down. "We don't need to do this. Let's just go inside and talk."

The Estarian twitched. Sean didn't hesitate.

BAM.

Sean shot him.

The blaster propelled the Estarian back inside the hut, the sound ringing out through the settlement. There was a scurry of unseen activity in the neighboring huts, and hushed, panicked whispers.

Giles shook his head at Sean, mortified. "Shit, Royale."

Giles pushed his way through the doorway to find his friend on the floor. He squatted down to help him, realizing with some relief that he was still alive. He reached for the wound on the Estarian's left shoulder, trying to stop the bleeding. He was so preoccupied, he didn't see Robin raise his other hand with the pistol in it.

There was another shot from the blaster, and the Estarian's entire left arm disappeared in a bloody mess.

Giles jumped back, shocked and splattered with blood. It took several moments for the ripple of horror to leave his body, allowing him to process what had just happened.

Gathering his wits, he turned to see Sean inside the doorway, holding his blaster. "The fuck?!" Giles shouted back at Royale.

Sean shrugged. "He was going to shoot me. I had to stop him.

Plus," he flicked a switch on the weapon and put the safety on, "he's a wanted criminal in the Inner System. He goes by several names; one of which is 'Mac Kerr'. His crimes were horrendous."

Giles felt sick to his stomach and was still in shock, trying to absorb what had just happened. He had blood on his hands, and though he had been intent on stopping the bleeding, it was now a null task.

He scrambled up from his spot next to the dismembered body. "You're an asshole," he growled as he got to his feet. "That was my friend," he said, pointing, stepping around the body to move further into the hut.

Sean rolled his eyes. "You mean, your 'frenemy'?" he corrected, watching Giles disappear into another section of the hut.

Giles now moved quickly and with purpose. He first went to the kitchen and started washing the blood from his hands and face. Then he wiped down his atmosuit jacket and tidied himself up.

Next, he started searching through the rest of the hut, intent on finding the prize they had come for. "You gonna help me look or just stand there?" he shot across to Sean, who had pulled the body further into the hut, and closed the door. Sean looked out of the window, checking for any signs of life.

"Sure," he responded. "But we don't have long. That was two shots fired. I'm pretty sure it's only a matter of time before the locals or the heavies get wind of the news, and come to even the score."

Giles pulled his head out of a cubbyhole in the wall. "I'll say," he agreed, putting his hand inside and feeling around for a switch or a trap door, anything that might give away where the amulet was being held.

"Shit," he exclaimed, sitting back on his haunches. "Robin was the only one who knew where the damn talisman is."

Sean shook his head as he searched the surfaces and cubby-holes built into the mud hut. "You're delusional if you honestly think that someone who tried to have you killed was going to just hand over something that you traveled across the galaxy to retrieve."

Sean kept his eyes scanning and his hands moving, checking deftly and professionally, just as Giles had been doing. His blaster tapped against the back of his legs every now and again as it lay strung over his back, ready for action at the slightest sound of a threat.

Giles scowled in Sean's direction. "You don't know that. And now we'll never know," he added poignantly. He slumped back against the cubby he had just been searching, his legs outstretched in front of him. "We're fucked. That was our only fucking lead."

Sean ignored the sentiment and kept searching.

Gaitune-67, Hangar Deck

The Empress was ready to leave the hangar deck, locked and loaded. The normal air of camaraderie and excitement had been replaced with a general anxiety about the impending mission.

Maya had sat next to Jack upon boarding, feeling that she needed something to take her mind off what she was about to do.

Jack had appreciated the company, but wasn't about to get into a girly heart-to-heart about life regrets and shit. That just wasn't how she executed missions. *Eyes on the prize*, she told herself as the engines fired up and the remaining team members scuffled to take their seats and buckle up.

"You ready for this?" Maya asked sympathetically.

Jack frowned and nodded once. "Of course. This is what I've been trained for. This is what we do."

Maya trained her eyes straight ahead of her, conscious not to push it. Jack was strong. And proud.

And the last person she wanted to piss off.

Paige glanced over to her from the other side of the cabin where she sat with Pieter. She smiled weakly, understanding what Maya was trying to do.

Crash's voice came over the intercom. "A warm welcome back to our frequent flyers. Today, you have qualified for platinum status; the prize for which is an all-expenses-paid trip to the ass-end of nowhere, where you will be invited to bomb the fuck out of a rogue space terrorist. If you would like to decline this option, please talk to your flight attendant now. Otherwise, sit back, relax, and enjoy the rest of the trip. Your planet thanks you for your service."

There were a few giggles and chuckles at the announcement, and *The Empress* lifted up off the deck.

In the cockpit, Brock was concentrating hard, listening to the ship as she took off. "You can feel the extra weight, can't you?" he said to Crash, his eyes darting over to gauge Crash's reaction.

Crash nodded.

Emma's voice filled the cockpit. "I can indeed. Though I understand that gentlemen should not comment on a lady's weight. Ever."

Brock chuckled. "When did you get a sense of humor?" he asked her.

"Boy, I've had a sense of humor since before you were born!" she retorted.

Brock shook his head gently as he pulled at his harness, checking it was secure. "But seriously," he persisted, concern playing around his eyes. "Is this extra weight going to be an issue?"

Emma flicked on her video feed on his console. She shook her computer-generated head. "Nope. It's an extra strain on take off, but once we're moving, we'll be fine. We just need to take it into account when we come out of warp, as we'll have a little extra momentum."

Crash was intently focused on his console and taking *The*

Empress out of the hanger. He didn't show any signs of even hearing the conversation.

Brock needed to make sure it was handled, though. He frowned and leaned forward, toward her video image. "So, you're doing all those calcs and stuff, so that he doesn't have to, right?" He thumbed over in Crash's direction.

Emma nodded. "You bet your sweet ass I am!" she told him.

Brock's shoulders dropped as he relaxed and sat back in his seat. "Well, okay, then," he surrendered.

Aboard *The Empress,* Near Chom-X9

Within half an hour, they were pulling out of warp, the teams each in position.

Joel looked over at Jack. "You sure you want to do this?" he checked with her.

She glanced back at him. "Bit late for second thoughts now," she smiled nervously underneath the bravado.

Joel adjusted his seating position awkwardly. "Well, that's probably true," he agreed.

Emma came on over *The Little Empress*'s intercom. "Okay, boys and girls, we're out of warp. Dock doors opening. Please start your engines, and be ready to reverse out slowly. And I mean *slowly*. No showing off."

Joel and Jack flicked immediately into ops mode. Jack set a bunch of switches, and Joel checked his instruments before starting the engine of *The Little Empress*. Both their faces were expressionless.

Joel's hand hesitated over a holocontrol. "Do we have permission to fire as soon as we get a clear shot?" he checked with Emma.

"Affirmative," she responded. "You're cleared to engage at will. This is your op until we collect you. Leave the comms open; I'll be on the link for both ships to coordinate."

A moment later, *The Little Empress* reversed out of the dock of *The Empress*, a baby spaceship being birthed from its mother.

Jack's expression turned stern. "Weapons online and locked on target," she confirmed. "Approximate distance from target, 8300km."

Joel checked a couple of dials, and straightened up as he watched *The Empress* pull away and then disappear into thin air. "We're on our own now," he said, the feeling of dread behind his words hanging suspended in the air.

"Let's do this," he added, trying to disperse the spell he had just cast with his idle comment.

Chom-X9, War Room

Former-Lord High Marshall Shaa had taken a seat at the head of the table in the only console chair in the room. He sat back, arrogant about the power he held, almost daring someone in the room to challenge him.

It was true. This was a recruiting mission; a drive to bring investors and allies on board. But to show weakness or any hint of it being an equal partnership right now, in these early stages, was to set the stage for discontent later.

No. Better to show them who's pulling the strings upfront. Then they'll be under no illusions as to how this will to play out.

"Allow me to share something else," Shaa said, changing the direction of his discourse. "As you are probably aware, I have long been an advocate of staying ahead of the technology curve. When I ruled the Zhyn Empire, I had the foresight to develop a new computing language that would remain a secret from the Federation. It allowed us to conduct our business in private, as well as fortified us against their cyber intrusions."

He pulled up another screen for them. All eyes in the room moved from Shaa to the new hologram appearing in the center of the table.

"Today, you are witnessing an extension of the commitment we made to stay ahead of the curve. The base has just been alerted, through traditional radar means, of a ship that has entered into our space. However, we were aware many minutes ago that this ship was on its way, via our advanced early warning system. Now we have confirmation of its presence, we are adequately prepared to defend ourselves."

Silence fell on the room as Shaa shifted forward to perch in his seat. He drew a deep breath, admiring the image onscreen of the ship that had just made it into their firing range.

The voice of the Yaree off to his right interrupted his thoughts. "But how do they even know you're here? We thought this place was off-grid?"

Shaa didn't answer the inquiry. He didn't even glance up to acknowledge the questioner. Instead, he connected his holo with the control room. "Lock on!" he instructed.

The control room came on over the conference room audio feed. "Locked on, sir."

"Fire!" came the order from Shaa.

The guests watched intently, acutely aware that they were no longer watching a simulation, but a real feed of anti-spacecraft guns firing upward into the orbit of the planet, at the ship that had just appeared.

Shaa looked very satisfied with himself. "This literally is the case of 'forearmed is forewarned'." He chuckled at his own joke, oblivious to the horror in the eyes of those watching from around the table.

Aboard *The Little Empress*

Joel moved the stick forward to take *The Little Empress* further in. "How are you doing getting a lock on something useful there?" he asked, not taking his eyes from the console.

Jack hesitated. "I'm... Okay. I've got something. Looks like a cluster of buildings surrounded by weaponry. It's probably - "

At that moment, the computer picked up some anti-aircraft radiation signatures.

"Scratch that. It's definitely hot. Locked on, firing."

Two seconds later, missiles left the armaments on the sides of *The Little Empress*, and navigated their way down to the surface.

Joel pulled the stick to the right, banking the ship on its approach. Jack flicked a second switch on her joystick and deployed the decoys to draw fire, just as Sean had taught her on her first outing in *The Little Empress*.

"How are we doing?" Joel asked.

Jack paused before responding. "They're taking to the decoys. We're okay," she confirmed.

Suddenly, there was a loud, deep *bang*. The ship vibrated through the hull from the shock. Joel felt their trajectory being altered and felt the resistance on the stick, even despite the minimal atmosphere they were encountering.

"What the - " he started.

Chom-X9, War Room

Shaa was marveling at the destruction unfolding on the holo-screen. In a matter of moments, the puny ship that was taking fire from his superior armaments would disappear from the screen completely.

There was a beep at the door, pulling Shaa's attention from the screen. His guests, however, seemed somewhat relieved at the interruption.

"Come," he called. The door slid open, mechanically whirring on its heavy iron innards. One of Shaa's soldiers appeared and stepped purposefully into the room. Without further invitation, he made his way straight to his master.

Shaa didn't look at the Zhyn; he regarded him merely as part of the functioning of his operation, like a butler in a house where the staff moves unseen and unacknowledged until their message becomes relevant.

The man whispered in Shaa's ear, and then took a pace back, awaiting a decision.

Shaa raised his eyes from the screen, contemplating the new information. A second later, he rose from his seat and addressed the assembled delegates.

"Gentlemen, it seems we have a second craft appearing on the other side of our little planet."

As if on cue, the ship appeared on their live feed. Shaa continued. "At this point, I know you would normally like to join the fight, but, all things considered, it would be prudent for you to leave now."

There was muttering and a flurry of subdued motion amongst the people around the table.

Shaa continued to relay his instructions without pausing. "Sergeant, have our guests escorted to their ships so they can get away from here. Gentlemen, get a safe distance away as quickly as you can. It is best you are not caught here, or known to have been here. Tell no one of our discussions or what you have seen here today. I will be in touch."

The guests around the table found their way to their feet and then to the door, looking back only to ensure that their escort was following them. A mix of fear and confusion mulled around them as they ushered each other along the corridor. The sergeant clicked his heels and saluted Shaa before attending to his gaggle of charges.

Shaa nodded his dismissal and then turned his attention back to the screen. Once the doors to the conference room closed, he hit his holo, connecting him to the control room. "Report!" he demanded.

·　·　·

Aboard _The Empress_

"Sit rep?" Molly prompted from her console in the cockpit.

Crash checked the visual, and then the console. "We're okay. We're about five thousand kilometers out; within target range, and probably as close as we can get without materializing into the planet."

Molly nodded. "Okay. Engage as soon as we get a lock on."

A moment later, two missiles left the bottom of the ship and streamed their way to the surface of the moon.

Molly watched, trying to see if there was any discernible difference in the visual. "Did we get the target?"

Pieter shook his head. "It hit, but there are three other anti-aircraft weapons locked onto us. He must have distributed them all over the surface. We need to get closer to see what's happening."

The visual showing the other side of the planet suddenly lit up.

Molly's forehead tensed in anxiety. "Emma, whose lights are those? Is that _The Little Empress_ firing?"

Emma's voice came through on the cockpit intercom. "_The Little Empress_ is firing, but those aren't her missiles. Those are coming from the surface."

Molly felt her stomach lurch. "How are her shields doing?"

Emma reported. "She's been compromised. Shields at fifty percent."

Molly was on her feet, her hands gripping the console on the arm of the chair. "Shit. Tell them to abort. Get them out to five kilometers. We'll pick them up."

Crash looked instantly nervous. "There's no way we can gate in that close to them; not without risking colliding with them. Or worse."

Molly had visions of the Tardis landing around them - or the Tardis landing within the ship - and realized that she really should only concern herself with reality in these moments of high stakes. She shook the thought from her head.

"What other options do we have?" she pressed.

"We could warp over there," Crash suggested.

Molly shook her head. "We'll be drawing even more fire." She paused. "Oz, ideas?"

The optimum solution is for Emma to pull them out to a safe distance while we gate to a safe distance from them, further out of Shaa's range. Then we can travel in to collect them the same way we we did the drop-off.

Molly nodded, not entirely satisfied, but ready to make a move. "Okay. Let's do that. Crash, make the jump the second we've set the course."

Crash nodded. "Acknowledged," he said, setting up the coordinates.

Aboard _The Little Empress_

There was another _bang_, and this time the ship was knocked upward. The planet below disappeared from view as they tipped backwards into space.

Jack poked at her console. "We've been hit. I don't know what happened." She replayed the camera from beneath the ship. "Looks like their missiles split when they reach a certain height. We've been hit by two of them."

Joel tried to retrieve control of the ship. "Emma, if you're there, a little help would be great."

"Joel, I'm here. Molly's orders are to retreat. I can get you stabilized, just hang tight. This is going to take a few minutes. The ship will continue to rotate for a while longer; I hope you don't get spacesick…"

Joel glanced over at Jack. Jack shook her head and smiled nervously. "We'll be okay. Thanks, Emma. Glad you've got us."

The next several minutes were the longest minutes of Jack's

life. Despite knowing Emma was working to get them stabilized, they had little bearing on which direction the surface missiles were coming from. That meant they had a smaller chance of being able to counter them, let alone get out of the way.

Jack continued to focus on the task, though. "I'm laying down decoys to see if we can avoid taking another hit. Shields are at forty three percent," she reported.

Joel continued working furiously to find a way to help them regain control, simultaneously racking his brain as to what he could do once Emma got them out of the spin.

Chom-X9, Control room

Shaa stormed into the control room. Glancing at the hangar deck monitor as he entered, he noticed the group of his would-be associates making their way hurriedly to their various spacecraft. Unless more combatants showed up, they would likely get away without drawing any attention; particularly if they followed the emergency flight path his team had already figured out for such a purpose.

Shaa's attention moved to the main screen showing the two ships attacking from different directions. "Fools," he grunted out loud. "They think they can waltz into battle with me and win? Who do they think they're fighting against? Some half-baked cocksucker?"

There was a titter of activity and agreement amongst the personnel manning the control room. Six defected Zhyns worked furiously to coordinate their defenses around their 500-km-radius rogue moon.

"Your Highness," one of them announced. "We're receiving reports that some of our anti-spacecraft weapons have been destroyed."

Shaa felt the frustration rising in his chest. "Onscreen!" he commanded.

The secondary holoscreen lit up, displaying visuals of one of the anti-space gun towers, half destroyed and billowing black smoke. A moment later, it flicked to give a different angle showing a small fire. Then it switched showing a different tower in another location, this time surrounded by thorny vegetation.

"Switch to firing from the poles," Shaa commanded. "Something tells me they would rather withdraw than risk their own deaths."

The Zhyn responsible nodded and then relayed the order to the operations deck.

Aboard *The Empress* Actual

"Gate complete," Crash announced, immediately pushing the ship forward in the direction of *The Little Empress*.

Emma's voice interceded. "I'll have them stabilized from their rotation in another thirty seconds. I'll plot a course to pull them around. Better them maneuver around you this time, despite the risk to their shields."

Molly frowned and stood up, looking over the consoles that Brock and Crash were working on. "Anything we can do to protect them from here?"

Brock raised his hand. "Yes! Maybe..." He poked at the console some more, and then suddenly fist pumped the air. "We can extend our shields to include them. It will take a lot more power, and we'll have to drop them to bring them up at a different distance, meaning we'll be-"

"Do it," Molly ordered without hesitation or needing to hear any more.

Brock busied himself with the task as they drew closer.

A rally of missiles suddenly launched from the planet, heading straight for *The Empress* and *The Little Empress*.

Molly's mouth dropped open. "Holy mother of fuck..."

CHAPTER EIGHT

Ansan Settlement, Northern Province, Teshov

The whole hut had been searched, top-to-bottom and then bottom-to-top. There was one more place Sean hadn't looked, and he disappeared from Giles's awareness. He came back several minutes later.

"Not on the body, either," he reported.

There was movement outside the window. "We're going to have to move," he told Giles. "We're not safe here."

Giles was displaying signs of shock: pale complexion, catatonia. Sean marched over to him.

"Don't make me bitch-slap you, soldier. We have to move. NOW!" he barked.

Giles came back to his senses as if woken from a dream. He rubbed his face with one hand and scrambled to his feet. Sean helped him up, glad that he wasn't actually going to have to slap some sense into him and then explain a shiner to the others when they got back to base.

The two started for the door.

Giles finally noticed the blood that had splattered all over the walls, just inside the hut. He shook his head and stopped. Sean had his blaster in-hand, ready to open the door for them to make their move. He glanced back at Giles. "Ready?" he asked.

Giles shook his head. "No." He paused, scratching behind his ear. "There's... there's somewhere else we can try before we go back to the ship."

Sean glanced nervously at the door, straining to hear if there was anyone on the other side. "We're going to be drawing some heat, you realize that?"

Giles took a step back, and then turned deeper into the hut. "There's another way out. We need to go in this direction, anyway," he called back.

Sean followed him through the little hut to another door that they had missed when they conducted their search. Giles opened it, carefully checking out of the window, and then stood back to let Sean conduct a proper visual and lead the way.

Sean stepped out first. The area behind the hut was quite different; like a back alley, without an alley actually having been constructed. There were the backs of a few other huts, and an area for various forms of waste. It smelled. Really bad.

Sean ventured further out, sweeping his blaster from side to side as he checked points of potential ambush. Seconds later, he beckoned for Giles to follow. Giles stepped gingerly out, and then pointed in the direction they needed to go, out across more sand.

It took them several minutes to clear the huts, and then several more to get out across the sand dunes and drop down onto a cliff face. Despite the drop below them, the rockiness of the cliff was actually a welcome change from the soft, unstable sand under foot.

Giles led the way now, moving agilely across the rock, wending his way down and around the natural crater on the edge of the desert. Occasionally, they would come across signs of life: a vine that had wrapped itself around a rock in the shade, or a tiny scorpion that scuttled away at their movement.

Sean looked up at the sky, remembering his time out here in the past. "Hasn't changed. Still just as oppressive as ever," he grumbled.

Giles kept moving, seeming to enjoy the activity, now that they were away from the threat of the locals. "I dunno. I think it's beautiful, in a morbid kind of way. And when it's not so hot, it's almost charming..."

Sean didn't have the energy to argue. He pressed on, focused on the mission. "Where exactly are we going?" he asked.

Giles glanced back, and then ahead. "Just a little further around this cliff face. There's a cave; Robin would use it to hide his stash. Weapons. Chemicals. Delicate toys or contraband. It's sheltered from the heat and any prying eyes; or satellites, if any authority came a-calling."

Sean frowned as he navigated his way over a protruding rock. "You mean you knew he was bent?"

Giles shrugged. "I guess. Yes. But I wasn't here to arrest people. I was here to study them."

Sean's features furrowed. "So you were studying our criminals?"

Giles talked as he clambered along the rock, careful each time he placed his foot. "More like the social dynamics between them and the other groups here on the planet. You see, all these groups are intricately entwined. When you come away from the judgment, you can see that they make up a delicately balanced ecosystem - socially, spiritually, and, indeed, economically."

Sean wasn't exactly following the socio-babble, but he spotted the cave entrance just up head. "This it?" he called forward to Giles.

"If memory serves," Giles called back, reaching for a rock in front of him to balance himself. Sean was aware of a sudden movement from Giles's direction, and looked up just in time to see him lose his footing and disappear out of sight.

There was a flurry of rock and sand as Giles dropped. Sean's heart jumped into his mouth as he rushed forward, realizing that Giles was hanging onto a vine that had been protruding from the cliff.

Giles let out a shout, scrambling for something else to hold onto. He kicked at the rocks to try and get a foothold, anything, to try and take some weight off the vine which was already ripping away from its roots in the rock.

Sean scrambled forward, anchored himself against the rock, and reached down to offer the dangling scientist his hand.

Giles looked up with panic in his eyes, blinded by the dust and sand. Sean grabbed at his arm and steadied him, keeping him from bouncing against the cliff. Giles found a completely inadequate foothold, but enough to give him contact with the cliff face.

"It's okay, mate. I've got you. You're not getting out of this adventure that easily." Sean's face showed the strain his body was under, holding them on the tiny track and preventing Giles from falling to his death.

Giles noticed in that moment of extended time how in his element the marine was, now that there was a physical threat to deal with. He found himself envying the calm. Envying the tolerance for pressure. Envying the life that seemed to spark inside of Sean as soon as there was trouble.

Addict, Giles realized.

The man is a danger addict. And that is what makes him such an asset to the General.

It all became so clear.

Giles watched everything in slow motion as Sean talked to him, giving him instructions to find a better foothold; to release the vine and grab onto the rock; to transfer his weight onto Sean's grip and make the transition upwards. Sean was calm and clinical. Exacting. Like he was merely teaching a child to rock climb.

"That's it, mate. One last push, and you want to haul yourself up and over onto the track, such as it is. See if you can use that white rock there to pull your leg over. Hook it first, and then pull; careful about straining, though. Just turn your hip over. You got it?"

Giles grunted and then swung his leg up as instructed. He turned his hip, noticing that, had he not, he wouldn't have had the strength in his inner thigh to make the maneuver to safety. He marveled at Sean's insight... almost as if he was just observing himself being in mortal danger.

A row of rocks represented some semblance of a path they were following, and Giles lay facedown against them. He was breathing heavily, regaining his strength... and his balls, which he was sure had dropped down the cliff face when he initially slipped.

He could hear Sean recovering his breath, as well. He turned his head and looked up, his body flooding with gratitude. Sean was wiping the sweat from his forehead with his sandy atmosuit. Sean shook out the arm that he'd used to pull Giles up.

Giles grinned. "Thanks, man," he panted.

Sean chuckled a little. "Anytime, mate." He paused and looked out across the crater, and then back in the direction of the cave. "You think you can make it the rest of the way?" he asked.

Giles started getting to his knees, but his body had gone limp, and the fear from what had just happened was catching up to him. He nodded anyway. "Yeah. Think I may just crawl, though," he said, carefully trying not to glance down at the drop, even though every curious bone inside him wanted to see the carnage he had narrowly escaped.

Sean nodded and scrambled to his feet, keeping an eye on Giles behind him to make sure he was following.

They made their way carefully to the cave, and arrived panting, relieved to have made it and to be out of the heat.

Giles, already on hands and knees from crawling, collapsed on the soft sand and rolled onto his back. Sean made his way deeper inside, and found a wall to slump against while Giles recovered from his near-death experience.

"So, do you think we need to worry about booby traps?" Sean asked, glancing into the darkness of the cave, waiting for his eyes to adjust.

Giles rolled over onto his front, now thoroughly covered in sand. "Dude, you really have watched too many of those old tomb-raiding movies!" Giles laughed to himself, the relief of being alive still settling into his bones.

Sean glanced back at him. "Can never be too safe," he said. His tone was more commanding, as if Giles had said something completely inappropriate.

Giles chuckled a little.

Sean rolled his eyes as he scrambled to his feet again. "You realize your good humor is a result of the scare you just had, right?"

Giles sniggered. "Yep. But I intend to enjoy it; and every moment from here on in. No more complaining from me, no, siree."

Sean ventured deeper into the cave, carefully eyeing each step before he placed his foot, aware of every single thing around him. His eyes now adjusted to the darkness, he could make out outlines of things. A desk. A picture on a wall. A seating area. He pulled up his holo and projected a low-power flashlight from it, to illuminate the area without destroying his night vision.

Giles had made it to his feet, and wandered over to join Sean while dusting himself off. He nearly tripped over an edge as the sandy floor of the cave transitioned into some kind of flooring. Catching himself in time, he looked down and stamped his foot. "Looks like he's upgraded since I was last invited down here," he commented.

Sean wandered onward, finding a passageway off the main area. "You remember this?" he asked indicating into the doorway.

Giles nodded. "Sure. That way lays his prison, where he puts people who have pissed him off. The passage off to the right of there goes to the walk-in safe."

Sean nodded. "Guess I'll start there, then," he decided, wandering off to explore.

Giles stood in the middle of the main area and looked around. Then he pulled up his holo as Sean had done, and started searching the place methodically.

Aboard *The Empress*

Brock, Crash, and Molly watched the forward screen as the green-lit missiles headed in their direction. Not a few kilometers ahead of them, *The Little Empress* languished; suspended in space, still rotating on an off-kilter axis, attempting to regain control from the last blast it took.

"Looks like they've been deploying decoys," Crash commented, raising his arm to feebly indicate the projectiles coming from *The Little Empress*.

Brock shook his head. "It's not enough," he said, barely peeling his eyes from his console. "Come on, come on..." he muttered to the array of controls in front of him. "Come ON!" His frustration levels rose and Molly glanced down, vaguely aware that he was working on something.

Crash turned to read off a screen Molly couldn't see. "Three seconds till impact," he reported.

Molly held her breath.

Emma's voice interjected. "They could withstand a couple, but not more than three of those missiles."

Molly tried to take in what Emma had just said. *It isn't possible...*

Brock hit a final switch, only then looking up to watch the screen.

Molly braced herself, not quite sure she had put it together right. *Is Joel's ship about to be destroyed? Is that what Emma is saying?*

Her heart was in her mouth as the implications of the missiles hitting *The Little Empress* dawned on her.

And then their own ship shuddered.

"What was that?" she asked, still watching the screen and noticing that *The Little Empress* was still intact.

There was another shudder. And then another.

"It's working!" Brock shouted. "It's working!"

Molly was confused, and then she saw the green flares as the missiles hit the forcefield around not just *The Little Empress*, but their own ship as well. Her mouth opened in shock, and then a smile. "You did it?" she half-asked, half-celebrated, her hand finding its way to Brock's shoulder.

Brock was celebrating with a little hand jive. "Oh, yeah. I did it!" he confirmed. "It was tight, but I managed to drop our shields and then, thanks to Emma's uber processing power, we were able to recalculate and bring them back online around *The Little Empress*."

Crash rolled his head to look at his copilot. "Nice job, Slick," he said. Brock raised his hand for a high-five, and Crash hit it.

Molly became aware of her legs going weak, and realized she needed to sit down. She stumbled over to one of the console chairs opposite where she had been sitting before. "Emma, report?" she asked.

Emma responded immediately. "Shields at eighty seven percent, and holding. *The Little Empress* is nearly stabilized, and the course is being plotted to bring them in. Expect them to dock in four minutes and twenty seconds - as long as they leave the flying to me, now."

Molly sat back in the chair, which tipped her backward in the bucket seat. She closed her eyes. "Make it so," she ordered.

Relief flooded through her body. She hadn't thought that she could actually lose Joel, and then there it was: a semi-routine mission turned nearly fatal. *Of course I would have been devastated to lose Jack, as well,* now that she considered it. *Or any one of my team. But...*

She shook the thoughts from her head, savoring a moment of relief before she slipped out of the console chair and left the cockpit.

In a daze, she found herself running down to the cargo bay as quickly as she could.

Kerr's cave, Northern Province, Teshov

"Royale! I've got it!" Giles's voice carried through from the other room.

Sean had been working on trying to crack the safe for the last twenty minutes. In the dark, and the stifling air, he worked through one mechanical combination after another, trying to get the damn thing open.

His frustration was only heightened when he heard Giles's voice announcing that it wasn't even necessary. He scrambled to his feet and stretched his back a little before moving into the main cavern.

Giles sat at the desk, looking through some papers. He barely glanced up as Sean returned. "It's there," he said, nodding at a lump of metal on the desk in front of him before returning his attention to the papers.

Sean looked suspicious. "And yet, rather than whooping and cheering that we accomplished the mission, you're engrossed in some old school papers?"

Giles looked up. "Yes," he replied simply. He gathered up the papers and folded them into a rectangle several times smaller, then shoved them into the inside of his jacket.

Sean had picked up the talisman and was inspecting it by the glow of his holo. He turned it over in his hands, trying to figure out what was so special about the lump of metal, which had holes in it.

Giles rounded the desk. "Shall we?" he said, indicating the cave mouth.

Sean shrugged and popped the talisman into his own inside pocket, and zipped his jacket up a little. "Sure. I'm ready for a cold shower and a beer."

The two men headed out of the cave, leaving the darkness behind them.

Onboard *The Empress*

Molly waited for the cargo hold doors to close before she attempted to hit the airlock button. She stood watching Joel and Jack shutting the ship down, talking as casually as if they'd just done a routine run, or a training exercise.

Once the cargo doors closed to the outside, the button lit up to her left. She thumped it and leaned on the door, trying to hurry it open. It retracted sideways. She watched the gap widen until it was big enough for her to just slip through. She stepped into the chamber and waited impatiently for the air pressure to stabilize on the other side of the second door so she could gain access.

Joel and Jack had disappeared from view of the cockpit's windows. She stamped her feet impatiently, her emotions heightened by the adrenalin.

Finally, the second door opened, and she stepped quickly out onto the cargo hold's gridded floor, grateful for the thick boot soles that protected her from the metal grating underfoot.

A moment later, Joel appeared from around the rear of *The Little Empress*. He walked casually, still talking to Jack. "Well, that was an epic fail," Jack was saying.

Joel scratched at the back of his head, and then looked up, noticing Molly. He looked surprised that she had come all the way down to greet him. He looked back, to see if there was something on the ship he had forgotten, before wondering if she had come to greet them.

She walked toward them, her pace quickening. She was intently focused on Joel, but remembered herself, and included Jack when she spoke. "I'm so relieved you're both okay," she called as they approached. "You gave us quite a scare!"

Jack's eyes widened in agreement. "Yeah, we gave ourselves a scare, too. I think I've earned a cold one," she said, slapping Joel on the upper arm before hurrying off, leaving the two friends standing on the deck.

Joel looked down at Molly, his face damp with sweat and anxiety. "It was a close one," he acknowledged.

Molly nodded, slowly recognizing that her brain had stopped working because she was overwhelmed. Joel didn't press her or put her on the spot. He just quietly swung his arm over her shoulder and walked them back to the airlock. "It's over now. Apart from the fact that we have to find another way to take out this High Marshall *Drudeili.*" He chuckled to himself and squeezed his arm around Molly's shoulders.

The two headed off down the corridor together in comfortable silence.

CHAPTER NINE

Onboard _ArchAngel_

"They must have had some way of knowing we were coming. No way they could have had their weapons locked on us at such a distance so quickly. They knew _precisely_ where we were gating in. It's the only explanation."

Molly paced up and down the lab, talking out loud to herself, allowing the others to hear the thoughts that were churning in her mind.

Pieter had his holo out in front of him, but without a specific bounded problem to solve, he resigned himself to waiting for Molly to decide on the best course of action.

Paige and Maya sat quietly, trying to look helpful, but coming up with nothing. It really wasn't their area.

Defeat hung in the air.

Joel wandered in, his hair damp from the shower, looking a little brighter, but still stressed out. "I've sent the others to get some rack time," he announced.

Molly barely registered the comment.

"Oz," she asked. "Can we check in with ADAM to see if he has any insights? Any reports of tech that can do this?"

"On it," Oz answered over the room's audio.

Joel took a stool next to Paige. "Why are we in a lab?" he asked. Maya shrugged. Paige leaned closer to him to whisper. "I think it helps her think better."

Oz's voice came over the audio. "That, and it's out of the way of prying ears that may be interested in the operation. No one would think to look for us here... unless they got the memo."

Joel raised his chin. "Ahh," he said, understanding. "We suspect a mole."

Molly turned to look at him, her ears pricking up. "We can't rule it out," she muttered. She turned back to stare at the spot on the wall she had been studying. Joel noticed that she disappeared from behind her eyes and went somewhere else. "We need to know what their edge is. Then we can figure out a way around it," she mumbled.

Four pairs of eyes were locked on to her. Not that she was aware.

Molly's mind kept churning. "Or we need another way to get close enough to take them out. Longer range missiles."

Joel straightened in his seat. "I guess if we had either drones or a longer reach, we could be outside of the orbital range and it wouldn't make any difference if they see us coming. Unless they scramble jets, there won't be anything they can do."

Suddenly there was a familiar figure leaning against the doorframe.

"Well, that's assuming they don't have a boatload of jets on standby. Which they probably will." It was Sean. He uncrossed his arms and wandered into the lab.

Giles appeared behind him, walking in casually as if they were just joining a briefing for a routine mission.

Molly did a double take, suddenly putting together who they were, and where they had been. "Did you get it?" she asked, looking at Sean.

Sean pulled up a stool and sat down on the long side of the room, perpendicular to where the others had accumulated.

He nodded in Giles's direction, and Giles wandered over to one of the central benches and threw something metallic down onto it. "Piece of cake," he announced with a casual half smile.

The talisman clanked and clattered on the surface before coming to a rest. Molly looked at it for a moment.

"'Piece of cake,' my ass!" Sean scoffed.

Giles shrugged. "All in a day's work," he chirped. "So I hear you may have a mole. And a problem blowing up a moon?"

Molly studied him carefully, still unsure of what to make of him. "Maybe. We just don't know."

Giles raised his eyebrows and turned to face Joel, who was watching the newcomers carefully. "The thing with the long range missiles won't work. He'll adapt. He *will* send out fighters," he said, nodding in Sean's direction. "And if there is a mole on board, he'll know you're coming even before you leave the ship."

Joel folded his arms. "So what are you suggesting? I'm assuming your criticism is coming from a place of having an actual way forward?"

Arlene appeared, and all eyes turned to her, the thought of a mole now planted in their psyche. She looked awkwardly around the room, feeling judged and surveilled.

"Hi," she said nervously. "ADAM told me you were all down here." She looked at Molly, trying to be natural under the spotlight. "How did it go?"

Molly turned casually and sat down on one of the lab stools, behind the central bench. "Fine," she told her, noncommittally. "Apart from the blowing the fuck out of Shaa. That bit was a bust."

Arlene suddenly understood at least part of the mood that hung in the room. "So, what's your plan?" she pressed, looking around at the others who looked less than gloomy.

Molly idly picked up the talisman and turned it in her hands.

"We're trying to figure that out. Sounds like your boy Giles has something to add into the mix, though," she said, looking up at him.

Giles animated himself. "Yes, yes I do," he said, glancing at Arlene and switching into professor mode. He paced the width of the lab to the windows on the far side of the room, away from the group. Arlene ventured into the room and took a seat next to Sean.

"I've studied this Shaa fella from his public addresses. He's a megalomaniac. Narcissistic. Driven by power. Ruthless. And at the same time, completely insecure."

Giles turned to face the group. "His weakness is not his military. Not his defenses. His weakness is... his ego."

Molly leaned on the desk, suddenly paying close attention, the talisman forgotten - at least by her. Had she been paying attention to Arlene, she would have noticed the woman's pupils dilate when she spotted the metal object Molly had been idly playing with in her fingers.

Giles continued. "So the thing that Shaa wants the most is affirmation that he is on the right track with his grand plan. Deny him that, argue with him, reason with him, and all you'll get is more resistance from him. And, in the case of a dictator with a large stash of armaments, this will be very painful for all involved. However," he began pacing again, "what you have is an opportunity to find your way to his side, simply by affirming what he believes to be true."

Molly frowned, not quite seeing how this was going to help her blow him up.

Giles turned to face her now. "You'll want to choose someone from the Federation, who isn't a threat. But who could be of use to them for intel. You need someone to surrender to him, to make him think that he's won them over; someone who can convince him that they've switched sides. That will be the biggest stroke to his ego. Indoctrinating someone from within the ranks, and promising them the world… that's easy - but to have turned someone to his cause from *outside* his circle? That will give him ya-yas till kingdom come."

Molly stroked her chin, carefully considering the information.

Joel was the first to speak. "So what you're saying is that we need to put someone on that rock, and let him think they're defecting?"

Giles nodded. "Basically, yes."

Sean chuffed, folding his arms and straightening his legs out in front of him, and then crossing them as well. "Well, that ain't me!" he declared. "The guy sounds like a right lunatic."

The others just sat silently, watching and waiting to see Molly's reaction. Giles wasn't done with his discourse, though.

"What you really need is someone who would have credibility; someone who is *in* the Federation, but not *of* it. Someone who could potentially have access to both sides of the story and have naturally come to the conclusion that he is right in his course of action."

Molly was still churning the possibilities.

Giles took a step towards the bench she was leaning on. He looked down at her, dragging her gaze up to look at him. "Someone like me." His voice was steady and balanced, but there was a glint of excitement evident in his eye - the glint that a drug addict would get when seeing his poison of choice.

Molly paused for a moment, frowning slightly, weighing the pros and cons. Giles started to offer more evidence, speaking just as she did, and he missed what she said.

He stopped. "Sorry, what?"

"I said 'okay, then'." Molly's face was expressionless, but there was a titter of resistance from the others around her. She looked at them each in turn, noticing the outrage on their faces.

"What do you propose, precisely?" she asked Giles, ignoring the protests.

Giles stepped back against the bench behind him, leaning the heels of his hands on it as he faced Molly seriously. "I'll need to make my own way over there. So I'll arrive in a stolen ship, I guess. I'll give myself up, and tell him why I'm there. He probably won't believe me at first, so I'll likely spend a few days in the brig... and then," he sighed as if he were simply talking about running another lecture course, "he'll start to trust me. I'll give him some intel to prove myself, of course, and then I'll figure out how to create a chink in his defenses so that you can get through."

Molly shook her head, letting her arms drop to the desk now. "How are we going to stay in contact with you?" she asked, her face showing she was ready to shut the operation down.

Giles looked over at Arlene.

Arlene shook her head. "No. No way. I'm not okay with this."

Molly looked confused.

Giles sighed. "Yes, we'll get to that; but technically there are devices you could implant into my retina and ear, that would do that quantum whatchamacallit thing you have, right?"

Sean uncrossed his legs and sat up a little. "Yeah, the tech exists," he admitted, glancing at Arlene, who had pursed her lips in resistance.

Arlene folded her arms. "It's too dangerous," she insisted. "The minute you even get into his airspace, you're going to be escorted to the brig. You won't even get to meet him. He won't take you seriously, and I'll bet if he's even half as intelligent as you think, he's got a file on every single person in the Federation that may be a threat to him. You, as the 'nephew' of the General, will be on that list. You mark my words!"

Arlene's tone was that of a mother scolding a child. Molly half expected her to start wagging a finger at any moment.

Giles remained neutral to her response, and looked back to Molly to adjudicate the discussion. "I can do this," he insisted calmly.

Molly leaned forward and pushed her stool away, standing up. "You probably can. I'm just not sure I should let you."

Giles opened his mouth to protest, but Molly held her hand up to stop him. "I need to consider this, and all our options. Oz will look into the tech, and I need to talk to a few people. We'll meet back here in two hours with a decision."

Giles looked defeated. "Okay. Fine," he said, throwing one arm in the air and shaking his head in surrender. "Back here in two hours," he confirmed.

The group began to disperse, and Arlene was the first to leave the room. Giles went after her. Joel loitered for a moment, but disappeared when he noticed that Sean was waiting around to speak to Molly directly.

Finally the others who had been chattering amongst themselves picked up their stuff and headed out. Molly had her head in her hands, her face hidden from the room. Sean observed she was likely thinking. Or talking with Oz.

He wandered over to the bench, and stood in the space where Giles had just made his case. He paused, collecting his thoughts before he spoke. "You're not seriously considering this, are you?" he asked her.

Molly lifted her face, her eyes weary - and one looking a little puffier than the other. "In the absence of anything better... yeah. I am."

Sean's face hardened. "You're going to send a guy with no military training, no skills, no experience, and no idea what he's doing into what could very quickly become a hostage situation?"

Molly watched him carefully without responding.

Sean leaned on the bench in front of her. "You know he calls Reynolds 'Uncle,' right? Have you any idea what kind of leverage that would give Shaa over the Federation?"

Molly blinked, but other than that, her face revealed nothing.

Sean's brow furrowed, and his skin took on a slight sheen. The coloring around his face and neck increased, showing his agitation despite his attempts to curtail his feelings on the subject.

Finally Molly spoke. "Look, something tells me that maybe he isn't as inexperienced and untrained as we might think. I've got a feeling he's learned how to handle himself; and he wouldn't have suggested it if he wasn't confident."

Sean practically rolled his eyes. "Yes, Yes he would. Civilians don't know how to assess their own abilities. They have *no idea* how they'll hold up in a hostile situation. They imagine they'd do this, and that, and get the bad guy; but really, they have no fucking clue. And men - men are *wired* to overestimate their ability."

Molly leaned away from the desk and folded her arms. "Says who?"

Sean shook his head in disbelief. "Says science! And all my own damn experience! I know. I *was* that guy... until I got my ass shot to pieces on an *Andskotans* mission for trying to be a hero."

Molly filed the data away, interested to see another side of Sean. But she wanted to wrap this conversation up more than anything. She sighed. "Okay, look. I'll think about what you've said. But I'm not promising anything. If we don't send Giles, then we'll need to find someone we *can* send."

Sean straightened up and stood back from the bench. "Okay. Well... I can look into finding a replacement," he agreed, his bluster dispersing as he turned away. "Someone who won't bring the Federation down as soon as they're turned into a hostage," he added as he strutted out of the door.

Molly, losing the will to live, leaned over the bench in front of her, and let her forehead rest on it for several minutes, exasperated with the whole thing.

Giles hadn't realized she had been following him until he became aware of her footsteps behind him in the corridor. He called back to her over his shoulder. "So, you're ready to work some of that old *Garlene* magic again?"

He didn't look up as he scanned his fingerprint to access his room. The door slid open and he stepped inside, taking off his jacket.

Arlene stormed in behind him like a hurricane. She brushed past him, entering the lounge area, and then turned to face him with her hands on her hips.

Giles's face dropped as he suddenly realized he was in enemy territory.

"And what do you think you're doing?" she demanded, her cheeks flushing despite her blue skin. "They have a whole army at their disposal! What do you think you're going to add that someone else can't already do?"

Giles knew better than to be a smartass at this point. "I thought I'd help out. You know. Get involved, help the mission... for the Federation."

Arlene's mouth was agape as she searched for the words to express her frustration.

Giles didn't dare move. He'd studied pre-reptilian behavior, and in that moment, he fancied himself as the prey to a velociraptor or something similar. Their vision was drawn only by movement.

If I don't move, she can't kill me, he reasoned.

"So you think you're just going to head on over to that known terrorist's paramilitary base, and hold your hands up, and *hope* he doesn't blow your brains out on the spot?"

Arlene shook her head in disbelief, not really expecting an answer to her question. "And if he doesn't kill you right away, you can bet he's going to torture you."

Giles shrugged. "What's a little torture between friends? We've all been there," he said poignantly.

Arlene ignored the inference, not in the mood to delve into the past. She shook her fists, willing herself not to strangle him and complete Shaa's job for him. "Giles! You don't get it! These guys aren't your tribal men with sticks, and stories of ghosts and demons. These are evil people who have guns and blades and a tendency towards mindless violence. And taking a beating in a backwater coven as a rite of passage is in no way comparable to what these people will do to you."

Giles bit his tongue, his brain urging him to repeat the words 'rite of passage' out loud in disdain. Instead he sighed, releasing his own tension, deeming that a look of surrender would afford him the luxury of movement.

He plunked himself down into the armchair. Arlene remained standing.

"So what do you expect me to do?" he asked looking up at her, his eyes genuinely seeking an alternative now. "I can't just let them send some half-baked squaddie in there. They wouldn't stand a chance. No one is better qualified to talk to this guy than I am."

Arlene forced herself to take her hands from her hips, perhaps prematurely. She immediately folded her arms across her body in defense and frustration. "Who's to say that we have to put anyone in that position? Heck, why do we even need to land to take him out?"

Giles shook his head wearily and turned it to one side, pressing his finger and thumb against the ridge of his nose. "You know, if you were monitoring me, we'd be able to do this. And in a fraction of the time it would take me to figure him out on my own."

Arlene turned and headed for a chair to Giles's left. She sat down in resignation. "You mean monitor and interpret while you lead him?"

Giles dropped his hand and turned his face to look at her. "It'll be just like the good old days," he said, a slight brightness returning to his voice.

Arlene sat back in her chair. Giles knew immediately that he had her. He smiled to himself, careful to not gloat about his small victory.

Adventure-moon here we come, he thought.

Aboard *ArchAngel*, Reynolds's office

"Come!" the General called in response to the rap on the door.

The door opened, and Sean Royale stepped inside. "Sir, thank you for seeing me," he started.

Lance was sitting casually on one of his sofas, reviewing information on his holo. He glanced up as Sean approached. "You made it sound important," he said with a half smile.

Sean wrung his hands, tension rippling through his arm muscles. "It is. It's about Giles."

Lance sprang up, closing the holo to give Sean his full attention. "Ah, right. What's the little bugger done now?"

Sean hesitated. "He's, erm... volunteered for a mission he shouldn't be involved in. Not least because he's a civilian and shouldn't be on the front line-"

Lance's voice tightened. "Front line?"

Sean regretted having to break the news to him. He swallowed. "Yes, sir. It's to do with the Shaa mission. We need another way in... in order to penetrate their defenses. It's - "

Lance nodded understanding immediately what Giles expected to do. "Out of the question. That's what it is. That boy..." he headed over to the drinks tray without even thinking.

He poured himself a whiskey and then offered Sean one. Sean refused with a polite gesture of his hand. Lance drank his in one go, and then poured himself another. He walked back over to the sofa and sat down. "He thinks that just because I have the resources at my disposal, I can swoop in and save him. Time and again."

Lance shook his head, lowering his gaze. "It's my fault. It's what I've always done. Saved him. Gotten him out of fixes. One time, I sent the whole damn Armada out to the boondocks, just to retrieve his reckless little ass."

Lance's face took on a more determined look; one that seemed to betray his age, despite his engineered genetics. "He'll have to learn the hard way. I'll have a word; but if he insists on going against me, there will be no rescue mission. You'll need to communicate that to him, too. He simply won't believe me if I tell him."

Sean shifted his weight awkwardly. "Yes, sir. Of course, sir. Although, forgive me if I'm speaking out of turn. Might it be worth restricting his movement, perhaps?"

Lance looked up, his glass halfway to his mouth. "You mean confine him to his quarters so he can't leave?" He forgot that he was about to take a sip, and instead set the glass down on the coffee table in front of him. He sucked air through his mouth slowly. "I suppose… Although, he's a little old for being sent to his room."

Sean shrugged, relaxing a little. "It's a military operation. It wouldn't be unreasonable for someone to be imprisoned for interfering with a mission."

The General bobbed his head thoughtfully. "Let me talk to him first. Make sure he understands our position. And if you might have a word in his ear, too, it would be much appreciated."

"Of course, sir," Sean agreed.

"Okay, Captain. Thank you for bringing this to my attention," Lance concluded, picking up the whiskey tumbler and drawing it to his lips.

Sean nodded, and left the General to his predicament.

CHAPTER TEN

Onboard _ArchAngel_, Ship Lounge

Giles looked out at the darkness from behind the glass. The expansiveness of space never failed to put him in a good mood. He remembered standing at a very similar window as a child, tracing the patterns on the flooring, and then looking up and being captivated by the eternal blackness beyond where he could place his hands.

Giles felt someone come up behind him.

"Heard a rumor today," a voice reported. Giles wasn't immediately sure that the comment was directed at him.

Lance came and stood next to him, joining him in looking out the window.

Giles turned his head to see his uncle next to him. "I'm sure it took Arlene all of thirty seconds to alert you to my intentions," he commented.

Lance rocked on his heels. "Wasn't Arlene... although, I'm sure she made her case to you in true Arlene fashion."

Giles chuckled. "Yeah," he agreed, shuffling his hand through his already disheveled hair. "She did. Though I do believe I have her on my side now."

"So you intend to go through with it then?" he asked. Lance watched for Giles's reaction carefully, hoping that he wasn't going to have to force the issue.

Giles nodded, shoving his hands into his pant pockets. "I have to," he said quietly, still looking out of the window.

Lance drew in his breath, wishing he didn't have to make his next statement. "You know, with everything going on in the Federation right now, I'm a target. Which means you're a target. And you're going to walk right up to the most prominent threat we've seen in decades, and hand yourself over?"

Lance shook his head. "You know I'd move heaven and Earth to keep you safe; but if you get taken... and you can't talk your way out... I'm not going to be able to send in an extraction team this time. Not right now. And not with these people."

Giles looked as though he was going to interrupt, but Lance kept talking. "Besides, we've already put Molly's team on taking the guy out, and there was something we were missing. She failed. Do you understand the significance of that? There's no safety net, if you do this. Apart from anything, this is all off the record. Molly's team doesn't exist. So if you go in there, with them, it means officially, you weren't there. No one will ever know where you went."

Giles nodded, churning the information in his mind. "I get that, Uncle Lance," he said quietly, still gazing out into the blackness. His eyes seemed haunted. Haunted by something Lance couldn't possibly fathom at this point. Giles blinked. "And I'm okay with it," he continued, more determined now. "And I have every faith in Arlene's ability to help me read the guy fast enough to get out."

Lance looked away from him, out into space himself. "And if you're wrong?"

Giles's vulnerability disappeared behind a layer of bravado. "Then have a memorial service for me, and make sure you say nice things."

Lance shook his head, sadness and worry in his eyes. He put his hand on the man's shoulder as if he were still a child. "I need to say this," he said, pausing to make sure his words were being heard. "I don't want you to do it. I want you to stay here, where you'll be safe, and - "

Giles turned and slapped his father's best friend on the shoulder. "Uncle Lance, now you're starting to sound like Mom."

Lance knew that the window of opportunity had passed, and that Giles was deflecting. He resigned himself to sharing the boy's humor. "Well, *hell*. Someone's got to try and talk some goddamn sense into you," he said, producing a half-chewed cigar from his pocket and placing it in his mouth.

The two men's ages seemed switched; the older one appearing to be young and boyish, and the youngest seeming middle aged. But the respect they shared, and the ways they communicated in their relationship showed they were closer to equals. They headed toward the bar to have a final drink together before the now-inevitable mission rolled around.

"So, what've you got?" Molly asked as she strode into the lab they were using as a base on *The ArchAngel*.

Paige and Maya were looking exhausted from the work, but their spirits were higher than Molly expected.

Paige scraped her stool backwards as she stood up. "We've made some progress on Chaakwa's case," she announced brightly. Her cheeks swelled with pride, as she managed to muster her signature grin.

Molly wandered over to where the girls were set up with their array of holoscreens all over the bench. "Show me," she said.

Maya and Paige ran through the various points of intel they had gathered, pinpointing each of the players who had been involved in the sinister demise of Chaakwa's father.

"Depending on how you'd like to handle this," Maya explained, "I think we can probably enlist some help from some of his old buddies on the force. Chaakwa was clear that she wanted to take them in and give them a trial, so they would be publicly found guilty, and exposed."

Molly bobbed her head as she reviewed a holo that Maya had just passed her. "I see. So she didn't go for putting a bullet through them?" she confirmed.

Maya shook her head. "Nope."

Molly smiled. "I like her..."

Maya and Paige exchanged glances, relaxing a little. They knew that violence had its place, especially in an outfit like the military; but still, they found it a relief that they weren't going to have to be down for the killing on this one. Even though some of the fuckheads downright deserved it.

Molly pushed the holoscreen back toward Maya. "Okay, finish the background checks on these guys, and see if there is a way to get them all in one place. This will be far cleaner if we can round them up and then hand them over in one go."

Maya nodded in agreement.

Molly turned to leave. "As soon as we get done with this business with Shaa, that's next on our agenda."

Molly breezed out of the room, pleased they were making progress on *something*.

So it sounds like you're going to go ahead and let Giles do this?

Yes. I think I need to. We've tried the overt assault, and we need another way.

And the fact that he isn't even on your team...?

It's a concern, of course. But we supported him in regaining that talisman, and I have a gut feeling our job isn't done with that yet... Plus, the guy is convinced he knows what he's doing. And I'm almost tempted to believe him.

And if he can't get out?

Then we find a way to get him out.

The odds of success on this are low. I can share with you the parameters if you-

That won't be necessary, Oz. I think it's something he needs to do... and that we need to let him do.

Well, you can't pretend to me you're not uneasy about it.

Of course I'm uneasy about it.

Molly continued down the corridor, heading back to her quarters. There was work to be done before they would be ready to deploy Giles in the morning.

ArchAngel, Medical Facility

Arlene busied herself with checking the implants that the ship's surgeons had inserted into Giles's eye and the side of his head by his ear.

Sean looked down at the middle-aged professor sitting in the chair in front of him. "I need to make sure you understand what you're agreeing to do," he said, his face the most serious Giles had ever seen it.

Giles nodded. "I understand. We've been over it."

Sean closed his eyes for a second before continuing. "But the tech on that ship... if it falls into enemy hands, it's programmed to self-destruct. The EI on board won't let it just stick around."

Giles breathed a sigh of frustration. "I know. I get it. You're going to have the ship drop me, and then gate out of there."

"Yes," Sean pushed, "meaning that you're going to be on that moon, all alone, with no means of escape."

Giles glanced over at the kit Arlene had him rigged up to for the testing phase. "We had better hope that this shit works, then."

Arlene, who had been ignoring the conversation until then, peered at him over her tinted specs. "This 'shit' will work. My concern is that you'll get killed before you can work your magic."

Giles shook his head against the headrest, and then relaxed

backwards, knowing that this was going to go on until he was actually landed and out of their safety zone.

Giles was struck by a thought. "You know, it makes no difference about the ship. Even if there were a ship there that I could use to escape, they'd have it, and the airspace, so locked down, there is no way I'd get out of there alive."

Sean glanced up at Arlene, who had paused what she was doing and was still peering at him. "He has a point," Sean agreed.

Arlene went back to the holoscreen of the diagnostics. Both men could tell she was anything but happy about the situation.

"Okay," she said finally. "They did a nice job with the auditory implant. I've got it hooked up with the existing language chip you already had implanted there, and I've run a few firmware updates on it. Should be an even smoother experience, with less lag. The retinal one is picking up the quantum comm perfectly, and, as instructed, they've buried the connection button even deeper into your arm than they would normally. If you need to hit it, you're going to need to really press deep in to get it. At least like this, it will probably avoid detection if they search you."

She took the tinted glasses off, and stood up from her chair next to him. "Your nanocytes will take care of the incisions. They won't scar, so there'll be no hint of the implants after you're healed."

Giles sat up, and rolled down his shirtsleeves. "Okay. Thanks, Arlene."

Sean, with nothing left to say, stood up as well. He waved to Arlene, and then walked silently out of the door.

Giles watched him leave, and then shrugged, not expecting any sympathy from Arlene, either.

Aboard _The Empress_

"You sure we're far enough out?" Molly asked.

Sean nodded. "Should be. I don't know of any tech that could see us from here."

Molly's eyes were fixed on the screen ahead of her. They were able to see the former-moon, with the odd ship coming in and out every so often.

"Looks like a lot of traffic," she commented.

Crash shifted in his seat. "Yeah. I've been watching their flight path; I suspect they're doing exercises, rather than actually going anywhere."

Molly mumbled her acknowledgment.

"There!" Sean said, highly animated and pointing his finger into one corner of the screen. "That's him."

Joel had been sitting in one of the console chairs further back in the cockpit. He got up and moved forward in order to see better.

Arlene punched some keys in her holo console, to the left of where the others had congregated. "That's him, indeed. He's on approach."

The team watched as *The Scamp Princess* approached Chom-X9. Occasionally, one of them would shift their weight, or check something on another monitor; but other than that, there was silence in the cockpit.

Eventually, Arlene broke the quiet. "He's landed."

"Put his readout onscreen," Molly instructed.

A moment later, they were seeing and hearing everything Giles was experiencing.

Joel leaned back in his chair to catch Arlene's eye. "Can he hear us?" he asked.

Arlene shook her head. "No. But I can open a channel to his implant when we need to," she confirmed.

They watched as Giles stepped out of the craft, moving slowly and carefully as he went. It took a few moments before he spun around, revealing the view onscreen of the tribe of Zhyns with blasters trained on him.

"By my Ancestors!" Brock exclaimed. "How many of them are there?" He only vocalized what the others were thinking.

Sean leaned forward on his console. "Yeah, and my bet is they didn't all come out to say hello."

Joel glanced over to Molly. "Looks like he has more than a few defectors. Seems like he probably has more of an army at his disposal."

Molly rolled her lips together. "Certainly explains a few things," she admitted. "You know, the intel that we receive may be helpful after all."

They watched as Giles was taken into the custody of the muscle-y, angry-looking Zhyn. He was cuffed at his wrists, and a restraining device was placed around his neck. They all recognized what that did, but no one said a word. Giles had made his choice, and there was no turning back now.

Molly glanced over at Arlene. "Now what?" she asked.

Arlene removed her headset and sat back in her console chair, watching the screen at the front of the cockpit. "Now," she told them, "we wait."

Jack sat cross-legged in the main cabin, keeping the others company. Idly she swung her foot up and down. "So you think you can track down all these fuckheads?" she asked Paige, more making conversation than anything else.

Paige glanced over at Pieter, who was immersed in something on his holo. He looked up and nodded. "Yeah, we should be able to…" he said absently.

Jack peered over and realized he had created a copy of the screen that was in the cockpit.

So much for keeping them away from the distraction of the main event, she thought.

Maya muttered something to herself.

Paige nudged her. "What is it?" she asked, looking over her shoulder at her holoscreen.

"Background check on one of our tangos. I really don't think this guy deserves to go into the system." She showed her holoscreen to Paige, whose eyes widened in horror as she read his rap sheet. "And they let him out?" Paige clarified, hardly believing what she was reading.

Maya nodded. "Every time. And each time, he has gotten involved in more murders. It's like the system is corrupt or something…"

Jack leaned forward, jarred by what she was overhearing. "Let me see," she said, reaching for the holoscreen.

Maya shared it with her and watched Jack's reaction.

After a few seconds of scanning the background summary, Jack spoke. "This shit can't be allowed to go on. I'll have a word with Molly, but when we bring these guys in, this one won't be handed over." Her eyes blazed with a passion that none of the team had seen before. She was possessed by anger; her whole aura pulsed with fury.

She passed the holoscreen back to Maya and stood up. Without another word, she strode off in the direction of the cargo hold.

Maya and Paige looked at each other, surprised by this glimpse of Jack. Maya broke the silence. "She has a point," she said, folding the screen away and moving on to the next thing.

Paige went back to her work, glad that there were fighters in this world.

Warriors like Jack, who cared.

Chom-X9

"You don't understand. I have important information for the High Marshall. I've come from the Federation. They don't know I'm here!" Giles shouted back through the dark, damp corridor as his new imprisoners slammed the cell door shut on him.

They had led him, not to speak with Shaa, as he had hoped, but rather, down to some kind of dungeon with metal walls.

He kicked at the door in frustration, and turned away, looking at the state of the place he'd willingly walked into. "Damn cliché of a dungeon, if you ask me!" he retorted to the silent Zhyn whose footsteps he could already hear walking away.

He wasted little more time on his emotions. In fact, once alone, his demeanor changed. He stood more upright, and calmly looked around the cell, checking for ingresses and vents, and anything else that might be either a help or a threat.

He searched around for signs of cameras, knowing in all likelihood he was being watched. Although, there was no need to overdo the play-acting for the cameras. Things would progress soon enough.

Finally, he noticed a little spot in one corner of the cell.

Bingo, he thought, careful not to gaze at it for too long. He'd found his camera. Now he knew where his audience was, he could carefully hide his conversations with Arlene...

Shaa's office, Chom-X9

"Your Highness, the prisoner we picked up yesterday is still asking for you."

The voice interrupted Shaa's train of thought.

Slightly irritated, Shaa turned from the window that looked out onto the open expanse of rocky terrain. "What does he want?" he asked gruffly.

Davon lowered his eyes and clasped his hands. "He's saying he wants to... er... defect, sir."

Shaa swung around. "On what grounds?"

Davon wrung his hands tightly. "He says he has information.

About the Federation. Says he was close enough to have intel that we would want."

Shaa waved his hand dismissively and looked back out of the window. "Yes, but *why*? And what could he possibly have that would be of use to us?"

Davon shrugged. "I don't know. Allow me to find out more." He bowed and started to leave.

Shaa's voice stopped him before he had made it to the door. "And who is he, exactly?" he asked idly.

Davon pulled up his holo. "Our records show that he is one of the long living ones. Son of Kurns, who we know has always been on the inner circle. Never had a way to get to him, though; he was always locked up tight within the empire."

Shaa shuffled his weight a little before turning back to his second in command. "Have him brought up here. I'd like to see this Son of Kurns. If he has anything interesting, he can share it before we dispose of him."

Davon bowed again, and this time hurried out of the room.

Shaa turned back to the landscape in front of him, imagining what it would be like, populated with other believers - other Zhyn who were prepared to go the distance.

Imagine what I could accomplish, then. The Federation wouldn't have a chance.

CHAPTER ELEVEN

Aboard _ArchAngel_, Lance's office

"It's been twenty four hours!" Molly's voice was a little higher than she had hoped it would come out.

Sean sat on one of the General's sofas, rubbing his face. Molly could tell he was worried, despite his assurances that Giles probably knew what he was doing.

She glanced over at him. "You've changed your tune," she said to him, a hint of accusation leaking into her statement.

Lance hovered next to his drinks tray, looking at the small group of worried friends who had appeared in his office. "As have you," he pointed out to Molly.

Molly put one hand on her hip, trying to find the words that would be helpful. Arlene sat patiently, waiting for her opportunity to weigh in. Joel sat next to her, very aware of her tension, contemplating the operational variables that might give them an edge.

Molly finally found her way to express herself. "I thought he'd be in and out by now. That was what we'd agreed to."

Arlene took her hands from her mouth. "It was never going to happen like that; that isn't how these things work. He's in for the long haul. And he knew that," she added.

Molly honed in on Arlene. "You knew what to expect?" She paused, watching carefully, reading Arlene's calmness. Then she saw it. "You've done this before. That's why you were both so confident. This is what you've been doing for the Federation for years - pretending that you're just out there, gallivanting and exploring and reporting back some cultural studies - but really, you're spies. You've been grifting our enemies forever!"

Molly shook her head in disbelief, not just in the revelation and her naiveté that she didn't see it before, but also at her surprise that she could see it now. It all seemed so clear, standing here in front of Arlene.

Arlene pulled her shoulders up, and then relaxed them; her hands now tidily perched in her lap. "You see that now because I'm allowing you to," she explained, as if reading Molly's thoughts. "It was too risky to let you know before then."

Molly glanced over at Sean. "And you! You don't seem surprised."

Sean wiped his face again with one hand; the other hand was on his knee as he sat forward on the sofa. He didn't speak. He just looked up at the General, and then down at the ornate rug under his feet.

Molly looked at Joel just to make sure she wasn't going mad. Joel seemed just as surprised as she was. She could feel his mind churning through the realization that they'd been played.

The General poured himself a drink, and then turned back to face them. "The point is he's in now. So what are we going to do about it?"

It had become Arlene's operation, by some kind of unspoken agreement. She drew herself up a little and took a deep breath. "The way this normally goes down - "

Molly looked down and shook her head, seething at the reminder of their deceit.

Wow; looks like you're having a reaction to the words 'nor-mally goes down'.

Well, do you blame me? I mean, how were we supposed to know that this is what they fucking do?

On the plus side, it sounds like they've got this.

Yeah. I'll count that blessing later. When I've finished reeling.

Arlene had continued with her narrative of what to expect. "... a few days for him to get an audience with Shaa. Or one of his henchmen. Either way, it's a waiting game until then."

Joel brought his attention back to the conversation. "And when he gets his audience?" he asked, shifting on the sofa to face Arlene a little more.

Arlene nodded. "Then, the real work begins. Giles has been fitted with the surveillance devices that we can hook up to the analysis software. This is going to help me determine exactly what kind of sociopath we're working against. Once we know that, and we have a complete profile, Giles will know exactly what to do to gain his trust, and in turn, how to take him down."

Lance looked at her briefly before returning to the task of studying the contents of his glass.

Sean suddenly sat up. "Okay. I guess that's it, then. Nothing more for us to do until...?"

Arlene thought through the timeline. "We're looking at a few days before we have a profile, and then it'll probably take a week or so before we see any significant changes in their dynamic. And that's assuming we get straight to Shaa, and not one of his goons. If we have to process through one of them to get to Shaa, it will add on a week or two."

Molly folded her arms. "So what are we meant to do until then?" she asked, looking now to the General.

Lance realized the question was directed at him, and pulled himself back from his own concerns about Giles. "Right... well," he said, putting his glass back down onto the drinks tray. "ADAM tells me your team has made some progress on that police captain's death back on Estaria."

Molly nodded, not entirely sure why that was relevant right now.

Lance looked to her, and then to Joel. "I suggest you take yourselves back to Gaitune, and work this case to its conclusion."

Molly's eyes widened as if she were about to protest, but Lance continued speaking. "If there is any change in the situation here, Arlene will make sure you are the first to know. And when things heat up, we'll have you back here to finish what you started." His voice was conclusive. Molly decided there was no point in arguing.

"Until then, go catch some bad guys, and make the Federation proud," he told her.

Molly unfolded her arms and noticed that Sean had relaxed in his seat again.

He knows more than he's letting on.

He does. I think he's seen Giles do this before. Or at least, he knew of it. I'll see what I can find out, if you like?

Thanks, Oz.

Molly walked over to the General and shook his hand. "Okay. Thank you for your hospitality, sir. I look forward to seeing you sooner rather than later," she said, her eyes darting over to Arlene.

She turned and headed out of the room, waiting outside for Joel and Sean to say their goodbyes and follow her out.

Chom-X9, Shaa's Office

"I hear you've been requesting an audience with me," Shaa prompted as he sat down in his console chair behind a makeshift desk.

Giles looked around the room, taking in as much detail as he could. His eyes came to rest on the former Lord High Marshall of the Zhyn Empire. "I have information in exchange for asylum," Giles said, monitoring his own tone to make it even and confident, without a hint of arrogance. He needed to play this guy just right.

Shaa steepled his hands. "Why do you want asylum?"

Giles was expressionless for a moment. "Because the Federation has become power hungry and corrupt. My ideologies no longer fit with their agenda."

Shaa regarded him skeptically. "And what do you think you can tell me that I don't already know?"

Giles lowered his chin a little. "You know who I am, right?" he ventured quietly, hoping the language chip was doing its job, and setting the right tone in his statement.

Shaa rocked gently in his chair. "I do. But that doesn't tell me what you know that might be of strategic use to us. In case you hadn't noticed," he continued, waving his hands nonchalantly about him, "we have a lot of things already covered."

A smile leered over his lips, lopsidedly showing his contempt for others, and the arrogance for what he had achieved.

Giles lowered his chin a little before answering. "I can give you all kinds of information. Like where the weak points are in their defenses, and the sequence of their runs into the base. I can also tell you all kinds of things about how their systems are built. You know I can. You know who my father is."

Aboard *ArchAngel*

Several thousand kilometers away, Arlene watched and listened as Giles led Shaa into their trap.

She tutted into the empty comms room. "Oh, no, you won't, wide boy. You will not be sharing that kind of intel." She made a quick note of his promises in case she had to give the General a heads-up, shaking her head at how cavalier he was with secrets that she was sure other service people would defend with their lives. "He's a law unto himself, that one," she said to the darkened communications room.

Empty food packets were scattered around her workspace and filling the bins. She had not left the place since the meeting with the General the day before, when they returned to the *Arch-Angel* after depositing Giles there. There was no way she was going to abandon him. She just wished he could find a way to gain Shaa's trust without putting the Federation in jeopardy.

Chom-X9, Shaa's Office

"Okay. I'm interested," Shaa confessed. "Interested enough to see what you have."

Shaa glanced down at Giles's wrists. "I see you have no communication device, or computer on you."

Giles rubbed at the place where his holo would have been, finding it difficult to move in his handcuffs. "Er, no, I don't. My holo was taken from me as soon as I landed. If I could have it returned to me, I can start drawing up the information I brought for you to review..."

Shaa nodded to Davon, who was hanging back by the door, watching the whole exchange. Davon acknowledged the order with a small bow.

Shaa turned his attention back to Giles. "I'm particularly interested in anyone who might be aligning themselves with the Federation. Anyone who is having talks with them, but hasn't been official in their intentions."

He leaned on his desk. "*That* would be of value," he added.

Giles nodded. "I can do that," he agreed.

Aboard *ArchAngel*

Back in her dark room, Arlene held her headphones closer to her ear in order to hear better. She shook her head. "You'd better be making this shit up, you motherfucker," she muttered to herself, making another note on her list.

She tapped a message onto her holo to ADAM.

I NEED TO APPRISE THE GENERAL OF DEVELOP-MENTS ON CHOM-X9. MIGHT WE SET A MEETING FOR A FEW HOURS FROM NOW?

>>SEND<<

Shaa stood up. "It looks like we have a way forward, then," he said. He pointed at the guards behind him, and signaled for them to take him back to his cell. "I look forward to reviewing your offering," he added.

The guards grabbed Giles roughly by the upper arms, and manhandled him out of the room.

Giles nodded his head towards the Lord High Marshall before he was whisked away. There was nothing to say; he had his in.

And Arlene had her baseline.

Chom-X9

Giles was shoved back into the holding cell where he had spent the last day. He fell forward as he was shoved in, and waited for the swish and clank of the metal door closing behind him.

He took a few paces forward, his awareness on the door without turning to look at it. Once he was certain it was closed, and the footsteps were moving away, he lay down on his rack on his right hand side with his cuffed hands in front of him.

He turned his head downwards so his lips would be hidden from the camera. "Did you get all that?" he whispered.

Arlene opened up the connection on his earpiece. "Yes, every word, you scoundrel. You realize I'll be reporting this in to the

General so that he can have reinforcements sent to wherever they're needed?"

Giles breathed in exasperation at the woman. "I'm in a holding cell at ground zero to the biggest terrorist operation the Federation has seen in our extended lifetimes, and you're giving me shit about a few little 'secrets' that the guy probably already has?"

Arlene frowned though Giles couldn't see it. "Well, at the very least, it's generating more work for me, mopping up after you."

Giles fidgeted, trying to get comfortable on the thin mattress, in his handcuffs. The metal bracelets were digging into his wrists horribly, but he couldn't risk sitting up and having their conversation detected.

"Did you get the baseline for a profile?" he asked again.

Arlene huffed over the line. "Yes. Of course I did. You're the last person I should need to remind that this is not my first rodeo."

Giles smiled. "Yes, I'm well aware of this. And, hey, if this works out, maybe I can convince you that it won't be your last either."

Arlene's lips, unable to be restrained by her brain, spread into a small smile. She was grateful that Giles wasn't able to see her, because he would certainly have counted that as a point. "Are you sitting comfortably? There's a lot to cover for this one."

Arlene pulled up a dashboard from the video footage of Shaa she'd used to analyze his reactions: facial expressions, choice of words, tone of voice, speed of speech in different points. "And remind me to circle back to the hot spots I noticed when he made his counter-offer of the intel he really wants. I have a theory I want to run past you."

Giles shuffled on his side again, his back aching already. "Okay. Go ahead. I'm listening."

Arlene began the rundown as if it were just last week they had worked as a pair, infiltrating a high-stakes game.

. . .

Aboard _The Empress_, En route back to Gaitune-67

Paige chattered away excitedly to Maya. "I can't believe that all this time, Arlene has been some super-spy!" Her eyes were wide as she tried to contain her excitement and keep her voice down.

Pieter poked his head up from behind their seats, joining the conversation. "Of all the people I have known, she'd be the least likely to be a super spy. I mean, Sean... he's all dark and mysterious when he's being serious. He's got skeletons. And closets by the shed load, for sure."

Sean yelled from the cockpit, "Yeah, and you'll show more respect, unless you want to be a skeleton in said closet!"

Paige, Maya, and Pieter looked at each other. Pieter lowered his voice to a whisper. "Yeah, and ears like a _fjandi_ bat!" he added.

Paige had clamped her hand over her mouth, but she didn't really want to suppress her ability to speak. "Yeah, I mean, Arlene - I thought she was just some dear old lady, and then she had all these Estarian super powers. And then this!" Her voice had accidentally gotten louder, and she returned her hand to her mouth and subconsciously ducked her head down.

Maya glanced around seeing if someone else might overhear them. "Yeah, and Giles! The doddering professor. Who'd have thought?"

The sound of their voices carried through the cabin. Molly reclined in her seat and reviewed the files that Paige and Maya had pulled together for her.

Joel sat on the other side of the aisle, going through the material at the same time. "So, you think we should get Chaakwa involved at all? I mean, it's a little risky for someone in her position. Not to mention... emotional."

Molly pulled her eyes from her holo. "Yeah. That's what I

thought. But when we first talked about it, it was clear she needed closure. She needs to be in on this."

Joel's face softened. "Yeah, I can understand that," he said, his eyes taking on a distant feel.

Molly dropped the holoscreen down and rested her arm. She looked thoughtful, and her eyes glazed over a little. She turned her head against the headrest. "Joel?" she asked, looking in his general direction.

Joel looked over again. "Mmm," he said.

"What do you do for fun these days?" she asked, her eyes still a little distant.

Joel looked out across the cabin, contemplating his answer. "Well, I use the gym, I guess."

Molly pulled her gaze up to meet his. "No, I mean fun. Not for health. Not for training. Not for work. Just... fun."

Joel folded his holo screens away. "Well, I guess I don't do anything. Not really."

Molly shifted in her seat and brought her eyes forward. "Yeah. Me neither," she agreed with a small sigh and a hint of resignation.

Joel twisted in his seat to look at her, crossing one leg over the other. "We should do something. Something fun; when we get back to Sark. Either on Gaitune, or even Estaria."

Molly frowned a little. "Something? Like what?"

Joel's eyes lit up. "Laser tag!"

Molly smiled and flicked her eyes upwards briefly. "That sounds like either a team building exercise, or a training disguised as fun." She grinned and nodded in the direction of the gang. "Though, it might be an idea for them, one weekend."

Joel's face was brighter now. "Yes, that's a point," he said, mentally filing it away.

There was a pause in the conversation.

"How about we go for a beer?" he suggested.

Molly shrugged. "Sure. Why not," she agreed simply. "In fact, I need to go to Estaria to see Chaakwa, once we've put together a plan. We could head down together."

Joel bobbed his head. "You're not worried about being seen? You are supposed to be dead, remember."

Molly smiled dryly. "I'll wear a hat," she said flippantly.

Joel chuckled. "You've already had Oz deal with that, haven't you?"

Molly avoided making eye contact. "Let's just say Oz is an excellent team player, who more and more is working under his own steam." Her smile widened, and Joel laughed.

"Well, it sounds like you have him well-trained," he remarked, pulling up his holos again, and settling in to get some work knocked out.

CHAPTER TWELVE

Gaitune-67, Base conference room

"Okay, any last questions?" Joel prompted. He looked around the conference table. The team was looking rested and back on the case, but the usual joviality was absent. "Don't all talk at once," he teased.

Brock grinned. "I got nothing. This one looks like a slam dunk."

Joel closed his holos. "Let's hope so," he said, the memory of their 'failed' and 'unresolved' missions still lingering. The details of this cop's mission were intricate and detailed, and they had to follow them to a 'T' to make sure they got the six culprits all to the same location at the same time.

Paige stuck her hand in the air. "If we're done, I have an announcement," she said brightly. A few of the team members around the table sat up a little, pleased for the change of pace.

Joel nodded, giving her the floor.

Paige glanced around the table, a little like a politician running for office. "Well, it's real short. Because everyone was so tired when we got back here last night, we are pushing our pizza dinner to tonight."

Maya leaned in. "We're also going to have a beer for Giles," she added.

There were approving grunts and affirmative sounds around the table. Brock sat up straighter in his chair, ready to be dismissed.

Joel looked to Molly, who acknowledged it was time to wrap up. He did the honors. "Okay, folks, there we have it. Pizza dinner tonight, and we'll give you an update on the Chaakwa mission as soon as we get intel confirmation from Pieter – who, remember, is your point person on this one. So, any questions, direct them to him. Any decisions," he looked at Pieter, "you run them up the chain to me. Got it?"

Pieter nodded once. He had slipped so low in his seat it was a wonder he hadn't fallen on the floor. Paige wanted to reach over and slap him.

Joel brought it to a close. "Okay, peeps. Let's call it a day," he said, circling his finger in the air in his normal 'move out' sign.

The weary participants were glad to see the end of a three-hour briefing. Each and every one of them loved their job, and adored the people they worked with; but three hours in a non-stop operations planning and briefing was just grueling.

Brock leaned over to Pieter before they stood up. "Makes you wonder whether Giles has the better option!" he chortled, looking at the time on his holo.

Pieter snickered, managing, through some kind of weird agility, to pull himself up onto his seat properly, and then stand.

Paige had already made her escape from the conference room, her high heels clipping along the corridor, heading to get changed so she could do the pizza run.

Gradually, the room emptied out but for Sean, Joel, Jack, and Molly. Sean had surreptitiously made sure that Jack knew to stick around.

When all the others were gone and out of earshot, Jack made

sure the door was closed, and wandered back over to the side of the conference room table where Molly still remained.

"This about the tango number six?" Jack asked.

Molly nodded. "Yes. And thank you for your message about that one. It was well worth us taking a proper look at."

Jack bobbed her head. "So, what's the verdict?" she asked bluntly, then glanced at Joel and Sean.

Molly pushed back in her seat to better see everyone. Sean had perched on the desk next to her, and Joel sat on her other side. Jack stood leaning against the wall.

"Well, we've all seen the file. I just want to make sure we are all in agreement." She looked at each of them in turn.

Joel was the first to answer. "Yes. I'm sure we are," he said, looking at the others to make sure he was accurate.

Jack shook her head. "In agreement about what?"

Sean and Joel exchanged looks, obviously having spoken about it together before they walked into the meeting.

"We'll take care of it," Sean said simply. "Once we leave the warehouse, we'll give the signal to Chaakwa and her team, and they will find the five. As far as they're concerned, the sixth guy was never there, and he'll never be found."

His tone was as straightforward as if he had been reading off a shopping list.

Molly wasn't disagreeing, but she had a look of curiosity in her eyes. "What will you do with him?" she asked.

Sean shook his head. "You don't need to know," he said in response to Molly, and then looked back at Jack, recognizing the pain and anger in her eyes. "Just know that it will be handled."

He and Joel exchanged another look; a look of agreement, sealing the bond of what they had volunteered to do.

Jack's shoulders relaxed as she witnessed this. She realized in that moment that they were willing to handle this; not just because they thought it was the right thing to do, but also so that she and Molly didn't have to. She was grateful for that - despite

ELL LEIGH CLARKE & MICHAEL ANDERLE

the fury that boiled in her blood whenever she thought of the heinous things the tango had done.

Estaria, Downtown Spire

"Okay, so just message me when you're done," Joel said as Molly slipped out of the pod in the middle of the alley.

"Cool. See you soon," she called back to him.

The door slid closed and then the pod shot back up into the sky. She checked her holo. Lunchtime.

She stepped out of the alley, looking left, then right. The precinct was just one block to her right, and Chaakwa took her lunch at the place just a few blocks up to her left. Molly started off down the street, noticing how surreal it felt to be back in this world. After all she had seen. All she had done. All the places she had visited, so far away.

Space was starting to feel more normal to her than this life she had left behind.

As she walked, her mind flicked back to her childhood, and then to her time in the military. The events that had propelled her out of the military and into the meeting with Joel; the time at the safe house, and then running around this planet trying to get off world. It felt like it had been a million years since that first day in the bar, when she had gone to him for a job.

And now...

She looked up, watching the shop fronts pass by as she kept her eyes peeled for the little mocha shop where she would find Chaakwa. She spotted the sign just up ahead, and walked purposefully towards it.

Just outside, she stopped, letting a mother with a stroller leave through the double doors first. The little Estarian baby was giggling and gurgling away, a toy in his little hands. Molly smiled. This world seemed so alien to her. Like a dream she'd had once, but could barely remember.

She stepped through the doorway and headed over to the counter, keeping a lookout for Chaakwa. She didn't see her.

"What can I get you?" the friendly barista asked from across the counter.

Molly looked up at the menu and sighed, remembering that she couldn't have mocha. "I'll have a tea, thanks," she said, trying to keep the disappointment from her voice. After all, it wasn't the barista's fault.

She paid for her tea, and looked around at the seated patrons. Suddenly an arm appeared from behind a plant and a pillar. It was Chaakwa. Molly waved back with her fingers, careful not to draw too much attention to herself.

Once her tea was deposited on the counter, she scooped it up, and headed over to join her friend.

"Greetings," she smiled, as she popped her mug on the table. Chaakwa got up and hugged her, taking her a little by surprise.

"Greetings. I was so pleased to get your message," Chaakwa explained with a definite note of excitement. "I take it you have news? A lead?"

Molly sat down, quite content to get straight down to business. "I do. Well, a whole plan, in fact."

Molly described the plan to Chaakwa. "There are six individuals that we know were directly involved," she explained. She pulled up her holo and showed Chaakwa some mug shots they had pulled from various authorities. "This guy gave the order." She pushed another image over to her. "This one pulled the trigger. This one is the head of the network that does this kind of thing, a lot, in the pursuit of their own power." Molly showed her one picture after another.

"This one..." she said, her tone becoming a little more serious. "This one did a lot of the groundwork to find where your father was most vulnerable. He had files on you, too. Photographs of you in your apartment; probably as insurance, but also... we think maybe for his own pleasure."

Chaakwa's expression barely changed, though Molly could tell that the information was disturbing to her. She hesitated to tell her more, but then decided it was better that she knew.

Her tone was soft. Sympathetic, almost. "We found other footage on his holo drive of many women. Maya did a background check on them. All were violently assaulted and murdered. The police haven't been able to connect the cases, because the MO was different each time - probably deliberately so. But this guy has been in and out of the system on suspicion of various things, and, basically, he's not a good person. He's served three sentences, and each time, has been released and gone on to commit more murders. More than even the police knew about."

Her voice softened, wishing she could make it easier on Chaakwa.

Chaakwa took a deep breath as if accepting the situation, and processing it. "So…"

Molly's face became more determined. "So, he's going to go into that room, just like the other five… But he won't be there for you and your friends to arrest. We'll take care of him. But you mustn't go looking for him. Nor share this with anyone." Molly held her gaze. "*Anyone*," she reiterated pointedly.

Chaakwa nodded her head, like a little girl in the head teacher's office. She pushed the holoscreen back to Molly, who closed down all the images and put the holo away.

Chaakwa listened to her explain the plan in rapt attention, hardly believing that Molly's team, in such a short time, had managed to not only track down all the relevant people, but also put together a workable mission.

Molly finished briefing her, and moved on to the next task: getting the names of friends of Chaakwa's father who might help to make the arrest.

"This has to be a small team of people," she qualified. "No current cops. You can't trust any of them. They might be on the payroll, or we'll be putting them in danger; out-of-service folks are probably less vulnerable. We'll vet whomever you think you might want to use before we take action."

Chaakwa agreed.

"And remember," Molly told her, "I'm already dead."

Detective Indius smiled. "And your team doesn't even exist. We just got lucky with an anonymous tip."

"Exactly," Molly concurred.

Molly took down the names. The two women looked at each other, smiling, and clinked their drinks together.

"How did it go?" Joel asked as Molly stepped into the pod.

Molly hauled herself up into the pod, holding onto the grab bars on either side of the door. "Great," she told him. "She was on board with all of it, and seemed to have taken the thing about the pictures well.

Joel helped her get settled before hitting the door button. "I suppose it helps, knowing that the man who has been stalking you is about to be disappeared," Joel mused.

"This is true," Molly agreed, looking out of the side window of the pod. "So, where are we going?" she asked, shaking off work for the day.

Joel gave a half grin, and looked a little sheepish. He ruffled his hair nervously. "I thought we might take a trip down memory lane, and head back to that bar over in the Irk'n Quarter in Uptarlung."

Molly squinted with one eye, trying to place the name. "The one where we reconnected?"

Joel nodded. "Yeah. I thought it might be fun," he added quickly.

Molly sat back and reached for her harness. "Hmm, funny. I was just thinking of that place when I was walking over to the mocha shop."

Joel frowned a little as he tapped the location into the head up display. "Oh yeah?"

Molly clipped the straps together and settled back, crossing her legs and getting comfortable. "Yeah. And about how far we've come since that day. I mean, heck... we're no longer outlaws, for one thing."

Joel chuckled. "Speak for yourself. You were the only one who was ever an outlaw; and technically, if they knew you were breathing, you still would be!"

"Fair point," Molly smiled, shrugging one shoulder and settling in for the ride.

Chenz' Bar, Downtown Uptarlung, Irk'n Quarter

Not long after, they arrived at the bar.

Joel opened the door for Molly, and she stepped inside.

"Wow... it feels just the same," she exclaimed in a near whisper.

Joel glanced around, his special skills detecting a disturbance in the force. "No, you know... I think they redecorated. I'm sure the carpets were darker before."

Molly giggled and slapped the back of her arm against his body playfully.

Joel pretended it hurt, and then ushered her towards the bar. They ordered drinks and took a seat.

"So, this is... *different*," he said, looking around and relaxing into the situation.

Molly bobbed her head, a little nervous now that they didn't have the seriousness of missions and work to talk about. "Yeah. It's... *different*," she agreed, unable to find a more descriptive word for everything she felt in the moment.

Joel looked thoughtful. "You know, it kinda makes you wonder about what would have happened, had we not decided to do the whole skills-for-hire thing together, doesn't it?"

Molly turned her lips down. "It does. Man, life couldn't have been more *different.*"

Joel smirked at her dig at their choice of words. Then he leaned over the sticky little table, and rested his arms on it; something he knew straight away he would regret later. "What do you think you would have done?"

Molly shrugged. "I dunno. Maybe ended up on the street? Or worse, computing for a living."

They both laughed.

A moment later, their drinks arrived, and they cheersed. "Don't you have parents here, though?" he asked, taking a swig from the bottle and looking a little more serious.

Molly tilted her head to one side briefly, before straightening up and taking a sip of her own beer.

Joel noticed her reaction. "Okay. So conversations like that are off limits," he noted to himself.

Molly smiled. "No. It's just..."

Joel waited. She struggled to find words. Joel fiddled with the bottle between his hands. "You never talk about them. But they're still alive, right?"

Molly nodded. "Yeah, they're still here. It's just I haven't seen them for a very long time. And..." She clammed up.

Joel put the beer down, and pressed her a little more, without looking at her. "And what?" he said gently.

Molly tilted her head again. "Well, I don't know how they would feel about seeing me again."

Joel frowned. "They're your parents. Whatever has happened, it wouldn't change that."

Molly raised her shoulders again, and studied the label on her beer, carefully avoiding eye contact.

Joel had another thought. "Hey, if you haven't spoken to them since before you left, they probably think you're dead."

Molly bobbed her head.

The area around Joel's eyes darkened a little. "You've considered that?" he asked, a slight frown playing across his forehead.

She nodded again with sadness in her eyes.

Joel shifted his beer bottle a couple of inches on the table. "Look," he said, choosing his words carefully. "I don't want to tell you how to run your life - "

Molly smiled. "So don't," she said confidently, lifting her eyes to meet his.

He grinned, picking at the label on his beer. "But..." he continued, very aware he was going to say his piece despite her comment. "Don't you think you should just let them know that you're still alive? You know. A phone call. Or something. I'm not talking about going and spending the weekend, or anything; but just let them know that their little girl isn't dead."

His suggestion seemed to have an impact. Instead of putting up her shields and deflecting, for once she let his words in. She nodded ever so slightly, before picking up her beer and taking another swig.

Joel noticed, and marked it as a victory.

She put her beer down and wiped the condensation from her hand on her pant leg. "So, Oz and I have been thinking about other stuff that might be fun," she said, allowing herself to change the subject.

Joel smirked good-humoredly at her tact. "Uh huh?" he grunted, sitting back in his chair; noticing that he was actually enjoying himself, just sitting and talking with her.

"Yeah," she said. "We're thinking about starting a university."

Joel frowned. "Right..." he said slowly, not quite sure if he had understood correctly.

"Yeah," she said. "To teach leaders how to be leaders."

Joel smiled at the prospect, considering the source of the comment. "Okay."

Molly noticed his smile. "What?" she said, hardly able to keep from smiling herself, at this point.

"Nothing," he said, the hint of his smile growing into a full manifestation. He hid behind his beer bottle, taking another swig.

Molly saw that he was toying with her. "I'm *serious*. This could be really great," she protested.

Joel tried to straighten his face. "Okay. Tell me. I'm clearly not understanding what you want to do."

She shook her head, a little frustrated. "Yeah. I'm not talking about leadership boot camp, like the military teaches," she explained, seeing where his thought process would be coming from. "I'm talking about something bigger. Imagine if the leaders of the world were all educated in things like diplomacy and negotiation. Imagine if they learned to put their personal feelings aside, and navigate toward solutions, rather than reacting out of pride or anger."

Joel nodded in agreement.

Her beer bottle stood forgotten, and her hands started punctuating as she spoke. "And now imagine that they were shown things like how to reach peaceful agreements. There are lots of cases to study where nations have succeeded against the odds - with multiple internal problems, as well as foreign policy issues."

Joel cocked his head, becoming more interested.

Molly found herself in a flow, talking about something she had been mulling quietly for some time. Something that she never thought would be a possibility - until her conversation with Oz. "And then imagine if they were versed in things like how to effectively govern, and distribute resources. How to make sure that no one race is suppressed or victimized. And then what if they spent time learning about how societies impact their physical environments, and how to preserve the resources, like the land and the water supply? How to not pollute their planets so that they have to go off and conquer others."

She realized she'd been ranting. She quieted herself, folding her hands in her lap.

Joel was leaning forward, nodding vigorously. "That sounds

fucking amazing!" he agreed. "And much needed, even within the Sark System."

Molly sighed in relief at his acceptance. She picked up her beer bottle again, and started picking at the label. "Yeah. I think so. So that is where we start. Oz and I are going to see about getting a course going within one of the existing universities to start with; you know, just a small course, and then grow the faculty and reputation. Prove the concept. Build some connections and so on." She bobbed her head as she spoke.

"Uh hmm..." Joel leaned back, looking off across the bar. A couple walked in and sat down a few tables over. They were canoodling and laughing. Joel was momentarily distracted. "It sounds wonderful... but doesn't this kind of thing take a boatload of cash?"

Molly looked up at him. "Yeah. This is true. But Oz did a rundown of the companies, and there is definitely money in there we can pull. And then there's my money..."

Joel pulled his attention back to her. "Your money?"

Molly bobbed her head. "Yeah. The trust fund."

Joel did a double take. "The trust fund?" he asked.

Molly took a deep breath, almost scared to share this with him. "Yeah... I have a trust fund put aside. Something my parents gave me before I left home. It's just... I never felt like I trusted myself to touch it. I mean, I didn't want to just live off of it; I wanted to make sure that I was capable enough before I started trying to do something with it."

Joel's face softened, and Molly could see an aura of pink clouds around him. "You mean you wanted to make sure that you were good enough, before you allowed yourself to touch it?"

Molly nodded, a rush of emotion sweeping into her chest, and disorienting her thinking. She sat silently, waiting for it to pass and grappling for something to say - or something to distract them from the subject at hand.

But the brain fog had descended.

Joel pulled away from the cold, damp beer bottle and put his hand on hers. "You were always worthy of that money," he told her. "But it's nice to see that you're starting to see that for yourself..."

Molly smiled weakly, and pulled her hand away. Overwhelmed, she suddenly needed to go to the bathroom. "I'll be right back," she announced. She trooped off, relieved to be away from the conversation that had gotten a little too intimate too quickly.

Indius Residence, Downtown Spire

"And are you sure about this tip?" Bob's voice came through her implant clearly. She could hear the concern in the timbre.

Chaakwa nodded even though he couldn't see her. "Certain," she confirmed. "It's a source I trust."

The sark had started going down as she arrived home, and it had taken her several minutes to pluck up the courage to connect the call.

She heard Bob's sigh of agreement. "Well, if you're sure, I'm in. I'll give Ron a call," he told her solemnly.

Chaakwa flicked her eyes upward, and did a quick count in her head. "Okay, so that will make four of us," she confirmed.

"Think we need anyone else?" he asked.

There was a pause on the line as Chaakwa ran through the possibilities in her mind.

"Chaakwa?" Bob pressed, wondering if the line had disconnected.

"No. We'll be okay," she told him. "I understand they'll be in no shape to give us any problems by the time we show."

She heard Bob's tone change, as he prepared to end the conversation. "Okay, well, if you're sure," he chirped. Chaakwa could hear voices in the background, like someone had walked into the room and was chattering away.

"Yes. Thanks Bob. I appreciate you doing this with me," she added.

The seriousness of Bob's voice had left him, and he was talking as if they were just arranging a bowling match. "Hey, it's what your father would have wanted. I'm glad we finally get to nail these sons of bitches."

"Me too," she agreed, pursing her lips together.

"Okay," he said. "Well, call me if anything changes; otherwise, I'll see you there tomorrow evening."

Chaakwa looked out of her window, over at the cityscape against the fading light. "Will do. Thanks, Bob."

The line clicked off, leaving her sitting alone in her darkened apartment.

She remained there quietly for a few minutes, lost in thought, when her eye fell on a picture she had on the sideboard - a picture of her and her father, when she was a little girl.

"This is for you, Dad," she whispered into the darkness.

CHAPTER THIRTEEN

Above a warehouse, Undisclosed location in Spire

Paige turned to Maya as they sat against a wall in the dusty loft of the warehouse. "I don't understand. How is he getting them to come in?" she asked quietly.

Maya smiled. "Ah, a trick my father used once. He basically led them each to believe that someone was plotting against them, and let their paranoia and mistrust of each other fuel their actions. Pieter's been working on the setup of the ruse since we got the green light a few days ago."

Paige frowned, her blue skin catching in the low light of Estarian twilight. "So how do you get them to show at a specific time?"

Maya shrugged casually. "Different stories for each..." she said, keeping her voice super low so as not to draw attention from Joel, "but with vague enough messages that they fill in their own blanks. That way, if they talk to each other, their suspicions just get compounded. They might think there is a meeting going down that they're gatecrashing, or that someone is plotting to take them out, or that they're there to take someone else out."

Maya grinned. "It's basically a clusterfuck waiting to happen once they all get here."

Paige's eyes widened in a strange mixture of horror and delight; she knew what these men had done.

Jack, Joel, and Sean stood in one corner, talking in hushed voices. Their full protective gear weighed on them as they waited patiently for the go signal from Pieter.

Joel glanced over at the young guy intensely focused on his holo. "Looks like it's working," he remarked.

Sean cracked his knuckles. "Yeah. I'm looking forward to getting my hands on these pieces of shit."

Joel glanced up at him. "Just remember that we're here to do a job."

Sean glared at him intensely. "I know," he retorted. "I've been doing this since before you were even-"

Joel waved a hand. "Yeah, yeah. Before I was born. You're the big bad." Joel motioned with his hands, pretending to bow to his superior experience. Then he stopped. "So how much before I was born?" he asked, flipping the conversation around.

Jack smiled. "I heard that he served with General Reynolds way back in the day," she said, watching Sean's agitation grow.

Sean found his composure. "Yeah, I heard that rumor... just after I heard the one about how I married a Noel-ni, and got promoted to Chief of the *Meredith Reynolds*."

For a second, Joel thought that they were about to get real insight into the past of Sean Royale; but then he realized that Sean was just toying with them.

"Guys..." Pieter called quietly across the loft space.

Joel headed straight over to where Pieter was sitting on the floor with his array of holoscreens. "Yeah. What's up?"

Pieter pointed at one of the screens. "Your sixth guy is just arriving, through the side entrance. It's locked, so my guess is he's going to head around the back to the next one. The others are all in there, but they're confused. A few of them have found each other."

Joel peered more closely. "That's the tango that was never here, right?" he confirmed, recognizing him from his mug shot.

Pieter nodded. "Yeah, I've been double-checking facial for each of them. He's your guy."

Joel scanned the other screens, giving them eyes on each of the other five. "Okay, great. And I guess this one," he pointed, "is the big boss of the network?" he checked.

Pieter checked another screen, pulling up the facial recognition profile. "Yep. The suit might give it away, too, once you see him in person."

Joel watched as two Estarians in one of the rooms started talking with each other. "Okay, we'd better get in there," he said.

Joel turned to the others. "Okay. We're good to go. Let's move out." He made his hand gesture to reinforce his words, and Sean and Jack started making their way down into the main warehouse.

Joel turned back to Pieter's screens. "Looks like the handoff recipients are here, too?"

Pieter enlarged the screen to show Chaakwa and her late father's police colleagues. "Yep. They're here. They know to wait for the signal, but if anything changes, I have a line to her holo. And I'll keep you in the loop."

"Okay, great," Joel muttered. He turned and left, leaving Pieter monitoring his screens as if nothing else in the world existed.

Three space cars showed up in the small warehouse parking lot, and four Estarians stepped out. One of them was a female wearing a suit and a protective vest. She immediately drew her firearm, and walked purposefully over to the main entrance.

The light was fading. It was time.

She strained her ears to hear inside, keeping her awareness on high alert. She took a quick glance over her shoulder to make sure they weren't being followed.

The other Estarians also wore vests marked with the official precinct emblems on the collar. But these weren't current police; they were veterans. Veterans from a time when you stuck with your own, no matter what; serving with someone made them as close to you as family. You had their back, and they had yours. No matter what.

And that was why they were here.

For family.

Bob caught up to Chaakwa, his firearm also drawn and ready. He whispered in her ear. "You sure it's time?" he checked.

She shrugged. "We have to be close enough to hear the signal," she told him.

He had a look of concern in his eyes. Concern for her. For what this whole experience might do for her. Or not, as the case may be.

He knew how he'd felt when he finally caught the guy who took his partner out twenty years ago. He had thought that it would make the pain go away, that it would put it right. But in the end, the bad guy ended up locked up, and his partner was still dead. That was just the way it was. Then the real battle began - the battle to deal with his feelings.

He looked at the young woman; a career, a life, still ahead of her. He hoped that for her it would be different.

Chaakwa turned, catching the eye of the other two vets behind them. She signaled for them to hang on before they took up their positions, acutely aware they didn't want to thwart the getaway of the team delivering this victory.

Chaakwa kept her weapon quarter raised, checking the safety was still on as she started to move forward.

. . .

Inside the warehouse

Sean and Jack crept down the stairs along the back wall of the warehouse. Sean came gracefully to a halt mid-step, giving Jack the signal to hold. He pointed directly ahead of them at the target that had just walked in through the back door. Then he pointed to himself. Jack nodded.

They continued their descent silently, as if the volume had been turned off in a bubble around them. When they reached the ground, Sean kept moving forward, without looking back. Jack turned and headed into the main warehouse.

She swept her weapon left and right, scanning the area in front of her as she advanced, on alert for any signs of movement.

"Door on your right," Pieter told her through her implant. She cautiously approached, keeping close to the near wall. "Two tangos. One has his back to the door," he informed her.

Jack took another two paces and paused, listening intently. She could hear their muffled voices through the makeshift construction of the office divider. She breathed deeper and then moved, swinging effortlessly around the doorframe, and, in one movement, taking out the nearest target with a single round.

The guy dropped, and she waited until he was out of her firing line before popping off another round into the heart of the second guy. His eyes were wide as he collapsed like a sack of potatoes in a heap on top of his comrade.

Jack clicked her holo twice to let them know she'd taken down the two. A moment later, she heard another click. That was three. *Probably Sean and his guy.* She swung her attention around to advance into the main area.

She heard a click in her ear. She kept moving forward. That left two more. Just two more tangos, and they were on to phase two.

She emerged from the narrow area into the wide-open space in the middle of the warehouse. There were boxes and crates all over the place. Spotting a heavy-duty forklift truck, she stole away behind it, keeping herself from view.

There was a scuffling, and then a pause. Then another click.

One more, she counted.

She turned back, and could see Sean emerging from the corridor, following her through. They made eye contact, but there was nothing further to communicate. She didn't have eyes on either Joel or the last bogie.

And then there was another click.

Sean's gait changed from one of extreme stealth, to that of a casual surfer dude heading home from the beach. He flicked the safety on his weapon, and lowered the muzzle.

Joel headed down the second set of stairs by the front of the building. He knew he had to move faster or else the front of the building would be unsecured. He moved as rapidly as he dared without drawing attention. Every step, he risked the sound of his boots on the metal grid resonating in the air and alerting their targets to his location.

He calmed himself.

Come on, Dunham. You've done this a million times before. Stay cool...

He made it halfway down the stairs, and spotted movement just underneath him. One of the perps had hidden behind a stack of crates, to watch another one, who was oblivious to the presence of anyone else. He stood around like a duck waiting to be shot.

It would be easy to just pick him off right now, Joel mused. But that would alert at least this one guy to the fact that they were being taken out.

He lowered his weapon and continued down the stairs. *Save playtime for the holo games,* he chided himself. *This is work time.*

He found his way to the ground level, and followed the path he had traced from his higher position; through the aisle of boxed goods, in the direction of the hiding tango. Quietly, he approached.

Shit, this guy is just oblivious, he thought to himself.

Five paces out, he could see he was still distracted by the other guy. He was crouched, in a vulnerable position. Joel smiled to himself and pulled out the rag he had laced with chloral hydrate and shoved in his pocket, just in case.

Three paces out.

Joel held his breath, now praying the guy didn't hear him. Didn't sense him. Didn't turn around.

Two paces out.

Joel's heart was in his mouth. At this range, he didn't have time to take off the safety and trank the guy; he'd have to smack him, and proceed with the chloral.

One pace.

Just one more step, he told himself. *One. More.*

Joel wound his hand around to the target's face, and clamped the rag over his mouth and nose, while putting his gun hand against the back of his head. He pressed the rag tighter.

One monkey, two monkey, three-

The Estarian's eyes rolled in his head, and all resistance melted. He went down, and Joel effortlessly released his grip.

Well, that worked. Now for tango number two.

He tapped his holo, sending a click to the others, and then crept back in the direction he had come, listening intently for any signs of life. He paused and stood straight, giving Pieter the signal that he could do with some guidance.

A moment later, Pieter's voice was in his ear. "You've got one hovering just inside the entrance way. He's on his holo. Distracted. Take a right behind those boxes in front of you, and you'll see him."

Joel nodded his thanks to the camera in the far corner and started moving again.

He carefully swung around to the right, and moved between the boxes. Then he saw the guy. It was an easy shot. He took it, and the guy collapsed. He clicked his holo again.

One more. The guy who is just standing in plain view.

Joel moved right again, heading into the main floor of the warehouse. He spotted his target, but then the Estarian turned and spotted him right back. His expression was one of shock, but before he could make a sound, Joel popped him twice in the chest.

The tango dropped to the deck, his legs folding underneath him as he was put under the trank's sleeping spell.

Jack flicked her safety on and lowered her weapon before venturing out from behind the truck. Leading the way, with Sean coming up along the corridor behind her, she continued her path through the array of boxes and crates to find Joel standing over the last guy he had just hit with a tranquilizer.

He looked up at them. "I think I recognize this motherfucker," he said thoughtfully. A hint of anger seemed to jar his jawline.

Sean came up next to Jack. "Where from?" he asked.

Joel bent down and poked the body with his foot. "Not sure," he said, shaking his head. "You meet so many people in this game… Might have just seen him on the system when we were searching for jobs, or checking out our competition. But for some reason, he has me pissed."

Sean shrugged. "Hmm. Well he's going to be going away for a very long time, so you'll have plenty of time to place him."

Joel straightened up.

Jack interrupted their navel-gazing. "Where are the other two?" she asked.

Joel thumbed backwards. "Back there. Got one with some chloral."

Jack frowned. "Why?" she asked confused. "Why not just stun him like we did the others?"

Joel shrugged. "Cuz I could. And I kinda wanted to see if it would drop him as fast. I think it was quieter than firing a shot."

Sean nodded. "Riskier, though."

Joel looked nonplussed. "Well, you know. Just experimenting. Need to keep evolving our game."

Jack grinned. "Okay, ladies. Let's get this wrapped up."

They all turned to retrieve their sleeping beauties, and execute phase two of the plan.

Rooftop across the street from the warehouse

I should be there with them.

You're meant to be dead, remember?

Yeah, but you took care of that.

Five of those guys are going into the system. Last thing we want are rumors, even in the prison system, of a phantom vigilante.

I think my exclusion has more to do with Joel trying to keep me out of harm's way.

So what if it does?

I'm the leader. I'm meant to be leading from the front.

No. You're the leader, and they need you alive. You die, and this whole team falls to pieces.

. . .

You're feeling guilty about Giles?

Yes, I am. He's rotting in some cell, maybe already dead, because I was a shit leader and I let him risk his life so that we could take out Shaa.

You made a command decision. And besides, he wasn't

taking 'no' for an answer. Even the General ended up letting him go.

The General has to think of the good of the Federation.

And now, so do you.

Not above my team. These guys come first.

Interesting how you're thinking of Giles as your team...

Whatever, Oz. Let's stay focused. Is that Chaakwa moving in?

Molly raised her holo to her eyes, and took a view through the telescope app.

Tell her to move back from those doors. They're not done yet... it's not safe.

Chaakwa headed up the steps, toward the front doors to the reception area. She approached slowly, knowing full well what she might be walking into.

Bob followed closely behind her, peering in through the windows as best he could from his vantage point.

She stopped dead. She could see a group of people through the doors, and there were a number of Estarians on the floor.

They looked dead.

Or at least unconscious.

She felt her chest tighten as reality dawned on her. *This is actually happening,* she thought, as her feet automatically moved her closer. She stood, mesmerized; the whole scene feeling surreal, like a dream. Or an alternate reality.

She couldn't make out the faces of the three figures that stood around those that had been captured, but she had a flash of recognition of some of the Estarians on the floor.

Suddenly her holo buzzed, pulling her back to the here and now. She glanced down.

STEP BACK FROM THE DOORS AND AWAIT THE SIGNAL. UNSAFE TO PROCEED AS YET.

It was from an unknown sender.

But knowing who she was involved with, she immediately knew it was someone on the team. Maybe even Molly herself.

Chaakwa gathered her wits and moved back, indicating for Bob to follow her. He did without question. They backed up about fifty yards before they stopped.

Bob glanced over at her. "Too soon?" he asked.

"Too soon," she confirmed.

Inside the warehouse

Joel looked down at the six stuppered tangos. "Sean, want to take out the trash?" he offered.

Sean grinned. "It would be my pleasure," he responded, grabbing the infamous tango number six by the scruff of his neck, and hauling him away from the group easily.

Joel looked satisfied that they were going to make a difference today. "Well then, I suppose it's-" His attention was pulled from the group. They were gathered just inside the building where they had their prisoners bound, but he sensed movement at the door, and spun around to see two figures through the window.

He recognized one as Chaakwa, and there was a second person behind her.

"Shit," he said. "Pieter?" he called into his audio feed.

"Already on it. Oz is telling her to fall back," Pieter responded over the shared channel.

Joel waited, watching them move away from the door. "Hope they didn't see anything," he said. When he was satisfied they were gone, he looked down again at their captives, noticing one of them was coming to.

"Okay, looks like a win for the chloral hydrate," he said, looking pleased that his impulsive action was actually paying off. "We need someone to scream," he explained for the benefit of the waking low-life. "That's the signal." He grinned and chivalrously opened his hand to Jack. "Would you like to do the honors?" he offered.

Jack smiled, pulling out her weapon. "It would be my pleasure," she replied, flicking the weapon into live rounds mode and removing the safety.

The tango's eyes widened at the realization of what was going on.

Sean picked up his perp, and slung him over his shoulder, then started walking purposefully in the direction of the back door. Joel followed, patting Jack on the shoulder as he passed her.

Jack grinned, looking down on her prey. It had been a long time since she had gotten to put some pain onto some bad people. She was going to relish this moment.

Outside, Chaakwa and Bob stood back as if holding a half-assed, invisible perimeter around the building. Bob shifted his weight. "Are you sure we haven't missed the signal?" he asked gently.

Chaakwa shook her head, taking her hand from her poised weapon just long enough to swipe a strand of hair back around her ear. "I'm - "

There was a gunshot from within the building, and then a blood-curdling shout of pain.

Chaakwa signaled to the other two to head around the back, and she and Bob charged the doors.

Inside the warehouse

No sooner had she fired the shot, Jack was on the move, running through the warehouse to meet the other two teammates out back.

Sean was already in one pod with the unconscious tango number six. Joel was waiting for her in the other pod. She bounded up to him and jumped in, holstering her weapon as she turned around and hung on. The pods lifted up in tandem out of the sight line of the two retired cops just rounding the corner of the warehouse.

Jack sat down and strapped in as the pod door finished closing. A moment later, they shot up into the stratosphere, on their way to execute phase three.

Joel tapped his holo to connect with Molly. She answered, her voice calm and subdued.

"It's done," he told her.

"Great job," she replied. "And thank you. This will mean a lot to Chaakwa."

Joel nodded. "Of course. We're off to dispose of some garbage, but we'll see you back at Gaitune shortly?"

"Yes," she agreed, her voice sounding distant.

Joel sensed something wasn't right. "You okay?" he asked. Jack glanced over at him, realizing that something else might be going on.

Molly stood on the rooftop, watching the various trucks and teams show up. "Fine," she told him. "Just thinking. I may be a while here."

Joel wasn't convinced that everything was 'fine,' but there was little he could do until they completed the mission. "Okay. Well, look, just stay out of sight, and get yourself off-world ASAP. You hear?"

Molly smiled to herself. "Who are you, my mom?"

Joel chuckled. "No, but you're not too - " He stopped himself. "Just get back to base, yeah? And we'll talk."

Molly muttered something in acknowledgment, and the line closed off.

Joel sat back in the pod.

Jack glanced over. "Everything okay?" she asked.

Joel winced a little. "I think so... but I'll be happier when we get this wrapped up."

The pods shot down onto their second location just as the last sliver of light disappeared on the horizon.

There was a *bang* as the door flew open, and two armed policemen ran in, sweeping the area.

They entered to find the five people they had been tracking for years - all in a circle, bound at their wrists and feet.

"Where's the other one?" Bob asked, following Chaakwa into the central area.

Chaakwa was careful to keep her face turned from him. "What other one?" she asked casually.

Bob frowned, holstering his gun. "I'm sure I counted six perps when we looked in the windows."

Chaakwa shook her head decisively. "Nope," she said definitively. "No. We've got everything we came for."

She put her gun away and signaled to the others. "Let's get these guys taken into custody and back to the precinct. They've got a lot of talking to do."

The other police officers pulled the criminals to their feet and took them outside to their trucks.

Chaakwa opened a holo call as she watched them leave. "Greetings. I need transport for five prisoners. And send a cleanup team. We've just performed a bust as a result of an anonymous tipoff."

She paused, listening in her audio implant. "No. No witnesses... Yes, one has a gunshot wound, so if you must send an ambulance, we can work with that."

She finished her call and turned back to survey the scene in stunned disbelief that, finally, after all these years, it was over.

Rooftop across from the warehouse, Downtown Spire

Molly watched as the press arrived: individuals, and a couple of news trucks. She watched the police cordon off the area, and set a perimeter to keep prying eyes, and evidence-destroying feet, out of the way.

It was getting cold now that the sark had gone down. She contemplated sitting in the pod; but then she'd miss everything that was going on. She'd miss the sandy air. The buzz of the traffic. The office lights coming on in buildings across from the one she stood atop.

No. She wanted to experience it all. Just because. And because on Gaitune, there was nothing.

Well, not *nothing*. But nothing like this.

She sighed, thinking again of Giles.

How much longer do you think it's going to take him to get free?

I haven't enough data to make that estimation. Arlene thinks it could be several more weeks.

Several more weeks of captivity? We have to do something. Let's set up a meeting with the team for tomorrow. Maybe we can find a solution.

Okay. But Arlene has been insistent that we leave them to it.

Well, maybe Arlene needs to understand that she doesn't get her way every time.

Meow.

Molly observed the chaos below turn into order as two figures arrived in front of where the press had been gathered.

Can we get ears on what's happening down there?

Yeah, I can tap one of the recorders.

Thanks, Oz.

"Ladies and gentlemen. Thank you for being here. Tonight marks the occasion of something I never thought that we'd see in this city: the arrest of five of the city's best-known criminals, who have escaped arrest for too long. Today, we took them into custody, and we intend to charge them to the fullest extent of the law."

Molly listened closely while watching the scene below.

She makes a good statement.

Yes. I've heard she's on track for a promotion. She'll have her own precinct in no time.

Was that us?

She may have had a little help.

Is that ethical?

Yes. I merely compensated for some of the patterns that I've seen happening against her as a result of the corruption. The previous captain kept her back; that cost her three years. Then there was the partner who was sabotaging her investigations. That cost her five -

You're kidding?

Nope.

Molly tried to imagine what it must have been like for her.

Then there's the fact that she is female in a paramilitary organization, where -

Molly shook her head. *I can only imagine.*

Let's just say she is due to get caught up on her promotions.

I'm not going to argue with that, then.

Chaakwa's voice continued to stream through Molly's implant. "I'd like to extend a special thank you to my colleagues at the precinct for supporting this long-term investigation, as well as our veterans, who came back from retirement to help investigate the tip."

Chaakwa indicated to the three older guys who were standing at the top of the steps with her, still wearing their vests so they were identifiable as cops.

They nodded across to her, swelling with the same kind of pride they had about their glory days. Today was a gift to them. Not just because they brought their friend's, their captain's, killers to justice, but because they felt what it was like to get out into the city and serve again.

Chaakwa noticed Bob wipe at his face, and then look down. She guessed that the old guy was tearing up.

She looked back out into the crowd of press that had assembled over the past hour, and continued with her statement. When she was done, she stepped away from the microphone that had been erected by the news crews, and started to move back towards Bob and the others.

Just then, she had a feeling she was being watched. She raised her eyes upward, to the roofs of the buildings nearby. She could have sworn she saw the figure of a woman caught in the light reflected from the structures around her.

She blinked and looked harder, but, dazzled by the lights of the press and the activity around her, she couldn't find the silhouette again.

"Thank you, Molly," she whispered under her breath. She paused for a moment more, wanting to see her again - but if she had been there, she was gone now.

CHAPTER FOURTEEN

<u>Kitchen, Gaitune-67</u>

"Well, I, for one, am pleased we got a win," Sean announced into the silence of the kitchen. Everyone else had their mouths full of cheesy comfort and nourishment.

Maya pulled her slice of pizza away from her face, trying to break the bond of mozzarella and clear her palette so she could concur. She managed a half-discernible "me too," before resigning herself to more chewing.

Paige hadn't sat down to eat yet. Instead, she was fluttering around the kitchen, making sure everyone had everything they needed.

Maya noticed, and this time managed to empty her mouth to speak. "Hey, why have you still got your jacket on?" she asked.

Paige spun round, a little flushed. "Erm. I'm... on my way out."

Maya frowned instantly. Pieter, who was sitting at the table with his back to Paige, spun around with tomato on his bottom lip. "You're going out?" he asked her, hardly believing the blasphemous words spoken on pizza night.

Paige straightened up and put a look of determination on her face. A second later, the determination crumbled. "I have a date," she confessed, her bottom lip shaking a smidge.

Maya's face lit up. "You dark horse!" she exclaimed. As soon as she could dump her pizza on her plate and wipe her hands, she was on her feet and around the table, hugging Paige.

Sean looked up, amused. He and Joel exchanged impressed looks.

Pieter looked put out. "How come you have a date? We don't meet anyone here."

Paige blushed again, her chest crumpling in on her. "I, er... I met someone on the net," she admitted. "He's probably a lunatic. And I'm sure he doesn't look like his picture, but..." She shrugged.

Maya rubbed the side of her arm brightly. "It'll be great. I'm sure he'll be interesting. Ignore them. They're just jealous they've been on this rock the same amount of time, and haven't managed to get dates."

Brock exchanged a telling look with Crash, who kept his attention on cutting up some pizza before shoving it in his mouth, so he couldn't be drawn into conversation. Brock smiled knowingly, and swung his head from side to side with a look of mock innocence in his eyes.

Paige fussed a little more with some napkins and empty pizza boxes.

"Leave it," Maya told her excitedly. "Go have your date. And then come back and tell me *everything!*" she commanded, marching Paige out of the door. They disappeared together through the foyer.

Pieter looked over at Molly who was watching quietly. "Did you know about this?" he asked her, almost accusingly.

Molly shook her head, her expression deadpan. She went back to her pizza.

Did you know about it, Oz?

Yes, I did.

Hmm.

I don't see that she's in any danger. I took the liberty of doing a background check on her suitor. Nothing interesting or untoward, that I can see.

Okay. Sounds fine, then.

You don't mind that I didn't tell you?

Of course not. She's allowed a life. And a private one. As long as she's safe, she can see whomever she likes. She doesn't need our permission.

Quite.

Pizza-eating and chatting continued; although, most of the rest of the conversation revolved around how Paige had managed to get a date, where her date might be taking place on this rock, and, of course, the more delicate issue of the prospect of any of them finding true love with the life they now lead.

There were a few awkward glances in Molly's direction, from more than one team member, but Molly was careful to avoid any kind of incriminating eye contact for the rest of the dinner.

After they were done and had cleaned up, each of them excused themselves to play video games, hit the gym, or do some other thing.

Molly made her way down to the ops room. Alone.

Gaitune-67, Hraðlestin Restaurant

Paige took a deep breath and pushed the button to the airlock on the restaurant door. The door slid open, and she stepped inside. A moment later, the next door opened and permitted her to pass into the foyer.

The scent of curry floated over to her, instantly making her calmer. And hungrier.

"Good evening, miss," the maître d' greeted her. "Table for…?"

Paige flushed nervously. "Erm… I'm here to meet a friend," she said, glancing around the small restaurant behind him.

She spotted a male Estarian with his back to her. He looked slim and athletic, and she realized she wouldn't be disappointed if that was him.

"He may be here already," she said, glancing more deliberately in the direction of the young man.

Just then, a woman appeared, presumably having used the facilities, and she sat down at the table with the guy Paige had been looking at.

The maître d' turned to see where she was looking, and then glanced around the restaurant. As he did so, another customer waved his arm in the air, catching their eye.

Paige exhaled quietly in relief. It was the guy she'd been video calling with. She chided herself for being so anxious, but reasoned that people weren't always the way they were on video.

The greeter gestured for her to follow him, and led her through into the dimly lit restaurant, carrying menus.

Her date stood up as she approached: Estarian, medium build, with a relaxed, almost causal feel to him. He reached out to hug her as she arrived at the table.

The maître d' placed the menus on the table, and left the couple to it.

"You weren't kidding when you said you were human-small," he said, beaming down at her.

She grinned. "Yeah, I thought it was best to forewarn you... in case you like your women tall." She shook her head, recognizing how silly and superficial this dating thing was on first meeting.

"Well," he grinned welcomingly, "It wouldn't matter to me," he told her. He invited her to sit down, and she slid into the chair opposite him.

"Let me get you a drink," he offered, waving to the waiter who was standing over by the kitchen doors. Paige picked up a menu and started to peruse it.

"What will you have?" he asked.

Paige couldn't see where the drinks were. "Oh, I'll have... a beer, I guess," she said, seeing that he was drinking some kind of draught.

He grinned. "You like beer?"

She nodded.

He turned to the waiter. "Let's get her one of these to try." The waiter nodded and disappeared. "If you like beer, you'll like this," he explained.

Paige smiled, scrambling in her mind for a conversation that might be interesting to him. "So, tell me more about the work you do here, Carl?" she suggested.

Carl looked a little self-conscious and ruffled his hair anxiously before putting his arms on the table, and leaning in. "Well, I run a shipping company. Which sounds kinda dull, but when you consider it is a secretive and secure shipping company, it becomes a lot more exciting."

Paige narrowed her eyes playfully. "If it's a secret, why are you telling me?" she asked.

Carl chuckled. "Because I want you to like me, and I figure that if a smart woman like you is going to like me, I should start off by telling you the truth."

Paige felt a bit odd. She wasn't used to this much attention from a guy who had his wits about him. Nor was she used to this level of honesty. "Well... er... great!" she said, not quite knowing how to respond. "So, I take it that keeps you occupied?"

Carl nodded, rearranging his utensils on the tablecloth. "Yeah, mostly. I mean, there's a lot of research and coordination... But the team handles most of the ops. I just get my hands dirty with the cyber security," he confessed.

Paige grinned. "Oh, that's awesome. My friends on the team I work with are cyber-geeks too." She clamped her hand over her mouth, realizing that not everyone appreciated being called a 'geek'.

Carl waved his hand. "It's cool, I'm down with being a geek." He winked at her.

The waiter returned with her beer. She thanked him, and picked it up. Carl lifted his glass too, and they toasted. "Here's to new geeky friends," he said brightly.

"To new friends," Paige repeated, clinking glasses with him.

They sipped their beer. "Oo. This *is* good!" she cooed excitedly.

Carl smiled at her enthusiastically. "Right? I couldn't believe it when I found it here. Last time I had this was on Ogg."

"Oh, you've lived on Ogg?" she asked.

They got embroiled in a conversation about his time on Ogg, and her manufacturing business, and so many other things, they almost forgot to order food.

———

Several hours later, having eaten and chatted the entire evening, they were still enjoying themselves. Carl waved for the check and paid.

"You know, Paige," he told her. "I'm so glad you agreed to come out with me. I mean, I don't know if you know this, but the chance of meeting such an accomplished woman in a *city* is pretty slim; but out here on this rock..." His voice trailed off, but his smile remained bright.

Paige lowered her eyes, a little embarrassed. "I'm just a glorified secretary," she admitted.

Carl frowned. "No, you're not. You're an interplanetary businesswoman. And it sounds like you're also the glue that holds that team together. And even though you can't tell me what it is the team does, it sounds like it's pretty high-powered and intense at times." He watched her, observing how self-conscious she was under the surface of her easy ways and entertaining conversation.

"You know what I think?" he offered.

Paige leaned on the table, pushing her half empty mocha out

of the way. "What do you think, Carl?" she grinned a little bashfully.

He leaned forward conspiratorially. "I think that you've forgotten to upgrade the picture you have of yourself," he told her.

Paige frowned. "On my profile?" she asked, thinking how old the picture was she was using.

He shook his head. "Nah-ah. I'm talking about the pictures you have inside your mind," he explained, tapping his own temple. "Your self-perception." He paused, taking a last swig of his beer. "I think you seriously underestimate what you're doing, and what you're capable of," he added.

Paige tilted her head, considering his words. Slowly, she started nodding her head. "You know what?" she said. "I think you may be right." A relaxed smile spread slowly across her lips, lighting up her face.

Carl put his glass down on the table. "I know I am," he added confidently, looking deeply into her eyes.

Paige flushed; stunned both by the revelation, and that someone was actually seeing her.

"I hope you'll allow me to take you out again sometime very soon?" Carl ventured.

Paige's eyes widened. "Of course!" she almost laughed. "I'd really like that, Carl. You're fascinating and fun and... Yes. I'd like that."

They finished their drinks and parted ways outside the restaurant. All the way back to the base, Paige played and replayed the highlights of the evening's conversations.

Gaitune-67? she thought. *Try Cloud-frikkin-9!*

Chom-X9, Giles's prison cell

There was a *clunk* at the door. Giles lifted his head, and looked over his shoulder as he lay on his rack.

He heard the familiar sound of the keypad.

Beep, beep beep... Beep.

Over the last several weeks, he'd contemplated the different keystroke combinations it could have been. Of course, all that would become irrelevant if it wasn't even a human digit code. It came down to a combination on the array that was easy to reach in the spaced repetition of the beeps.

He sighed, sitting up as the door slid open.

An ugly Zhyn guard, with a face chiseled by years of resentment, stepped into the cell with him. His friend put a foot in the doorway to prevent the door from sliding back.

"You're up, pretty boy," he said, holding out the cuffs and neck brace.

Giles shuffled off the bunk, over the metal ledge that dug into his thighs as he moved. He stood up, straightening himself out, ready for his manacles.

He eyed the neck brace. "Is that *really* necessary?" he asked, more as a test of the dynamic than wanting rid of it. Though it was uncomfortable. And threatening - knowing he could be shocked at any moment.

The guard didn't answer. He just moved forward and clipped the round frame around his neck like a dog collar. Then he roughly turned Giles around to cuff his hands.

Giles kept his temperament neutral. He knew when to push and when to conserve his energy.

The guard grabbed his ill-fitting shirt, and tugged him towards the door.

"Where are we going today, boys?" Giles asked congenially.

The second guard, who was waiting by the door, responded. "Boss wants to see you up top," he told him simply.

Giles nodded. "Probably wants my opinion on his next move," he said nonchalantly, watching for any reactions out of the corner of his eye.

The ugly guard pushed him forward, and followed him out

the door, fake laughing. "And why would he want your opinion?" he scoffed.

Giles stopped in his tracks and turned to face the Zhyn. "Why would he keep inviting me up there to talk with him? What do you think we do for all those hours?" He held the guard's stare, planting the seed of doubt in his tiny brain. Then, a moment before he thought he might be pushing it, he relented and turned on his heels, walking with an air of civility after the second guard.

Point to Kurns, he thought smugly to himself. *Oh, yes. I may be the one in physical chains, but at least I'm not chained by my personality and fears.*

There was a beep at the door, and Shaa called for them to enter. Giles was pushed through first, followed by the two meatheads.

"Good day to you, Lord High Marshall Shaa," Giles started, more for the benefit of the guards than for his relationship with Shaa.

Shaa grunted, and signaled to the seats he had set out. The guards pushed Giles over to them, and he managed to stumble a little ahead and sit of his own volition.

Giles nodded to the guards as if dismissing them, and then turned his attention to Shaa. "So what would you like to discuss today?" he asked.

Shaa waved the guards to leave, and they clunked out of the room, exchanging questioning looks about the dynamic they had just witnessed. Giles crossed his legs casually, leaning back in the hard wooden chair.

Shaa wandered over to sit near him, in a more comfortable, ergonomically enhanced chair. "It looks like there is an opportunity to invade the Kroll system."

Giles looked serious all of a sudden. "The Kroll System? What use would that be to you?"

Shaa puffed his chest a little. "Well, it would be a coup in that it's Federation-controlled space. And it would be fairly easy to take with the forces I've amassed already."

Giles rubbed his chin. "Hmm. I'm... I'm not sure what advantage it would be to you, though."

Shaa looked curious. "How do you mean?" he asked gruffly.

Giles pretended to look casually thoughtful. "Well, it will take resources to go at it, right? You'd have to commit troops and ships."

"Of course," Shaa confirmed.

Giles continued, shifting in his seat to try and get a little more comfortable. "And those troops and ships will be there, having to defend that area from the Federation taking it back. You'd have no one to guard here, if you commit those."

Shaa leaned up a little. "But no one knows we're here."

Giles pulled back on his arrogance to respond. "I found you, didn't I?" He carefully balanced his tone.

Shaa wasn't offended. "Yes, but you're *clever*," he said, with a twinkle in his eye.

Giles smiled bashfully, and then turned his expression to one more serious. "And the Federation has lots of clever people... which means you need to be smart. Much smarter than them."

Shaa *Harrumphed* and sat up, perching on the edge of his seat. "Of course you're trying to stop me - "

Giles relaxed his shoulders a little more, trying to show he had no stake in the game. "No, no. I mean, if you want to do it, then great. I'm behind you. But... let me ask you this. What is your end game?"

Shaa's face lit with passion as he pumped one fist into the palm of his other hand. "I want the Federation to suffer. I want the Zhyn Empire to be free again. I want to return the power to those who deserve it."

Giles nodded, pretending to listen carefully, his therapist face on. He was aware that he was just getting the official propaganda that the commander normally trotted out to his people. "Great," Giles ventured. "So what strategic advantage does it give you to control the Kroll space?"

The Zhyn fell silent; he was feeling stupid, but searching for a way to hide it. To regain his posture. His face crumpled up, and Giles could see the anger boiling up around his straining neck. Shaa muttered something under his breath as he rose from his chair and paced across his office, but Giles couldn't make it out.

Giles waited, counting in his head. *One Jah-Dune. Two Jah-Dune. Three Jah-Dune.* Then he spoke.

"I mean, I can see why it's an exciting opportunity," he began sympathetically.

He paused, pretending to think. "Although... how did you come by this information; the intel that led you down this path of thought?"

Shaa turned back to Giles, a look of frustrated confusion on his face. "I... I... My people told me that they were - "

Giles looked down into his lap, somewhat constrained by the cuffs holding his wrists behind him.

"What?" Shaa asks.

Giles looked up, an innocent but serious look in his eye. "Nothing..." he said, deliberately hesitating.

Shaa scowled. "What?" he said more forcefully.

Giles frowned to himself. "It's... It's probably nothing. I'm just being paranoid."

Shaa took a step closer, his scowl not letting up.

Giles relented. "Okay, it's just a thought that occurred to me. What if the Federation *wanted* you to think that area would be worth attacking?"

Shaa waited.

Giles continued. "Well, they might choose a place that was of little strategic advantage, lure you out there with the rumors it was lightly guarded, and then set a trap. Or, at the very least, have you overcommitted there, not guarding your base, so they can swoop in and..." He let the thought carry itself.

Shaa seemed to get the picture. He nodded, relieved that he was clever enough to have seen it coming. "Yes! Those sneaky assholes. But I'm too smart for them. I won't be drawn into -"

Giles's expression was still solemn.

Shaa noticed. "There's something else?"

Giles lowered an eyebrow, turning his head awkwardly. "Well... I'm just wondering. *Who* specifically gave you this information?"

Shaa waved one hand dismissively. "Why, Davon, of course."

"Davon," Giles repeated deliberately. "Daaaaaa-von," he said again, drawing the name out quietly, luring Shaa in.

Shaa took the bait.

"Why? What are you thinking?" he asked, his frown turning to an expression of mistrust and curiosity.

Giles used his therapist voice, and kept his tone flat. "You tell Davon everything?"

Shaa nodded once, decisively. "Yes, he's my - wait a minute. You don't suspect that Davon is a traitor, do you?"

Giles shook his head dismissively. "No no. I'm sure he's as loyal as the day you met. He's never given you any reason to doubt him, I'm sure." Giles looked in the direction of the windows, able to see only a glimpse of the panorama from where he was situated.

"How did you get on with that other issue we discussed?" he asked, changing the subject, knowing that his mere suggestion would work its way like a worm into Shaa's paranoid psychosis.

CHAPTER FIFTEEN

Chom-X9, Giles's Prison Cell

It was the middle of the night. Well, that's what Giles assumed, based on the fact that he was fast asleep when it happened.

At first, he couldn't be sure. There was a *bang* in his dream, but then as he came back to the reality of his metal cell, it echoed in his mind as if it might have come from this world.

He listened, waiting for another sign that he wasn't just dreaming.

He often dreamed of being rescued - of all of his isolation and discomfort finally being over. He dreamed of seeing Arlene, or the General's team, bust through the door to his cell, and reclaim him into the comfort of civilization. And books.

Oh, how he missed his -

BANG.

Bash, bash... Bash.

SLAM.

A sound like the slamming of a door rang through the cell. But it wasn't his door. It must be next door, the cell next to him.

He heard voices. He recognized the tone of the guards; the

low, gruff grunting they made as they barked their orders at their subordinates.

Then there was a cry. A lighter-sounding voice. Still Zhyn, but it was someone who didn't have any control. It sounded like pleading. Begging. Reasoning.

And then the guards' footsteps walking away down the corridor.

Giles was up on his feet, listening intently. He put his ear to the wall on the side he thought the noise was coming from. It didn't help. He stood back and waited.

Then there was a banging on what was probably the next door, and someone calling for help.

Giles moved quietly across the cold floor in his dirty, bare feet. "Hello?" he called through the door.

The banging stopped.

"Hello?" he called again.

There was a sniffling. "Hello?" the voice responded. "Are you a prisoner here, too?"

Giles's heart leapt. The only people he had spoken to over the last several weeks of captivity were the guards and Shaa. "Yes. Yes I am," he said, perhaps a little too enthusiastically for an outsider to understand. "Who are you?"

The voice responded a little cautiously. "My name is Anton d'Zyll. I came here to join the cause. But for some reason they won't have me. They're calling me a traitor."

Giles tilted his head in a half-shrug. "Well, technically, if you're here, you are," he pointed out, amusing even himself.

Anton was quiet. Giles could just about make out his breathing. He visualized him looking around his cell, trying to fathom how on earth he had gotten here. It was exactly what Giles had gone through.

How did I get here?

What events led to this point?

How could I have been so stupid?

Am I being punished by one of the gods or spiritual overlords I've offended in my travels?

He'd been through it all before realizing, after a few weeks, the 'why' wasn't important. He was here. This was it. This was his reality right now.

This is what he had to work with.

He waited, allowing the new prisoner to acclimatize. And then, after a few moments of consideration, he padded back over to his bed and lay down. Waiting.

Gaitune-67, Operations Room, 43 days after dropping off Giles

Molly strode into the operations room, allowing the lights to come on automatically as a result of her movement. This was a ritual she'd been doing several times a week for over a month; ever since the celebratory pizza dinner after the Chaakwa case.

She carried with her a lemon tea - a sad and constant reminder of her sabbatical from mocha. She made her way to her usual console, and placed the antigrav mug on the ledge where she didn't need to wave her hands. She prodded a few keys, and then sat back to wait.

"Greetings of the day, Gaitune!" A woman's voice chirped through her earpiece before the holoscreen opened up.

"Greetings upon you, Arlene. How goes it over there?" Molly was pleased with herself for engaging in social chitchat. She'd been forcing herself to start and finish with something personable, and noticed that people actually bothered to respond in kind. She still felt it was superfluous, but Joel had assured her it was appreciated.

Arlene's image opened up in front of her. "Oh, it's going okay. Giles is in good spirits today. He was given an extra meal by the guard. I think he's made a friend."

Molly felt a wave of sadness flood through her chest. It was her fault he was in there, no matter what Arlene told her. Molly picked up her mug and took a sip of the tea. "Any sign of him getting out soon?" she asked.

It was the same question she had been asking on and off for the last forty something days.

Arlene bobbed her head while moving it side to side ever so slightly at the same time. Molly could read her. She was being optimistic, but didn't really believe they were any closer. "He's making progress," she told Molly. "It seems that they're still having semi-regular chats."

Molly frowned. "What have they been talking about this week?"

Arlene became vague. "Oh, you know. Military strategy. How Shaa can tell if he should trust his men… Mostly Giles is just an impartial sounding board."

Molly shook her head as she listened. "And you sit through all this?" she asked.

Arlene nodded. "Oh yeah. Have to. It's all part of what we do. Although most of it is drivel, it gives us insight into how to manipulate him."

Molly sighed. "And so what are we looking for? I mean, to what end? Let's face it. It's not ever going to get to the point where Giles is going to be able to say, 'Hey, be a good chap and let my people come and pick me up,' is it?"

Arlene looked like she had been jarred out of her routine answers. "Well, no."

Molly raised her shoulders and then dropped them again. "So, what, then?"

Arlene sat back a little in her console chair over on the *Arch-Angel*. "We'll just stay alert for an opening," she explained. "It's all we can do."

Molly wrinkled her nose disapprovingly. "It's been a month and half he's been in that hellhole. We need to do more than look for an opening. I've got the team working on other options, but we need Giles to find something we can use."

Arlene nodded. "Well, he's gathering intel all the time, and ADAM is compiling a plan of the facility as Giles can reach different areas."

Molly frowned again. "Is there nothing we can do in terms of hacking the system to get access to the whole schematics of the place?"

Arlene glanced ahead of her, looking beyond the camera. "I'm not sure. I'm assuming that ADAM is doing everything he can."

Molly sat forward on her invisible console chair cum sofa. "Well, I'm a fan of AIs, as you know, but maybe there is something else we can do. Can you have a word with ADAM, and see if he can send us over whatever he has right now? Oz and I will take a look. It may be that it will help us with what we're working on at this end," she explained, careful not to infer that she thought that the world's oldest and most evolved AI wasn't up to the task.

Arlene nodded. "Sure. I'll pass it on to him," she agreed.

Molly changed the subject. "Great. Anything else since we last spoke?"

Arlene shook her head, but then remembered something. "Oh, yes. I told him what you said about the grindle-beast…"

"And?"

"And he says that you need to look up the mythology of Sark. He couldn't believe you hadn't read about it. He called you a heathen!" Arlene smiled with genuine humor and affection for Giles.

Molly scoffed, nearly choking on her lemon tea. "You tell him from me that not all of us are social voyeurs. And not all of us have spent the last century plus studying every fairy tale under the sun!"

Arlene chuckled away as she took a note. "I will be sure to let him know…" Her humor faded a little and she grew serious. "You know, he appreciates everything you're doing for him. You and the team. But especially the messages and social calls."

Molly smiled, a heaviness weighing in her chest. "Arlene, it's the least that I can do." Her voice became quieter. "I mean, I'm the one that let him go in there. I should have stopped him. Sean was right - "

Arlene leaned forward. "Hush now. Enough of that. Giles knew what he was getting into, and this is nothing that he hasn't done a dozen times before."

Arlene's face was firm now. "And you tell that Sean Royale to let it go. It's none of his business. He's not in command. You are. And besides, I've watched him make tougher judgment calls than this, and I'll tell you - he didn't always shine so brightly as he makes out. So you just tell him from me to leave it be."

Molly shook her head. "He hasn't mentioned it again since that day when we were there on *ArchAngel*."

Arlene looked satisfied. "Well, good then. Now, Giles also wanted me to let you know about your take on the 'Firefly nonsense,' as he calls it."

Molly and Arlene chatted away, passing the night and grappling with ways to keep the morale going. Not just for the team, but for themselves. And for Giles.

Joel passed by the ops room on his way up from the gym. He paused as he walked by the door, noticing the light on underneath. He opened the door, and stepped inside, seeing the top of Molly's head over one of the main console units. He strained to hear, unsure of who she might be talking with. He turned to leave, but heard the word 'Giles'.

He knew she felt guilty. He knew she had the team working on all kinds of angles. But he hadn't known that she was consistently in touch with Arlene.

He crept quietly out the door, and headed up to the safe house, wishing there was something more they could be doing.

· · ·

Chom-X9, Giles's Prison Cell

Giles awoke for the second time that night; this time, to the sound of sobs.

He remembered where he was, but was confused by the presence of another person. Then he remembered the new arrival.

He sighed with empathy, understanding how hard it must be for someone - especially someone who didn't have his experience and outlook. Slowly, he dragged himself up to a sitting position and leaned against the wall that his cot was positioned against.

"Hey, chap," he called as loud as he dared.

The sobbing paused.

"Hey, it's okay. My name is Giles. I'm probably the nearest thing to a friend you've got in here, so how about you talk to me?"

There was more silence.

Giles waited.

"Okay," Anton replied.

And just like that, Giles was back in therapist mode, talking with Anton d'Zyll: traitor.

Gaitune-67, Molly's quarters

Molly felt the pain of her insides, screaming with exhaustion, as she reached across the bed to switch off her holo alarm.

Shut up, dammit, she willed it, unable to even open her mouth to curse at it.

I believe you set the alarm with the intention of being up and at it early.

Molly's eyes flicked open as a shot of adrenalin and guilt flooded her neurology.

Fuck. You're right, Oz. I wanted to talk to Brock to see if there is any progress on the shield design.

You realize that you're literally running your body into the ground with all this push, push, push?

Molly ignored the comment. She knew Oz was right, but she didn't have an alternative.

I need to get going, she told him, slithering off the bed, and stumbling to her feet. She padded across the bedroom floor to the shower room, quietly wishing she could still have her morning mocha.

Less than thirty minutes later, she was downing a protein shake and heading to Brock's workshop. She could hear his music as soon as she opened the door at the top of the steps.

She made her way down the stairs, her protein shake in hand. Brock was there, busting a move while doing something on the bench holo. "Hey, hey, haaaaaay, lady. Looking boom-chica-wow wahhhh, this morning. How you doin?"

Fuck. I hate morning people.

Me too... Though I love Brock.

Yeah. Ditto.

Molly smiled as she approached his workbench. "I'm doing okay, Brock. You seem in good spirits..."

Brock swung his hips, still jigging about to the music. "I. Am. A-OK," he told her in his usual melodic style. "I'm just setting up some tests for that little engineering problem we're trying to fix. Might tell us a bit more."

Molly set her shake down on the bench and pulled up a stool. "Still no luck with the last idea, then?" Her face betrayed her with a tinge of flatness.

Brock noticed when he looked up. He became stiller, and more somber. "'Fraid not," he admitted. "The thing is, I'm trying to do two things at once... Figure out what frequency they used, to be able to blast through this Federation issue shield, and then try and find a way to counter it. As soon as I find one that could get through, then it becomes a candidate."

Molly bobbed her head sympathetically. "I know. It's a huge task. I'm sorry to put this on you, Brock."

Brock shrugged. "It's cool. We'll get there eventually." He

finished what he was doing on the desk holo and then turned his attention to her. "Any news on how he's doing?" he asked.

Molly shook her head. "It's pretty much the same. Awful conditions. Awful food. Arlene is helping him keep it together, but time is short."

Brock's eyes widened.

Molly nodded again. "Yeah. Sounds like any little slip-up and he's a dead man. We've already had a couple of close calls. Ancestors know how he's still alive, given how volatile that Shaa is."

Brock's eyes dropped a little. "I wish there was something more we could do. I mean, poor guy. A month and a half in those conditions would kill me," he said, his mind churning for other solutions.

Molly scraped her stool back as she stood up. "It's okay. You're doing all you can. I've got some other avenues we're exploring. Just keep going as fast as possible; we'll catch a break soon. We have to."

Brock nodded, and turned back to what he was doing. Molly picked up her shake and decided to head up to her conference room to get some work done. "I'll check on you later, but if you get anywhere…"

"You'll be the first to know," Brock called after her.

Molly waved as she strode out to the stairwell.

Chom-X9, Giles's Prison Cell

Anton tapped on the metal wall. "Hey, Giles. You still awake?" he asked quietly.

Giles grunted. "Yeah."

Anton's voice was tentative. "You want to finish telling me the story of the necklace?"

Giles frowned for a moment. "Oh. The talisman… Yeah. Sure."

Giles's recounting of his last outing with Sean had been interrupted by the guards bringing them food, and the story had been forgotten.

He shuffled onto his back and stretched a little, getting comfortable. He picked up his story where he had left off, and brought his new friend, Anton, up to date to when he had returned it to the *ArchAngel*.

"So, do you know what it is for?" Anton asked.

Giles chuckled. "Somewhat yes, and somewhat no." He smiled. "It's a puzzle. Literally."

Anton was quiet for a moment.

Giles started counting the rivets along the top of the wall, as he lay gazing above him.

"You know," Anton spoke up again, "it kind of reminds me of that children's song."

Giles's attention was piqued. "Where in the Zhyn Empire are you from?"

Anton frowned, thinking it was a strange, unrelated question. "Er, the Orn System."

Giles nodded. "The home of 'the Oracle of the Eleven Moons,'" he said cooingly, as if reading off a tourist's guide.

"How did you know? I mean, I'm guessing from your voice you're human, right? How do you know about the Orn System?"

Giles smiled. "Let's just say I'm an archaeologist."

Anton was confused. "A what?"

"I study civilizations. But forgive me, you mentioned a nursery rhyme that you were reminded of?"

"Right," Anton agreed. "It talks of a map or something. It's probably unrelated. It just made me think of it."

Giles was starting to feel relaxed. He had food in his system, and it wasn't too cold in his cell, for a change. He could indulge the idle chatter. "Can you remember the rhyme?" he asked.

Anton muttered a few things, and then managed to recall parts of it.

. . .

Eleven moons, a sight to reap,
> When all align, no time for sleep
> A shaft of light, where the ions flow
> Onto the shroud, the glow does go.
> When one beholds the moons of Orn,
> Be sure to look up at the horn.
> The crescent marks the spot to be
> When the time strikes keen and on the mark
> And when you read the map of gold
> In your hands you'll graciously hold
> The elixir of life
> The holy grail
> The reason we're on
> The rising trail.

As Giles listened, he moved from lying idly on his rack to sitting bolt upright, listening to every syllable.

After cajoling - and then forcing - Anton to repeat it several more times, he felt sure he had it committed to memory.

"Why do you care?" Anton asked him. "It's a kid's playtime song."

Giles tried to hide his excitement. "One of the things I've learned in my line of work is that nothing is *just* anything. I've also learned that the way for elders to transmit vital information down through generations is to disguise it as songs or stories, for those who are looking to see."

Anton was starting to sound sleepy. "Well, beats me what it's all about. I just remember learning it at school. We had a trip out to one of the moons, once. There was nothing there. So it's just a story. A story to get kids to go on a boring school trip."

Giles smiled, listening to the silence in the darkness as his fellow prisoner dropped off to sleep.

Finally, he had his next clue. He couldn't wait to speak to

Arlene again; although, she'd probably heard every word of what he had just discovered.

Falling asleep was the last thing he wanted to do right then.

Gaitune-67, Molly's quarters

Molly sat on her bed the same way she had in the old safe house – and, for that matter, all through college and the military. She did her best work when she was alone, thinking.

Not that she'd been truly alone for a very long time.

Oz? You there?

Yeah. What's up?

I'm looking at this data that Arlene had ADAM send over. Some of the stuff he's been gathering from Giles's holo via his quantum pearl.

Yeah?

Well, I know he's tried to find models to fit it to, and his problem is a lack of data; but what if we were to just pin down some assumptions?

You mean guesses?

Yes.

...

Oz?

Yeah, I'm here. Guesses based on what, though?

Errr...

You're going to say your gut, aren't you?

Well. Yeah.

You do understand that people like ADAM and I don't have guts?

Of course, Molly grinned to herself. *And that's why humans will never be redundant.*

Her brain tickled her as Oz giggled away. She couldn't help but laugh a little, too.

Okay, talk me through what you were thinking on your holo.

Several hours later, Molly closed her holo.

I think we've got something useful there.

Yeah, as far as the base is concerned; we're still missing too many chunks to pinpoint the positions of those other three space launchers.

Molly scrambled off the bed, her back and butt now aching from sitting in a silly position for so long. She stood, slowly, and then stretched out gently.

But what about the data from The Little Empress?

What do you mean?

Well, she took a number of hits, right?

Right.

And we know where those hits happened - on either her shield, or her body.

Yes. All that is recorded. Emma can have it sent over.

Right. And we know her position when these hits occurred.

Ahh. I see where you're going with this. And we will be able to find the rotation of the planet, and guess where it must have been for us to destroy the one launcher that we killed.

Exactly.

Got it. Contacting Emma for the data now.

Excellent. I think I need to go for a run.

Okay. Don't overdo it, though. It looks like we'll be moving out for a mission any day now.

I'll be fine.

Molly smiled to herself as she rummaged for her running gear. She'd need her outdoor clothing for this one. She'd been cooped up for far too long without a real break.

CHAPTER SIXTEEN

<u>Chom-X9, Giles's Prison Cell</u>

Anton had been quiet all morning, pacing and exercising, churning in his own mind.

Giles was waiting impatiently for a time when he could communicate with Arlene. It was incredibly difficult, now he had someone else within earshot.

It isn't worth risking getting found out, though, he reasoned. *That will be a sure way to get sent to the firing squad.*

There were footsteps coming down the corridor. They sounded more purposeful, angrier than usual. And he counted three – no, four - separate pairs.

Anton heard them too, and stopped whatever it was he had been doing.

Giles got up from his rack and stood waiting for his door to open to be hauled up to talk to Shaa.

There was the usual clunking and messing about around the door. Then the sound of the keypad. Then the door swung open, and Shaa stood glaring at him.

The Zyhn had a look of thunder in his eyes.

Giles was taken aback. "Lord High Marshall. To what do I

owe this pleasure?" he started, trying to maintain a degree of respect in his voice.

Shaa was not amused. "The Yaree Justicar has just assured me they are not in talks with Reynolds. You've lied to me!" he declared.

Giles fell back on his heels a little and then took a half step backwards. "That's not true. I assure you, I've seen them in the logs. The justicar himself was on the *ArchAngel* two weeks before I was brought in here!"

Giles's voice rose in panic as he protested his innocence.

Shaa was having none of it. He took another step into the cell, looking like he was ready to explode all over Giles. "First, the codes you gave us didn't work-"

"They changed them!" Giles interrupted in desperation.

Shaa ignored him, taking another step. "And now this. If I didn't know better, I'd think you were here to set us up for failure. Getting me to accuse my ally, and then risk my only gated ship in a fool's errand, making us think we had the key to destroying the QBS Tornado."

Giles shook his head, holding his palms up in surrender. "I swear to you, I didn't. The justicar is lying to you. Let's talk about this," he begged.

Shaa wouldn't accept anything Giles was saying. "You're going to be executed. My mind is made up," he informed him. "You're going to be tied up, out in the atmosphere, on the traitor's pole… without a suit."

Giles didn't quite understand the implication of that. He knew he could survive a short time out there without a suit, but…

"You're going to die a slow and painful death; the death of a betrayer. A spy!" The fury came off Shaa in waves, his full paranoia and inferiority complex triggered to its maximum. His neck pulsed as rage ran through his veins.

Giles knew there was no reaching him at this point. He stood there, stunned. Neutral. Allowing whatever was going to happen to happen.

"You eat your last meal tonight!" Shaa shouted as he turned and left the cell. "And this is only because I want you to suffer, knowing you are going to die in the morning."

The door slammed behind him, and the guards locked it up. Footsteps shuffled around, and then followed the High Marshall's along the corridor.

Giles was vaguely aware of words coming from Anton in the next cell, but it was all he could do to keep it together. His mind swarmed, trying to figure a way out of here.

Fast...

Gaitune-67, Ops Room

Molly sat down at her usual console, talking with Arlene. "So what have you got?" she asked her, anxious that they might finally be able to move forward.

Arlene was grinning. "Okay, so the data that you sent back to us - the stuff ADAM had collated originally - it looks like now, given the last data dump, and your suggestion about making some assumptions and backtracking where *The Little Empress* got hit, we can interpolate and build up a map of the place. Or at least, most of it, including where the anti-spacecraft guns are."

Molly sat forward in excitement. "You're kidding? That's fantastic!" she grinned in relief.

"Yes. It is. We know that one of the anti-space guns is under maintenance; that much we were able to pull through Giles's data. The others are a live threat, but..." she moved in her chair and pulled up some more data, sharing her screen with Molly, who jumped to her feet, splashing her lemon tea on her thigh as she moved.

Molly wiped at the hot liquid on her leg, barely aware of it burning her skin through her pants. "So is this telling me that we might actually have a window where we can't be hit?"

Arlene nodded. "It's also a gray zone for their radar, but only if we send something small enough," she added.

Molly could feel the excitement rising in her limbs. "Finally!" she exclaimed. "So you mean something like *The Scamp Princess*?"

Arlene shook her head. "We could, but she'd be spotted, more than likely. I was thinking something like the pods."

Molly's excitement died. "But the pods can't gate…"

Arlene smiled. "But *The Empress* can. We just load them up, like we did with *The Little Empress*, and get them as close as possible."

Molly took a deep breath, "-And just hope for the best?"

Arlene pursed her lips. "Yeah. Pretty much. But I think they'll go undetected for the most part, even on the approach."

Molly sat back down, considering their options.

A moment later, she leaned forward toward the console and picked up her abandoned mug. "I'm thinking that it's the best plan we've had in the past nine weeks."

Arlene smiled knowingly. "I thought you'd say that."

Molly bobbed her head gently, making sure she had all the information she needed. "Okay, let me talk with Joel and Sean, and see if we can put a plan together. I'm thinking we'll swing by the *ArchAngel* to pick you up, and then head straight out there as soon as we can mobilize."

"Sounds good to me," Arlene agreed. "Just let me know when to expect you, and I'll be ready."

Molly nodded, getting up from her invisible console chair. "Great. I'll be in touch."

She ended the call, took a slurp of her tea, and then strode out across the ops room floor to find Joel. It was late, but this was far too important to wait until morning.

. . .

Onboard *The Empress*

Joel's voice boomed through the cargo hold of *The Empress*. "Okay, folks, it's got to be just like we practiced. Emma is going to drop us quite a ways out, and then we ride in on the pods."

He glanced around, making sure everyone was paying attention. "Now remember, the pods don't have the same defenses as *The Empress*, so we're relying on Emma to use envelope maneuvers if we get fired upon. Given what we know about the missiles that they're using down there, there's an eighty nine percent chance that Emma can shake them off our tails. But it might get bumpy - so make sure you put your harness on. Every one of you."

Joel looked over at Sean poignantly. "It doesn't matter how used to the pods you are, you can't overcome gravity, and we need you operational when you land."

He widened his address to the whole group. "Once on the surface, we have one directive. Retrieve Giles. That's it. No being a hero. No trying to get payback on the Zhyn. We'll use the intel Giles has captured at a later date to come in and deal with these guys. But for now, we're here for extraction only."

Joel looked at the solemn faces as he gave the final pep talk and briefing to the assembled team. "Paige and Maya - you make sure you stay near your pods. Your reason for being there is to provide an extra chance for a ride, if you see an opportunity to grab Giles while we lay down cover. You have firearms, but you are not to go looking for engagement. Do I make myself clear?"

Paige and Maya nodded in unison.

Joel turned to the others. "Any questions?" he asked.

Molly stood up from her leaning position by the weapons rack. She unfolded her arms, catching Joel's eye. Joel thought she wanted to say something, but she shook her head.

"Okay, folks," Joel said, doing his wrapping up hand signal. "Let's move out. And go get our teammate back!"

He clapped his hands to make them move, and immediately,

there was a scuffling to pick up weapons and any final pieces of gear they might need.

Paige looked at the blasters on the racks and made an executive decision, picking up a small handheld instead. Maya noticed, and did the same.

Paige glanced over at the bigger blasters as she checked her weapon over and holstered it. "No way I can move - or be of any use at all - holding one of those," she reasoned.

Maya nodded. "Agreed," she said. "Heck, my arms and legs have gone weak just thinking about what we're walking into."

Paige put her hand on her chest. "I know. My heart's beating so fast. I'm so scared." Her eyes teared up.

Maya stepped closer, lowering her voice so they couldn't be heard over the engines and the clicking and snapping of weapons and clips. "You know, you don't have to do this. If it's too much, they'll understand."

A tear escaped from Paige's eye. "I know," she said. Her expression hardened a little. "But I want to do this. It's one of us down there, and… I need to be a part of it."

Maya nodded. "You're going to do great. Just keep breathing, and stay near the pod. We'll be back at Gaitune, eating fatty pizza and drinking ourselves into a hangover in no time."

Paige laughed a little through another tear that escaped and ran down her face. She swiped it away. "Yeah. This will be fun, once we get out there," she agreed, pulling herself together.

The two girls followed the starship troopers to the pods in the cargo hold. Jack and Sean were keeping their usual banter going.

Jack called over to Sean as they headed for separate pods. "I suppose you and Joel are in competition about how many bad guys you take out?" she asked.

Sean shook his head as he reached up to the pod to haul himself in. "No, we haven't talked about it," he said.

Jack grinned. "Wanna go head-to-head with a girl, then?" She had a mischievous look in her eye.

Maya approached Sean's pod. "My money is on her," she interjected, drawing a scowl from Sean.

His jaw set in determination. "Right. You're on!" he called over to Jack. Then he hopped up into the pod and turned to face Maya as she started jumping up. "And *you're* buying the beer if you're wrong."

Maya clambered into her seat and raised her hand for a high-five. "You're soooo on!" she told him, competitively.

Sean chuckled to himself as he sat down and started putting his own harness on.

Within minutes, Joel, Molly, Sean, and Maya, along with Paige and Jack, were strapped into their respective pods, and being guided out of the cargo hold into the space behind *The Empress.*

Molly opened a channel to Joel's pod, but said nothing. Joel noticed. "Molly, is that you?" he asked.

"Yes," she replied quietly.

"You okay?"

She nodded, and then realized he couldn't see that from his pod. His pod drew along side her and he caught her eye through the windows. She nodded again.

Joel watched her, waiting for her to speak. When she didn't, he did. "It's okay. We'll just leave the line open, yeah?"

Molly touched the glass on her pod, and then pulled her hand back. She nodded again, and then the pods were moved into a wide formation so they wouldn't be detected by the radar.

Molly was out on her own, surrounded by empty space, watching the approach of the former-Chrom moon.

Several minutes passed like that; the silence and isolation disorientating her. She thought several times that she could say something to Joel, but she had nothing to say. It was her fault they had to do this risky mission - and last time they approached this very base, she had nearly lost him.

Double whammy guilt.

I shouldn't have to keep reminding you that none of this is your fault.

So why does it feel so sucky?

Because you take these things on. You're compassionate, and now you feel the fear and the tension in your teammates, and it's a lot to process.

So how do I deal with it?

I think you just need to accept it as it is. Accept their feelings. Accept your own. And then focus on the task at hand.

I used to be so good at doing the latter.

These feelings and sensations are still very new to you. Give yourself time.

Molly gazed out, trying to see the other pods. She could see one faint dot to her right, and then maybe another one just beyond that, but much smaller and fainter.

Joel's voice came over the comm. "Okay, folks, we're nearly there. I've just had confirmation from Pieter and Oz that they've not detected us yet. We're now heading into the missile zone, so if they're going to see us, this is where it's most likely. Make sure you're strapped in. These maneuvers can get intense if Emma has to move you out of a missile track."

There was a flurry of chatter on the line as the others acknowledged the order, and then the silence returned.

Molly could see the atmosphere of the moon. It was light. Nothing like what you'd see on an inhabited planet. But it was there. The pod speed seemed to slow, and the surface of the moon became visible. Molly could just about make out the darker area where there were constructions. She strained her eyes to see if that was it, or whether it was shadow. Then she realized she could use the head-up display to zoom in. She leaned forward to poke at the screen.

Suddenly there was a scream on the audio channel.

Then another.

Emma's voice came on. "Missiles have been launched. Evasive maneuvers in progress. Please hold tight."

Molly looked to her right. She couldn't see anything.

Oz, what's going on?

Two of the pods have been targeted. Emma is trying to get them free of the scent, but it's tough. She can't move them too fast, or jerk them around too sharply, because of the human cargo.

Huh?

You move a human too quickly, and things start to come apart inside.

Molly's mind whirred.

And then suddenly, she saw one of the pods shoot out in front of her, out of their formation, tightly followed by a missile.

"Who's in there?" she asked out loud.

Emma responded. "If you're referring to the pod out in front of you, that is Sean and Maya."

"Shit!" Molly shrieked. "Help them. Help them. Get them out of here!"

Emma responded calmly. "I'm doing my best,"

Molly remembered the calculations. Eighty nine percent, they had said. That left eleven percent that any one of them might be hit. She wondered if that included the base line of the missile just malfunctioning. *Maybe that might give us an extra percentage point in our favor?*

The pod disappeared from view, behind the missile.

Molly's heart was in her mouth. She was aware of Joel shouting instructions over the audio, but she couldn't focus. All she could do was watch the missile.

And then there was an enormous explosion.

Her pod peeled off to the left. The explosion and the moon

disappeared from view beneath her. She could only see space, and hear screams of despair over the comms.

What's going on, Oz?! What's happening?

"Joel? Joel? Are you there? What happened? Joel?" she shouted.

Calm down, Molly. It's okay. The missile exploded behind the pod. Emma managed to fool the two missiles into colliding with each other.

What the - ?

It's okay. Maya and Sean are okay.

And everyone else?

They're fine.

Molly felt her chest ache. She couldn't believe what had just happened.

Okay, let's get down to the surface, stat.

Already happening. Landing in less than a minute now.

Okay.

Molly noticed her hands were gripping the safety handles inside her pod so tightly she thought she might pop the joints out. She tried to relax them, and noticed how sweaty and slippery her palms were. She'd wedged herself between the grips, and her feet against the pod walls, when her pod had veered. She collected herself, straightened up, and picked up her blaster.

It's okay. Everyone is okay, she repeated to herself.

It seemed like an eternity had passed by the time the pods touched down on the surface. She slipped her atmoshelmet on, and tapped her communicator to their open channel.

"Molly online," she said, hearing each of the others check in.

Her pod door slipped open, and she gingerly shuffled forward and stepped out, awkwardly scrambling with her blaster. She could see the other pods in an array nearby, and her team was emerging. She felt a strange relief to see they were all there, but a part of her wanted them all to get back in their pods and go back to safety.

That wasn't going to happen now.

Now they were committed.

Now they had to find Giles.

Within seconds, Jack, Sean, and Joel also had their boots on the ground, and the pods carrying Maya and Paige slipped up into a position above the base – too high to be seen at eye level, but not high enough to be picked up by radar.

Joel signaled for them to advance.

CHAPTER SEVENTEEN

Chom-X9

The whole moon was dusty. In some ways, it reminded her of Sark. Except Sark had colors. Reds and browns.

Here, everything was a pale bluish gray: the dirt beneath their feet, the sky, the buildings.

There were no fences around the building, like most military bases.

Probably because they think of this whole rock as the base, Molly remarked to herself.

The building ahead of them seemed like the main structure. It matched the details they had pulled together from Giles's data, at least. Molly recognized the shape when they landed.

If Giles was anywhere, it would be here.

Joel motioned for Jack and Sean to head around to the right. He and Molly were going to try and get in the front.

Sean and Jack disappeared from view around the other side of the building.

Molly glanced over at Joel. "So, what? We just walk up to the front door?" she asked.

Joel glanced over at her, and then put his hand in his pocket.

He pulled out something small and showed it to her. "Nope," he told her. "We blast the door out. At the very least, it will break any air seals they have, and cause havoc – meaning Sean and Jack will have a distraction."

Molly nodded. They approached, and Joel set the charge. "Okay, start heading that way around the building. We're going to need another way in," he told her.

Molly started moving as fast as she could. The gravity was about half of what she was used to, and she suspected it was probably artificially enhanced, as well. The rock didn't seem large enough to retain even this much atmosphere.

Yes, it's artificial. I'm adding in data to our schematics as we go. He's using the same language as on the secret bases, so it's taking a little time to process.

Great. As soon as you have a hint as to where Giles might be, let me know.

Roger that.

Molly heard the explosion behind her and spun around. An orange ball of fire was emanating from the door area. She breathed a sigh of relief as she spotted Joel pressed up against a pillar that was jutting out from the side of the building, only a few yards behind her.

She smiled, and turned to keep moving. "You coming?" she asked him, over the communicator.

Joel chuckled. "Yeah, suppose so," he said. "Let's check out the area that Giles's location seemed to track to the majority of the time. I've got a feeling that just around this corner, there is another entrance. It looked like a passageway or corridor on the schematics."

Molly nodded, still moving forward. Then she saw movement up ahead. She ducked back around the corner she had just rounded, and pressed herself against the wall. Carefully, she ventured a look.

There were three Zhyns dressed in what were probably

civilian clothes, but carrying weapons. They were talking, and one of them ushered the others inside. They disappeared through a door.

The same door they were heading for.

Molly saw their chance, and moved to follow, praying they wouldn't turn around and see her.

Is Joel following?

Yes. He's catching up to you.

Good.

A moment later, Molly was racing toward the sliding metal door, and shoving her foot in its path to keep it from closing. It kept moving. She put her hands on the edge, and pulled it back. Finally it relented, allowing her through.

She glanced back, hoping that Joel wasn't too far away. He rounded the corner, and then raced to catch up. "Come on," she whispered urgently.

She slipped inside, keeping her body in the way of the sensors. The corridor was basic. It reminded her of something from the archives of the Estarian military. Functional. Metal. Cold. Brutal.

She prayed they would get to Giles in time.

Joel reached the door and slipped in behind her. He grabbed a rock from just outside, and put it in the path of the door. The metal panel closed to the rock and then stopped, wedging the rock in place, keeping the door ajar.

Molly gave him a thumbs-up for the good idea, and then started down the corridor, holding her blaster out in front of her. Joel followed doing the same.

Jack's voice found its way to Sean's ear through his helmet communicator. "We've got a life sign just up ahead," she told him.

Sean frowned. "Out here in *this* atmosphere?" he queried. "Are you sure?"

Jack confirmed. "It's weak, but definitely there. And definitely human."

Sean managed to make eye contact with Jack as she turned back towards him. "Giles?" he asked.

Jack again faced the direction they were heading. "Maybe. We should check it out," she said, moving forward more purposefully.

Sean matched her pace, and the pair advanced quickly as a unit. Sean moved forward, sweeping his blaster in front of them. Jack came behind, walking backward, making sure their collective asses were covered.

As they got closer to the life sign, Sean broke into a run. "It's him!" he called. "Get Paige down here with a pod."

Jack flicked to the general channel. "We've located Giles. Paige, Maya, can you bring the pods down to our location?"

Paige acknowledged. "On our way."

Sean ran out into the clearing to find Giles slumped in the dirt, on his knees and tied to a post. "Mate, you okay? You're okay. We've got you," he said, knowing his words weren't heard beyond his helmet.

Giles's complexion was gray, and his body looked puffy. Sean dropped his blaster into the dirt and tried to hold Giles's head up; his head just lolled.

Sean checked his eyes. "He's lost consciousness," he said, observing Giles's slumped body, held up only by his hands, tied behind him around the pole. "He's suffering embolism as a result of the low pressure. We need to get him inside."

"What are you doing?" Jack hissed at him, when she turned to see him removing his helmet. It was the last thing he heard from her, with the comms disappearing. He put his helmet over Giles's head, and tried his best to get it to seal.

"Come on, mate, breathe," he told him.

He switched his comms on his holo over to his implant. "He's not breathing," he told Jack. He looked up from his crouching position. "Where are those damn pods?"

As if on cue, the four pods descended in the clearing between the building and where Giles had been tied up.

Sean busied himself getting Giles's hands free, and then pulled him up. The pod doors slipped open, revealing Paige in one, Maya in another, and two empties.

Sean carried Giles over to one of the empty pods, and hauled him inside, closing the door as fast as possible. "Jack, get Joel and Molly out of there. We've got Giles. We need to move out."

Jack acknowledged, and jogged off in the direction of the other side of the building, staying on high alert for any signs of Zhyns.

Chom-X9, Inside the base

Molly and Joel crept as quickly and quietly as they could down the corridor. There was commotion, and alarms were going off. Every now and then, they had to freeze and flatten themselves behind structures in the building as numerous Zhyns ran past, heading to the front door where the explosion was still causing problems.

Molly glanced down at her holo map, and then gestured to Joel, pointing out a stairwell. Joel nodded.

As soon as the area was clear, they set off toward the stairwell, and then down the steps as quickly as they could.

They reached the next floor down. Molly looked back at Joel questioningly.

Oz, I dunno if this is it.

We've too much data missing to know. Try it, and then be prepared to back up.

Okay.

She pushed through the doors and headed down the corridor.

She could hear chatter and activity ahead. She stopped, and began to retreat.

This area is too populated.

I'm picking up the network now. That must be the control room. It's going to be swarming -

"Stop right there!" A Zhyn had just come through a door further down the corridor, and he trained his blaster on them.

Joel immediately fired, knocking the soldier back, and drawing the attention of his colleagues. Joel and Molly tried again to retreat. "Let's get out of here," Joel called to Molly.

"No arguments from me!" she said, returning fire.

Joel pushed against the door, but a shot came within an inch of his head.

A Zhyn had managed to get a clear shot on them. "Stop! Or the next one goes through her head," he said.

Joel paused, then backed up off the door. The Zhyn signaled for them to put their weapons down.

Molly started moving slowly to do as they were told. Joel followed.

Shit. Now what?

It's okay. We always find a way. Just stay alive. Do what he says.

Molly started to stand up, her hands above her head.

"Not so fast, mother fuckers!" She heard a human voice beyond the cluster of Zhyns assembling. And then, before she knew what was happening, there was another scurry of blasters being fired.

For a few seconds, neither she nor Joel knew what was happening. But when the blasting stopped, they saw a heap of blue Zhyns on the floor, and Jack standing at the other end of the corridor. "Thought you might need some help," she said smiling. "You ready to get out of here? We have Giles."

Molly processed the information quickly, and picked up her blaster. "Great. Was the way you came clear?"

Jack nodded. "Yes. Let's go."

Molly and Joel started down the corridor to follow Jack, stepping unceremoniously over the Zhyn bodies that Jack had just dropped.

Joel smiled. "Good shooting, soldier," he told her.

"Come on, mate. You need to breathe," Sean managed to get Giles propped up in the pod. His skin was puffy; incredibly puffy. He couldn't tell how long he'd been out in the low-pressure atmosphere, because this place was unfamiliar to him. It looked like it was either a form of torture, or they really did intend to leave him there to die.

"Giles, come on," he pleaded. "Those nanocytes should be getting to it." He patted Giles's cheek lightly, trying to encourage him to come around.

"Emma, what can you tell me about his condition?" he asked, reeling off the symptoms.

"I suspect he's been out in this for over half an hour, given what I can tell from the atmospheric readings. He should regain consciousness shortly. You're right about the nanocytes."

Sean sat back, slightly reassured.

He looked out of the pod and saw the others milling around the site. He switched to the general channel. "Hey, get into the pods. The pressure is too low to be safe for more than a few minutes," he told them, gesticulating to the girls.

Maya and Paige looked over, and then scurried into one of the pods together.

"Emma we need to get Giles to proper care ASAP. Any news on where the others are?"

Emma responded. "Let me find out," she told him.

Just then, Giles's eyes started to flutter.

"Hey, hey… Giles. It's Sean. Are you awake?"

Giles started to come into his body, and sat himself up a little more comfortably. "Hello. Oh... my. You're... you came..." His voice was raspy and dry.

He coughed.

Sean tried to help him up. "It's okay, mate. Just relax. We're going to get the others back out here, and then we'll all head back to *The Empress*."

Giles's eyes flew open, and he sat up straighter. "No. We can't go yet!" He was struggling to speak, and move. His body was still suffering the effects of lack of oxygen and pressure.

Sean tried to get him to settle down. "It's okay. We'll be out of here soon."

Giles tried to sit forward and stand. "You don't understand. We need to get Anton out of the basement, and then I need to blow this base." Giles managed to sit up. Then he half stood, and hit the button to leave the pod.

Sean tried to grab him. "Giles, there isn't time. This place is swarming with - "

Giles was stumbling out of the pod. He had Sean's helmet in his hand as he pulled away. He fell, and rolled into the dirt. He immediately scrambled up to his feet, picking up the helmet again, and half ran, half stumbled back toward the base where he had been held captive all this time.

Sean jumped down, grabbing his blaster. "Shit!"

He glanced over at the other pods, to the girls. "Get the pods in the air again. We'll be right back," he commanded into the holo on his wrist. Maya and Paige nodded mutely through the glass of their pod.

A second later, the pods lifted up into the air and vanished. Sean ran to catch up with Giles just as he disappeared through a lower basement entrance and down some steps.

CHAPTER EIGHTEEN

Chom-X9, Inside the base

Giles made his way down the corridor. Sean could tell from his awkward gait that he was in excruciating pain, trying to keep moving and breathing.

It also meant that whatever it was he was trying to do must be important.

Sean followed deftly, keeping alert for any signs of Zhyn. The alarms were still going, making hearing anything useful incredibly hard.

Giles veered off down another corridor, and then into a warehouse area. Then he dropped down another flight of stairs, and continued down into the darkness. Sean followed, noticing that Giles had thrown the helmet on his head. Then he realized why.

"Hello? Sean? Molly? Can anyone hear me?" Giles's voice intruded on the group communication channel.

Sean was about to respond via holo, but then Molly answered. "Hello? Is that - ?"

"Yes, it's me. Giles. Thank you for coming for me," he said ridiculously politely, given the situation they were in.

"You're welcome," Molly responded, confused. "Where are you?"

Giles's voice was intermittent, and he was panting. "I'm in the dungeon. I'm just about to rescue an associate of mine, but I need you to help me out if you're still in the building."

There was a pause. Then Molly's voice answered.

"Yes, we're still here. What do you need?"

Giles was direct. "For you to overload a service generator so we can blow this base into the ether."

Another pause.

"Molly?" he asked.

Sean listened, taking in every word that might help them get out of there sooner.

Molly's voice came through his helmet again. "Er. Yeah. Isn't that a bit extreme? I mean, we need to take out Shaa and decommission this place."

Giles's breathing was still heavy, and Sean noticed his movement had slowed. "No, it's not extreme. This is the only chance we'll get. We need to take it. The Federation is in acute danger if we don't. I need you to trust me. Can you do that?"

Something told Sean that perhaps Giles wasn't the type to need rescuing after all.

He could also hear movement at Molly's end. She was panting a little, now. "Okay, what do you need?" she asked.

Giles started explaining. "There is a weapons store near where I was being held. They have their ventilation systems and generators way too close to the weapons store to be safe. I'm also sure I smelled IRFNA - which means that it has probably corroded through whatever missile it was loaded into. This means that one little spark may cause the whole thing to go up. All it takes is for that stuff to mix with any rocket fuel that may be around, and it's curtains. If we can direct some of that explosion into the ventilation system, we can get the whole base to blow."

He paused. "I'm advocating causing an overload of the generator, and one of the ventilation systems in the basement. The two explosions should fuel each other."

Molly hesitated. "An explosion of that magnitude will take half the moon with it."

Giles's voice was steady and confident. "Believe me, that's the better option."

Molly sounded like she was resigning herself to the task. "Okay. We need to get everyone out of here before we do it."

"Right," Giles concluded. "I'm going to get Anton out of here, too. You get your people back out to the pods. I'll be along shortly. Let me know when you've got access to their facility's system."

Molly grunted something, and the line went dead.

Giles rounded another corner and found his way back to his old cell. He went straight to the one next to it and leaned against the wall, waiting for Sean. "Have you got something on your holo to access this keypad?" he asked. "It's a four digit code, if that helps."

Sean nodded, letting his blaster swing by his side on his shoulder strap. He connected his holo in, and started punching away at some keys.

Eventually, the lock popped and the door slid open.

Giles peered around the corner, still catching his breath, his puffiness returning to almost human levels now. "Anton?" he said, looking over at the shocked imprisoned Zhyn. "I'm Giles. I'll be rescuing you today."

Chom-X9, Storage cupboard

"Come on, Molly. Fast as you can..." Jack called in, exchanging nervous glances with Joel as they kept guard on an out-of-the-way storage cupboard.

How we doing, Oz?

Nearly there. Okay, we've got it. So what did he say? That he wants to overload the air con unit at the same time as the generator?

Yeah. Can you pull up the schematic and overlay it with where we think he was being held?

Sure. It's onscreen, on the panel.

Molly shuffled closer to the maintenance panel just inside the cupboard. It was difficult to see, and fairly low tech compared with what she had seen on the Zhyn bases.

Okay. So I think if we can reroute the power from the one on the floor above, it will probably be enough to cause an overload. Can you find a way of setting off the air unit?

Sure.

Molly clicked onto the general channel. "Giles, we have access. Tell me you're out."

Giles's voice came through her helmet. "Not yet. Might have to just blow it, anyway. Give me two minutes, and, if you don't hear from me, just blow it."

Molly frowned, looking frustrated. "I'm not blowing it until I know you're safe. I didn't come all this way and risk my team, to just blow you up."

Sean's voice interrupted. "It's okay. I'm here with him. If I have to carry him out over my shoulder, we'll get out. Might need three minutes, though."

Molly froze. "Sean. Why are you in the building? I thought it was just Giles?"

"He was in no fit shape to even walk on his own," Sean explained. "It's okay. We have his friend and we're heading out. Just hope we don't bump into any of these Zhyn on the way…"

Just then Molly heard firing on the other end. "Sean? Sean! SEAN!"

There was a scuffling on the line, and fire being returned.

A moment later, Sean's voice reported in. "Yeah. Yeah. It's okay. Keep working. I'll tell you when we're out."

Anton helped Giles move as fast as they could down the corridor. Sean strode ahead of them, taking out oncoming Zhyns.

Bam. Bam. BAM... He dropped one after another.

They rounded the corner and started up the stairs. Giles was breathing heavily again. He grabbed hold of the banister. "Sean, you and Anton go on without me. Keep going. I'll catch up if I can."

Sean turned around. "No way," he said flatly. "Now get moving, soldier."

Giles rolled his eyes comically. "You do realize I've never been a soldier."

Sean ignored the comment, and bounced on up the stairs to make sure their way was clear.

Giles tapped the connection switch on his helmet, connecting him to Molly again. "Molly, can you put us on a closed channel?"

He waited.

Molly answered. "Yes, we're alone now. What is it? Are you out, yet?"

Giles's voice was serious. He sounded like he was still moving, but struggling. "Whatever happens," he told her, "you need to do this. You need to destroy this base before you leave. For the safety of the Federation."

His voice quieted in shame. "They've had me too long... I told them things. You need to protect those secrets. Get your people out, and then blow this joint."

Molly shook her head. "No," she said adamantly. "We'll find another way."

Giles winced in pain. "There is no other way. It's now or never," he told her, panting.

Molly rested the forehead of her helmet against the wall next to the panel. She couldn't believe the situation she was in. All her people were in the building still; and yet, if she got taken out before the base was blown up, the Federation was at more risk than when they had allowed Giles to come in the first place.

Shit. Shit, shit, shit, shit, shit... Impossible fucking decisions!

She heard blasters firing just outside the door...

Molly poked her head out to see that Joel and Jack had dived around the corner, and were picking off the Zhyn as they approached and left themselves exposed.

Molly waited. She looked at the console. She should blow it. Operationally, she *should* blow it.

The Federation was at stake. Ancestors only knew what Giles meant when he told her that he had had to tell them things. He'd been a part of the inner circle for forever. He could know all kinds of vulnerabilities.

Her mind flicked to Arlene, wondering how much he'd shared with her. If he had told her everything, then maybe there was a way around it; like changing codes, or routes, or strategies. Arlene had already been a stickler for that.

But then, if it were that easy and he'd already told her everything, he wouldn't be so insistent that they blow the base, and everyone in it.

She took a deep breath. She was going to have to blow it.

Her finger hovered over the console.

Oz? Are you there?

Always.

You know that I have to do this?

Yes. It's the right thing to do. Protect the Federation. It's what we all signed up for. We knew the risks.

Molly couldn't believe that this was how her life ended. How her team ended. There was so much more they needed to do - things they needed to tell each other. Places they needed to go...

She felt her finger trembling as she reached forward.

"Molly? Molly, we're out. Get out of the building." It was Giles's voice. "Sean and Anton are out. We're getting into pods."

Molly breathed a sigh of relief.

Molly? Good news. I've managed to rig this on a time delay. You've got five minutes from when you hit that button.

Molly couldn't believe the turnaround in just a few seconds. She breathed a sigh of relief, and noticed that the shooting had stopped.

Joel appeared at the door. "Ready to get out of here?" he asked, smiling and pumped from a good shooting match.

Molly pressed the button on the console, her whole arm now shaking and weak. She hoisted her blaster over her shoulder strap, and slipped out of the cupboard.

Jack was already halfway down the corridor. "Let's move," she whispered loudly.

Joel and Molly jogged after her, rounding the corner just seconds later. Molly looked up, and could see the door they had come in through. It was still wedged open.

Nearly there, she told herself. *Nearly there. Just a few more -*

Molly could hear footsteps coming down the corridor they had just left.

She turned to see. Joel put his arm out as he jogged along, refusing to let her stop moving. She could hear him shouting.

"Go go go!" he shouted at her.

Everything was happening in slow motion.

She turned back around, feeling that a blaster was going to fire at them in any second.

Jack flew out of the door and disappeared. Joel was still shouting, pushing her on. She stopped resisting, and pushed herself onward as hard as she could. There was an empty pod just ahead of them. She squeezed out of the closing door, and into the pod.

She turned, looking for Joel behind her. The door had closed again, and he was trying to pull it open.

"Joeeeeel!" she screamed from the pod.

Joel appeared behind the door, getting it open. He slipped through and ran forward. She could hear the sound of blasters going off behind the door. It was just a matter of time before the horde of Zhyn came rushing through the door to finish them.

Joel was in the pod like a shot, and half a heartbeat later, they were being whisked up into the air with a g-force that made her stomach lurch.

Thrown back in their seats, and slumped down by the force of their rapid ascent, Joel and Molly looked at each other with expressions of fear, which turned to relief. Which turned to laughter.

"That was close!" Joel chuckled.

Molly shook her head. "That was fucking..."

Words escaped her.

Joel nodded. "It was..."

The g-force lifted, and they were able to sit up. While they strapped themselves into their harnesses, Molly was desperate to check something.

She opened the general channel, and removed her helmet, letting the audio come through the pod comm.

"Did we all get out?" she asked urgently. "Roll call, everyone..."

Two by two, her people checked in.

"Maya and Sean, checking in," Maya's voice reported.

Paige was next. "Jack and Paige, present and correct."

Giles responded. "Giles and Anton, now free!" he exclaimed, the relief in his voice palpable.

Molly smiled at Joel. "Molly and Joel, also safe. Well done, people. Great job. Emma, let's get back to *The Empress* as soon as we can... We want to be a long way from here before anyone notices what's going on."

"Right you are," Emma responded, as an almighty explosion rocked the surface below them.

Molly peered down through the side window as Emma whipped them out of the atmosphere. The orange cloud of fire reacted with the air, triggering a tirade of explosions from the weapons held in the bunker below.

"Quite the fireworks display," Joel said, looking through the window past her.

She nodded. "I'm just thankful we all managed to get out," she said, not daring to mention the decision she was nearly forced to make not moments before.

Aboard *The Empress*

Molly gazed out of the window from the little corridor next to the cargo hold. She looked back to the blast over the planet, as a mushroom cloud of destruction billowed up and the store of weapons continued to burn.

She felt someone come up along side her. The energy was tentative. Gentle.

"*We* did that," she muttered, her mind still there on the moon.

"We did." It was Giles's voice that answered her.

She turned, surprised to see him. She expected it would have been Joel, or Sean, or maybe even Arlene. She'd forgotten that Giles was an actual person, and not some entity that she communicated with through Arlene.

"We did," he repeated, "because we had to." His skin had returned to normal, and his breathing seemed unhindered now.

He stood calm and present. More present than she had seen him, even before his capture. His clothes were filthy, and torn in places. Molly could only imagine what he might have been through and not reported through Arlene.

Molly looked back out at the devastation they had wreaked. Her eyes were sad, but she mostly felt numb. "I know," she agreed readily. "But just because we had to, or because it was the choice we had to make to protect the people we care about, it doesn't mean that we get to absolve ourselves of what we've done. We don't get to devalue life just because it was the only decision we could make."

Giles didn't make any attempt to argue with her. She took a breath, thinking, and then continued. "Life is valuable, even if events have made some living people our enemies."

She half expected some kind of justification back from Giles, but when she looked up at him, he was smiling. "Molly Bates, I'm grateful there are people like you in the world," he said simply, placing a hand on her shoulder.

He looked at her long and hard, as if considering his next words.

"I also must thank you for your entertaining repartee during my enslavement." His eyes misted up.

Molly looked back at the moon as their ship carried them away. Giles continued. "Arlene was great. Obviously. She kept my mind busy, and never let me give up hope. But getting your messages through her..." his voice cracked a little, and he paused to collect himself. "They were the highlights of my days."

Molly didn't know what was happening.

She felt her insides tighten as she processed Giles's words. Her chest weighed heavy; still with guilt, but now with all these other confusing feelings. Her mind grabbed at the next thing she needed to do to keep everyone safe.

"I need to go and check on the team," she said flatly, excusing herself from the cargo hold and double-stepping it up to the main cabin.

Giles turned his head as she left, listening to her leave through the door behind him. He lifted his weary hand, placing it on the wall by the window, allowing him to lean and watch the moon disappear from view before they gated back to their home system.

CHAPTER NINETEEN

Aboard *ArchAngel*

The bar was filled with the sounds of jovial celebration and chatter; the kind of chatter that people engage in when they are relieved just to be alive.

The energy around the two big tables in the lounge area was excited, fresh, and hopeful. Even Jian, Shun and Zhu had come down to help the Sanguine Squadron celebrate their victory.

A few tables away, two figures were hunched quietly over a table, nursing their beers. Their demeanor was a far cry from the relief and excitement that the others were experiencing. Their expressions were those of responsibility; of knowing things that the psyche shouldn't have to contend with. The relief of survival was a drug they had used regularly in the past, and now, older and wiser, they found themselves with weightier considerations.

"Does Molly know?" Arlene studied Giles carefully as she awaited his response.

Giles rotated his beer bottle on the table between his thumb and forefinger. "About the *ArchAngel?*"

Arlene nodded. "Yeah."

Giles took a deeper breath. "Only what I said out loud on the surface, when I was out of my mind, suffocating and trying to get her to go through with it."

Arlene looked off over the empty chairs and tables in the bar area. "Well, at least she went through with it. This could have been a lot worse." She paused and looked back at him. "Does she know I know?"

Giles shook his head slightly. "Nah. I doubt she's even thought about it. Besides, you stopped the codes, right?"

Arlene nodded. "You're damn right, I did." She looked at him like a nana would look at a grandchild who had dropped a carton of milk. She took a swig of her beer.

A contemplative silence fell between the two for a few moments. Then Arlene had another thought. "You think she'll ask you about it again?"

Giles shook his head and looked down at the table. "I'm not sure. I mean, the threat has been neutralized..."

Arlene interjected quietly. "It's a court martial offense."

Giles nodded seriously, a look of brokenness playing across his features. "I know," he said, pinching the bridge of his nose with his thumb and forefinger, and leaning his arm on the table. "I know..."

Arlene pursed her lips. "Well, you were under duress. And it got the result in the end. Maybe it will be okay. I mean - " Her attention was caught briefly by a roar of laughter from the team. "How else were you going to stay alive? You had to give them something."

Giles rubbed his face. "Yeah, but at the same time, I wasn't sanctioned to be there."

Arlene clenched her fists and her expression hardened. "Yes. I'm sure Reynolds will lean on that fact, but when push comes to shove, you did the thing that he would have wanted doing, but that he couldn't send you to do."

Giles looked emotionally defeated. "I guess," he said. He started to shuffle out of the booth. "I think the best thing is to move on with the talisman investigation. It will be a distraction from people asking too many questions. And," he glanced up at the bar, noticing Molly heading toward it, "it will get us out of here for a while..."

Arlene mumbled her agreement, and looked to see where Giles was looking. She turned back to her beer. Giles shuffled up off the seat and patted Arlene's shoulder as he walked over to the bar.

"Yeah, so Molly is in the cupboard, doing Ancestors knows what, and Jack is like, 'we have incoming'. All serious and shit." Joel's voice carried through the lounge, retelling the story. "And I'm like, *shit*! I'm glad this lady is here, cuz honestly, I don't think I could have taken that many of those guys on my own!"

Jack's face lit up. "Well, that reminds me!" She looked over at Sean, her eyes very deliberate. "What was your count?"

"Oh, yeah, you two had a bet!" Maya chipped in.

The hub of the laughter and the exchange faded into the background for Giles.

He leaned on the bar, releasing his empty tumbler onto the surface. "Another, please, barkeep," he said, hanging his head. He was barely looking up, but was very aware that Molly was directly to his left.

"So this is your post-mission ritual?" she asked. "Being miserable and drinking to celebrate your narrow escape from death?"

He turned to see her sitting in a seat, nursing her drink, and gazing up at the screen behind the bar.

Giles smiled dryly. "It is. I find it helps counter all the exuberant celebration that other people do. Conservation of decorum, I call it."

Molly grinned. "Well, I'm glad you're back. And safe," she said raising her glass to him.

The barman finished refilling Giles's tumbler, and he raised his glass in return, and drank. He shuffled up onto a stool, leaving a space between them. She turned her attention back up to the screen, watching the information scroll through.

Molly still had an air of seriousness about her, despite being here with her team. She looked over at him again. "How did you cope? I mean, stay sane, all that time?" she said, shaking her head in amazement as she considered what he must have been through.

Giles looked down into his glass. "I'm not sure I did, honestly."

Molly's stare bore through his temple. He deliberately didn't return the look. "I mean, the guilt kept me focused. Knowing that I'd put myself in that position, arrogantly thinking it would be a breeze. And, I mean, don't get me wrong, it could have been a whole lot worse; but I did things. I said things. Things I regret. And I'll never be able to take them back."

He noticed he was opening up to her, and wished he could stop his mouth. But a part of him wanted her to know. Plus, if she understood, then maybe she wouldn't put it in her report.

Molly bobbed her head.

She looked down at her own drink. "You know, I couldn't live with myself. Knowing what I'd let you do. How I'd casually let you sacrifice yourself. It nearly killed me." Her voice was flat, but Giles could tell it was just her way of dealing with the intensity of what she was trying to explain.

He turned in his seat and looked her directly in the eye. "Now you listen to me, Molly Bates. I put *myself* in that situation. If anyone is to feel guilty, it is *me*."

His voice was determined, and stern. "And there's another thing. You made the call of a leader. You let me make my own decision. Just like Lance did. That's the mark of a *true* leader; someone who empowers people to do what they need to do for their own conscience. Not a dictator who tells people what they can and can't do, like they're children. It's true, you can't run a militia or a nation without some structure… but I'm here to tell you - you made the right call."

Molly's chest tightened again, and she felt her solar plexus get heavy. This was a lot to take in, as well as feeling the intensity of her emotions, on top of what she was picking up from Giles. His words were sincere. That much she could feel. And he was passionate about what he was telling her. His guilt was just as real as hers, too.

She wondered how old he really was.

She turned back to her drink and took a swig, draining it. She plunked the empty glass back on the counter, her mood changing instantly.

"We should do tequila shots," she said more brightly. "That's the solution to all this seriousness."

She waved the bartender over, and ordered up a series of shots for them. Giles took one last swig of his grown-up drink, smiling, bemused.

"Tequila it is, then," he agreed, placing his tumbler on the counter again.

The team had gone to get pizza, and Arlene had slipped away to do whatever Arlene does when she wasn't trying to get Giles out of captivity.

Molly and Giles, several shots later, were propped up at the bar. The bartender shift had changed, making them feel like *they* were the constant there, not the staff.

Molly rested her sleepy head on her hand, her arm on the bar. "So tell me more about this talisman that you risked your arse for the first time?"

Giles adjusted his posture to subconsciously mirror her position. He played with an empty pistachio shell. "Well, it harps back to one of my pet theories I had when I was younger and less cynical."

Molly smiled, encouraging him to continue.

"Well," he explained, "we know that this talisman has great significance in the Estarian culture. But I suspect that there is something similar in the Zhyn culture, too."

Her eyes narrowed. "You mean a talisman?"

Giles nodded. He turned his body, looking for another drink. He found a glass of soda, the ice melted and looking unappealing. He pulled it around in front of him and started sipping it. "Yeah. I think I know where it might be, too."

Molly frowned.

Giles's eyes were tired. He was a little drunk, despite his nanocytes - which he suspected had been working overtime recently. A smug smile spread over his lips. "Yup. When I was in the prison, the guy in the cell next to me told me a nursery rhyme..."

Molly grinned mischievously. "Wow, you must have been bored!"

Giles nodded, grinning in agreement. "Yeah, but from what I could tell, it was a part of their folklore. Or so they thought. They even ran school trips up to the place the rhyme referred to: The Moons of Orn." He paused, taking another sip of the lukewarm soda. "Anyway, I think that's where they have the Zhyn talisman hidden."

Molly shook her head, skeptically. "It's a long shot..."

Giles suddenly became animated, slurring his words a little. "Yeah, but think about it. You're this mega advanced race, and you want to make sure that, when your children get to the point of having evolved, they can know their history, or signal that they've 'arrived'; how better to seed in the instructions or information they need?"

Molly looked serious but fascinated, as she shifted her head in her hand slightly. "Through stories and nursery rhymes."

Giles clicked his fingers, but they made no noise. "Exactly!" he said. Molly caught a glimpse of him switching into his lecture mode. She smiled to herself.

"So, what? You're off to find that next?" she asked. "The next Giles Kurns adventure?"

Giles looked deflated and turned his body back to the bar, hanging his head over his soda. "Depends. The General didn't think it was relevant when I highlighted it in my report."

Molly felt for the guy. "Why not?" she asked.

Giles shrugged. "I guess he just thinks it's another one of my harebrained adventures. That I want to go cuz it will be fun, rather than it being of use to the Federation."

Molly turned to the bar too, signaling another round of tequilas. "So why do you think it would be of benefit to the Federation?"

Giles sat up a little straighter. "Well, for one, if this theory is in any way accurate, it would mean that there is another race out there. One more evolved and established than even the Kurtherians... Maybe." His eyes widened in excitement.

The two continued talking well into the wee hours, and through another shift change at the lounge.

The next morning, Giles woke up with a funny feeling in his stomach... like he'd spilled all of his secrets to someone.

But he also had the feeling it was okay. The weight on his shoulders had been lifted.

Aboard *ArchAngel*, Reynolds's office

"You know I've heard this before from him..." The General eyed Molly carefully. "What makes you so sure?"

Molly lowered her eyes. She didn't feel comfortable sitting on sofas, talking with the General like they were buddies or something. She preferred him on a holoscreen. A few thousand light years away.

She collected her thoughts. "You know, sir. I'm not sure. I have a feeling in the pit of my stomach, like it's all related. The talismans, the Moons of Orn he told me about, the Estarian traditions, and realm-walking. Even the stuff that I've been experiencing since my... upgrade."

Lance frowned a little. "You think it might give you answers as to what you've been experiencing?"

Molly nodded before forcing herself to look him in the eye. "Yes. I think it might be related."

The General wiped at his face with one hand, contemplating the new information. Finally, he started bobbing his head.

He got up, straightening his uniform. "Okay. I'll see what I can do. However," he said seriously, looking back at her. "You know that new leaders get one fuckup."

Molly frowned with one eyebrow, tilting her head forward to hear better. "Sir?"

"Ah, you've not heard that one yet?" he smiled, folding his arms. He stepped back a little to see her better. "You get one chance to potentially fuck up. Is this what you want to use it on?"

I thought you already used that chance?

Shut up, Oz.

Molly disappeared from behind her eyes, computing the probabilities and the options in her head. Then she seemed to return. "So if I'm right, do I get to retain my chance?"

Ha! Unless they find out about all the fuckups you've already made that they don't know about yet!

Oz, for the love of -

Shutting up.

Lance chuckled, his chest bouncing a little and jostling his folded arms. He uncrossed them. "Yes, Molly. You get your chance back if you're right on this..." he conceded playfully.

Molly nodded earnestly. "Well, okay then. I'd like to use my chance on this," she informed him, standing up to leave. "Do you want to tell him, or shall I?"

The General dropped his head, looking at the ground, contemplating. "Allow me... on this one. I need to make a few things clear to him, if he's going to do this."

Molly bobbed her head as she rolled her lips awkwardly trying to figure out how to end the meeting.

Lance made it easy for her. He extended his hand for her to shake. "Thank you for your service, Molly Bates. You did a great job out there… and I'm forever grateful to you for bringing Giles back in one piece."

Molly took his hand. "Sir, it was a pleasure to be able to put this right," she said.

For a moment, the two servants of the Federation looked into each other's eyes in mutual understanding of what they were trying to achieve together, and in their relief that Giles had been returned safely.

Molly broke the gaze first, and Lance released her hand. "Let me know when you're safe back at Gaitune," he added, realizing that he probably sounded more like her mom than her commanding officer.

Molly mumbled. "Of course, sir. Thank you." And with that, she made her exit across the office to the sliding doors.

Lance watched her go.

"ADAM," he said, after the doors had closed.

ADAM responded over the intercom. "Yes, General?"

"Get Giles up here, would you?" he asked, turning to his private office.

"Of course, sir. It looks like he's just getting up, after a night drinking with Ms. Bates."

Lance shook his head, taking a deep breath as he disappeared from the reception room. "Of course he is…" he muttered, a slight smile playing across his lips.

EPILOGUE

Mocha shop near Spire Police Precinct, Spire, Estaria

Detective Chaakwa Indius picked up her mocha at the end of the counter, and, with her toasted sandwich in hand, turned to head out.

She caught a flash of blonde hair over the top of a booth against the far wall. She did a double take.

Can't be... she thought.

It had been several weeks since that night when she and her father's friends had arrested the men responsible for his death. She hadn't had the chance to thank Molly. She was obviously staying out of sight - save for that appearance on the rooftop of the building across the street.

Chaakwa shook her head to herself. She was seeing things. It was her mind playing tricks on her, because she felt it was unfinished business. She strode down the length of the counter toward the doors, glancing back just to confirm it was someone else.

The woman had her head turned from view, but as Chaakwa's gaze stayed fixed on her, the woman turned her head. Chaakwa slowed her walk, and then stopped.

It *was* her.

Without thinking, Chaakwa turned around and wove her way through the tables cluttered with people and mochas. She slipped quietly and uninvited into the booth, her sandwich forgotten on the seat next to her, and her mocha placed on the table.

The woman turned and looked at her. "Was wondering how I might get your attention," Molly said, smiling at her.

Chaakwa was lost for words. She sat looking at Molly, with her mouth moving, but no sound coming out.

Molly waited patiently, understanding all too well what it took to deal with words and emotions at the same time.

Eventually, words started coming from her throat, her voice cracking. "Molly," she started. "I can't begin to tell you how grateful I am to you. What you and your team did for me - for my father - is incredible. I'm... Thank you."

Molly lowered her eyes, feeling them well up with her own emotion. When she looked up again, she could see Chaakwa was choking up, too.

"Chaakwa, it was my pleasure," she told the detective. "It was an honor to help you bring these people to justice, and we certainly owed you one for everything you did to help us bring down the Syndicate. I just wanted you to know that this wasn't a favor. You earned this. And you helped us take those men off the street so they can't hurt anyone else."

Chaakwa nodded her understanding. The two women looked at each other for a moment longer, and then Molly slipped out of the booth.

"I'll be seeing ya," she said gently. And then she disappeared across the mocha shop and out the door.

Chaakwa sat for a few moments, relieved that she'd had the chance to thank her friend for everything she had done. She had justice. And closure. She could get on with her life.

She shuffled back out of the booth, mocha and sandwich in hand, feeling like a new person.

. . .

FINIS

AUTHOR NOTES - ELL LEIGH CLARKE

AUGUST 27TH, 2017

As always I'd like to thank the Yoda for his unwavering support and encouragement - especially through my health being sub-par these last few months. His pep talks, chin wags (and even posting on the fb page) have meant the world to me. As you can probably gather from these notes and on the fb page, we have a laugh - and that is what makes the work not just doable, but fun.

It was Yoda's idea to go and sign up at the co-working space, WeWork, to get me out of the apartment and interacting with people again. It was he who encouraged me to go buy a piano to help balance out the writing part of my brain. When I couldn't figure out how to have caffeine without crashing, he helped me figure out the decaff to half caff ratio.

It feels like every time I have a problem, or I'm just too tired or I'm feeling stuck, he's there to solve the problem and to make everything ok again. And when I'm excited about new story lines, or something cool that has happened, he's always there to add to the giggles. (And take an Author Note to tease me about later). Thank you Yoda. You're like my fairy godmother... partner in crime, and best friend all rolled into one.

(No doubt he'll have something to say about the fairy

godmother reference - but I'm sure everyone else understands what I mean.)

I would also like to thank the rock star JIT team, and Zen-Steve their coordinator, for their incredible efforts in catching typos and story-flaws. Thanks also to Jen McDonnell for her incredible support and her editing skills.

We work on incredibly short turnaround times and yet she's still able to pull a rabbit out of the hat every time. She's even taken over fielding a bunch of the JIT corrections for me too, which today alone has allowed Yoda and I to plot out three new books. Thank you!

I'd also like to thank my Icelandic friend, Trausti Traustason this time for creating an audio file to help our narrator pronounce the Icelandic in Book 1. Dude, you're a life saver. I had no idea what to tell her when those words appeared on our list of things she wanted to clarify!

Massive thank yous must also go to everyone who also took the trouble to Up Vote us on our SXSW proposed panel. We'll keep you posted with what happens with that, but for those who didn't see, we submitted a panel where we would talk about the power of story to change the world.

I took a peek at a bunch of the other proposals and none of the others I looked at had anything near the levels of support you guys gave us with your shares and comments. Thank you sooooo much! <3

And last, but by no means least, gratitude bombs must also go to you, the fans, for reading, awesome reviewing, and leaving your kind words on the 'Zon. Your enthusiasm and interaction both on the 'Zon and the fb pages keep us writing - for so many reasons. Thank you!

Ellie and Dr. Mojito

As you may have seen on the fb page, the Author got referred for a couple of root canals, having had a filling fall out recently.

Arriving at new practice, she was greeted by the receptionist and talked through a form. For some strange reason she started telling the Author about how the Doctor was really good at making mojito. The Author cannot recall how on earth this came into the conversation.

Anyway, it was mentioned, and after the promise of Mojitos at some point one Friday afternoon after an appointment, he henceforth became known between MA and the Author as Dr. Mojito.

Ellie vs the Wittering

[Edit Mike: *What the fuck is Wittering?*]

Have you ever noticed how dentists witter on?

They have their quirks... because well – captive audience. And of course with all the instruments and braces and suction devices in one's mouth, they rarely get any feedback or retorts because their audience can't respond.

Until Ellie...

Dr. Mojito: Oh my god... I've never had a patient who talks back so much!

Ellie: 'ell 'ith all 'is crap in 'y 'outh it 'akes it 'ifficult 'o 'alk.

Dr. Mojito: You seem to manage just fine.

...Hysterical laughter from Ellie and Mojito's assistant.

The Count of Dentistry

I think we agree that root canals can be sucky.

The drugs they give to numb out... not so much. Turns out he may as well be giving me laughing gas.

Of course, Dr. Mojito realized this only too late and ended up giving me an extra shot to make me sleepy (my theory) even though I said the pain wasn't too bad... He said he wanted me feeling nothing at all because he didn't want the Author moving at all.

Ha!

More like he didn't want the Author laughing. Or talking.

Dr. Mojito: *(Counting the teeth he needed to work on)*. One two, and then three. See I can count...

(Ellie edit: see what I mean about the general wittering...?!)

Dr. Mojito: well, at least to three. I went to school you know. Pause.

Dr. Mojito: well, 32.

Ellie: why 32?

Dr. Mojito: laughs. Because you have 32 teeth!

Ellie laughs her head off, despite all the instruments in her mouth. Assistant pauses doing whatever she was doing, waiting for laughter to stop.

Mojito stands there waiting with instruments, waiting for Ellie to hold still.

Ellie continues to giggle.

Assistant starts giggle. Still waiting to put instruments her mouth.

Mojito starts laughing...

...

...

Ellie starts to regain her composure.

But then Mojito sniggers, and Ellie's off again.

...

...

...

Five minutes later, still no dentistry is being done.

Through fits of laughter, Mojito calls to the girl on reception: Is there anyone in the waiting room?

Ellie: 'hy?

Mohito: Coz I don't want them hearing this. They'll be wanting some of whatever you've had!

Ellie sets off laughing for another round of giggles.

Dental Porn

So, after 4 hours in the dentist's chair for one tooth, the procedure eventually comes to a close. Dr. Mojito has another x ray taken.

Dr. Mojito: That is a nice root canal.

Ellie: What makes a root canal "nice"? I mean, a root canal is a root canal, right?

Dr. Mojito: No. This is an American root canal. (Having a dig at British dentistry...)

Ellie: (*Not convinced*). Yeah, I don't see it.

Dr. Mojito: Seriously. Look at the curves on this... (*Points at his work*). Rather than this straight line crap. Root canals aren't straight through the tooth like that... (*Points at an existing one, on another tooth on the x ray.*)

Ellie: I bet you guys have websites where you sit admiring root canals at night.

Dr. Mojito disappears into his office laughing so hard he's crying...

Ellie and Hot Chocolate Therapy

Ok, so there's the guy who works in the café on site where I live.

Several months ago, when I first moved in, I was in there, and I needed things like the wifi password. I had problems understanding him. He's one of these guys that is too cool to speak properly... He gives the impression that it's cool to mumble.

You know the type right?

Anyway, I dove in for a latte on my way to the airport this one time, and I needed help with counting out change. I explained, I still haven't got used to your money here yet...

Mumbling guy: Oh you're not from around here.

Ellie: Er. No. Didn't my English accent give it away?

Mumbling guy: No. I just thought you were from North California.

(Ellie, secretly facepalms in her head, but maintains a polite smile.)

Ellie: Nope. Definitely from England.

Mumbling guy: Oh! I thought there was **something off about you.**

(Ellie cannot believe it!)

Ellie to MA later on: I just…

MA: Yep.

Fast forward to my return from a recent dental appointment.

Ellie goes to get a hot chocolate.

Ellie: Make it as chocolately as you can. I'm suffering.

Mumbling guy: oh why?

Ellie explains about the dental work, hand over her half numb face.

Ellie: also, I think the drugs have made me a little loopy – so it's that. I'm not drunk or anything.

Mumbling guy: Oh, drunk or no, it's no different from how you usually are.

Auterior vs ulterior

As you may have seen we've been involved in pitching a panel to SXSW to discuss how story can be used to change the world. One of the panelists is my friend and story guru, John Truby, (JT). I'd asked him to share what we're doing with his email list, to help us get enough votes in.

He told me all the reasons he didn't want to.

So I offered to write the emails.

Then straight away he said yes. With a grin suggesting it was all a ploy to get *me* to do the work…

So off I went to write a sequence of emails his team could just load up, and I sent them over to him.

A few hours later, I got a message on fb…

JT: I assume the use of the world auterior is a pun you intended?

Ellie: what pun?

(Getting undressed so she could finally get in the shower, after a morning writing emails).

JT: the word is ulterior. I thought auterior is a pun on the word auteur.

Ellie: hang on, looking up meaning of auteur.

(Stands in bathroom half naked, looking up on google on her phone what the word means...)

Auteur: a filmmaker whose personal influence and artistic control over a movie are so great that the filmmaker is regarded as the author of the movie.

Ellie: Oh fuck. That is clever as hell. Put it in italics. ... Yes it was totally deliberate. ;)

JT: Right.

Ellie laughs her ass off...

Heads up.

As you may have seen at the end of Michael Book 2 there was a section where the Duke hired a scientist to figure out how to kill Michael. Behind the scenes, that was actually MA trying to get Ellie to figure out how it might work.

As a result of this, and a bunch of conversations where MA was complaining about having so much to write and wishing he could have someone help him, we kinda came to the conclusion... why don't I help write the remaining Michael books?

And so it will be. We've already started plotting the last two books and I think I speak for MA as well when I say we're excited about how this is shaping up. MA will keep you posted on time lines but all being well we should have this next book out pretty quickly with the two of us writing in tandem on it.

And I'm sure the Author Note will be fun.

Speaking on Author Notes, we're going to try something out. MA and I on video talking about some of the stuff we'd normally just save for author notes. It may be hilarious. It may be an epic fail. Who knows. What we'll do though is throw the video up on the Lawn Fairies site later this week, and you can let us know. If it works, we'll keep going... and it may even turn into a podcast.

Here's the site: www.LawnFairies.com

The video wont be up right away... but give us till the weekend. We'll also announce on the fb pages too.

Ok. That's it from me. See you soon!

E x

AUTHOR NOTES - MICHAEL ANDERLE

AUGUST 26TH, 2017

First, THANK YOU for not only reading this book, but also reading to the end, and my author notes as well!

Second, Sumbitch CLARKE! I really didn't need to finish reading this book, with tears in my eyes (but apparently, you made me do it anyway.)

At the moment, I'm not sure what 'Clarke' is writing in her author notes. Hell, I'm not sure she remembers she has to DO author notes.

Heh heh heh.

So, in support of her awesome and emotional rollercoaster ride of a book, I'm going to pull out a few author stories... Ones that I find funny!

A note to protect the (mostly) innocent. Ell has been to the dentist 3-4 times for root canals, and has been "messed up" most Friday/Saturdays since the last book.

#WeWereTalkingAWhile...

So, I think the setup for this is we had been talking a while, and I (probably) said something that caused her to ... well, hell if I know. Anyway, here is the next few sentences:

Ellie: I should probably stop talking, now.

Then, she doesn't stop talking and <u>continues</u> on as if she didn't make that comment at all.

She notices me making a face...

Ellie: What?

Mike: Hopes dashed.

Ellie: Can you see me flipping you off? (In the English version 1.0 way)

#DuelingDoctors

Ellie becomes super excited on the Zoom talk.

Ellie: Tomorrow I get high again...

Mike: *(Completely confused, pauses talking)* ... Come again?

Ellie: I get to go see Dr. Mojito (a dentist)... Wait, don't write that - Dr. Awesome will get jealous...

Mike: Oh *HELL* yeah... (Laughing as he types up the note.)

#EllieIsHigh...IThink

Ellie is talking about a way to use Scrivener that I suggested.

Mike: Do you want to show me your screen?

Ellie: Yes, wait no - you might want to copy my work.

Mike: I'll think I'll put my name on it anyway

Ellie *kills* herself laughing.

<Ellie has had little sleep (which perhaps explains the maniacal laughter)>

Ellie: You've already done that (that which I copied above) I don't think you are allowed to do that.

Mike: Why not?

Ellie: There should be some terms and conditions to these author notes!

Mike: No.

Ellie: Hashtag IndieOutlaw - *Don't you fucking regulate me.* (*More* maniacal laughter).

#CaliforniaIsGreat-ButItIsn'tAllAmericans

For Ellie - Trying to be modest, Ellie calls it being "British"

Then, she goes on 'talk' how everyone here is American (not British), and obviously we must not *do* modest.

Ellie: My experience is you don't.

Mike: You are in California; Californians are genetically predisposed to not be modest.

(I've lived in California (Lake Arrowhead, Orange County, Family in Los Angeles) and I've met very humble people, but it is much more rare to find them in LA - just saying.)

#EllieIsAnnoyedThatImFocusedOnSomething

So, I'm focused on something relevant, and Ellie believes I'm not paying attention to whatever she was discussing. In her passive-aggressive style, she says...

Ellie: "Hi my name is Michael Anderle and I have a squirrel addiction."

Mike: *bitch!*

Then, after our laughter dies down and I explain how I was actually paying attention to the conversation, (but whatever)... I say:

Mike: I'm not sure I actually said 'bitch.'

Ellie: You *did*.

Mike: Well, at least I'm consistent.

Ellie: (Absolutely NO pause) We call that *unimaginative*.

Mike: (pause)... *bitch!*

cue more maniacal laughter.

#MikeDoesntDoEnglishShows

So, I'm working in the kitchen and Joey Anderle pops in (before he left for college). He notices that I'm on a conference video call with "British Lady" and he waves. Then, I share with him one of the headphones I'm using and he starts talking with Ell Leigh Clarke.

Then, they go off on some tangent about shows that I've got no clue about. Joey then asks British Lady a question.

Joey: What do you think about the new Doctor? (Doctor Who)

Ellie: ...The female?

Ellie: Well, I don't know I haven't seen her act yet.

Joey: You haven't seen Black Mirror? You know, the BBC series.

Ell: No...

Half a second pause...

Joey: (Deadpan) You fake British person.

#EllStillCusses

Ell is on Zoom, a version of Skype (Video Call). I'm showing her three fingers (as in, I counted something three times.) If you read Ell's comment's with a British Accent, it is ALL the more humorous...

E: What is that?

M: Three fingers, you said fucking 3 times in one paragraph.

E: I don't have a problem with that.

M: But, you don't want to be seen as cussing.

E: I just want to be fairly represented.

M: If anything, I underrepresent your cussing!

See, just for the record, I'm being nice to her and her potty mouth problem!

#EllieIsMolly

So, she is explaining a problem she had with the first visit to the dentist, where she is tipped backwards and spends two hours "needing to pee."

Then, when she can finally get out of the chair, and expects to make a dash to the restroom, suddenly there is no need.

Well, this causes her to wonder about this situation and looks at it from a engineers (designers) perspective. She figures out if you were going to put a sensor in the bladder, where is the obvious location?

Ellie: So, I figure the sensor is at the top of the bladder! So, when when the doctor tips the chair back down, the sensor isn't tripped anymore.

Mike: That is such a Molly comment.

Mike: I *have* to write this in the author notes.

#GeekIsWhatIDo

So, Ellie is at WeWork in Los Angeles, stickers all over her laptop (Dr. Who quote, Tardis sticker etc.) AND she is wearing a t-shirt with six spaceships on it (Millennium Falcon, U.S.S. Enterprise, Serenity, Planet Express, Tardis, Battlestar Galactica) with the caption "Choose Your Spaceship."

She explains she had a moment where she realizes for her whole life, she has been this geek, feeling like she was one of the fringe.

Now, she is a science-fiction author. It all makes sense and being geek *IS HER WORK.*

How cool is that?

#ItsFuckingHotInLA

So, we are trying to get through a scene or something and it's August in Los Angeles (So, hot!)

Ellie: I have to go close the door, one second. (She leaves.)

Ellie: (She gets back) Sorry, but I have to close the door because I was causing too much noise.

Mike: What, are you a #PartyAnimal that your neighbors are complaining?

Ellie: No, I'm talking with you.

Mike: (thinking to himself) *How the fuck does someone talk to loud they bother the neighbors?*

#MichaelIsCynical

Ellie is commenting that she often feels she doesn't know the world much better than "9 year old her." I make some comment that perhaps, just perhaps, I might have a clue at 50'ish.

Ellie: Do you feel like you have your view of the world sorted?

Mike: Gives 2 examples...

Ellie: So you use cynicism as a way of imposing order on your world?

Mike: Well, it sounds messed up when you say it that way.

Ellie: That's an author note...Write it up, bitch.

#PhysicistDoesntKnowEverything

Mike is talking about something, and spouts some numbers and something else that sounds like it's sciency.

Ellie: Look, Physicists don't know everything...And that whole thing about being able to do math in our heads? It's also *not* true.

Mike: Ellie, you are fucking up my world view.

Ellie: It's ok, it needs a reality check.

So ends the Author Notes from books 05 and 06 (some of those didn't make it into the last book.) THANK YOU for supporting what we do, because we can't do it without *YOU* reading!

BOOKS BY ELL LEIGH CLARKE

The Ascension Myth
* With Michael Anderle *

Awakened (01)
Activated (02)
Called (03)
Sanctioned (04)
Rebirth (05)
Retribution (06)
Cloaked (07)
Bourne (08)
Committed (09)
Subversion (10)
Invasion (11)
Ascension (12)

Confessions of a Space Anthropologist
* With Michael Anderle *

Giles Kurns: Rogue Operator (1)

<u>Giles Kurns: Rogue Instigator (2)</u>

The Second Dark Ages
with Michael Anderle
Darkest Before The Dawn (3)
Dawn Arrives (4)
Deuces Wild
with Michael Anderle
Beyond The Frontiers (1)
Rampage (2)
Labyrinth (3)
Birthright (4)

BOOKS BY MICHAEL ANDERLE

For a complete list of books by Michael Anderle, please visit:

www.lmbpn.com/ma-books/

All LMBPN Audiobooks are Available at Audible.com and iTunes. For a complete list of audiobooks visit:

www.lmbpn.com/audible

CONNECT WITH THE AUTHORS

Receive updates from Oz by registering your holo/ email address here:
ellleighclarke.com

Facebook:
http://www.facebook.com/ellleighclarke/

Michael Anderle Social

Website:
http://kurtherianbooks.com/

Email List:
http://kurtherianbooks.com/email-list/

Facebook Here:
https://www.facebook.com/TheKurtherianGambitBooks/

www.ingramcontent.com/pod-product-compliance
Lightning Source LLC
Chambersburg PA
CBHW020409110726
47899CB00006B/1911